Metaphysical Tales

AWP-3

Library of Congress Cataloging in Publication Data

Garber, Eugene K.
  Metaphysical Tales. AWP-3.

  CONTENTS: The Poets.—The Lover.—The Host.—[etc.]
I. Title.
PS3557.A63M4   813'.54   80–26057
ISBN 0–8262–0325–6

The stories in this book have appeared in substantially the same form in the following journals and are reprinted here with permission.

"The Poets," first published by the University of the South in *Sewanee Review* 86, 1 (Winter 1978); "The Lover," in *Shenandoah* 27, 3 (Spring 1976); "The Host," in *The Hudson Review* 24, 4 (Winter 1976–1977); "Malagueña," in *Paris Review* (forthcoming); "The Women," reprinted from *The Literary Review* 23, 1 (Fall 1979), published by Fairleigh Dickinson University; "The Melon-eaters," "Selections from the Assassin's Memoirs," and "White Monkey Man," in *Iowa Review* (1 November 1977); "The Black Prince," in *Denver Quarterly* 8, 4 (Winter 1974); "The Prisoner," in *Antaeus* 28 (Winter 1978); "The Child," in *The Georgia Review* 32, 4 (Winter 1978); and "The Gamblers" is reprinted with permission from the *North American Review*, copyright © 1977 by the University of Northern Iowa.

Drawing on title page by Cheryl Lavers

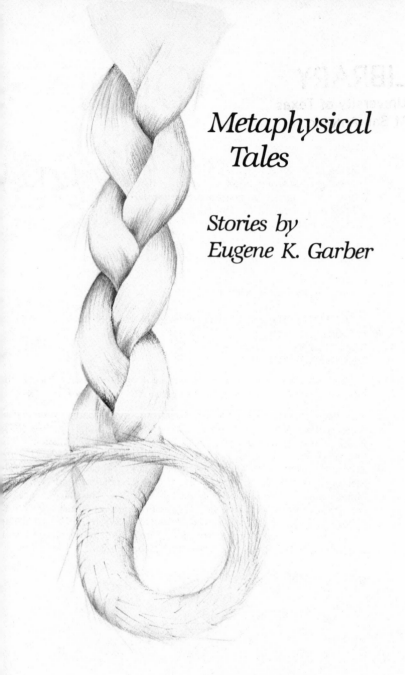

Metaphysical Tales

Stories by Eugene K. Garber

University of Missouri Press

Columbia & London

1981

For Bobby

Foreword

This remarkable collection introduces a writer of extraordinary skill and vision. In prose pieces that range from the wildly surreal to the *almost* credible, Eugene K. Garber invents dream landscapes that meld disconcertingly with our own and populates them with people—lovers, scholars, mystics, obsessed storytellers, "interlopers" of one kind or another—whose voices fairly quiver with the difficult audacity of their music. They sense themselves doomed—or are they redeemed?—by the ineludible mythologizing instincts of their souls. They are *possessed* by a curious sort of *dispossession:* they cannot resist substituting for this "rich round world of ours" the mesmerizing stratagems of the imagination.

Mystics, fools, besotted lovers, artists upon whom a sort of cosmic curse has descended; elderly men who live solely (and recklessly) in their heads, adolescent boys intoxicated with the first incursions of desire. There is a saint of a kind who so refines himself of the human that he becomes a feral man, and then a "monkey god" in the cosmology of a tribe of unfortunate savages, and then a tree, and then—nothing at all. He craves a "sufficient reduction"—what, in another context, might be called "devolution." He speaks in the tone of the great mystics; he echoes Pascal: "Imagine what I foresee—a jungle so wide that every place is its center, so dayless and dreamless that its moments all congeal into a perpetual present. I know that when I first enter it, I will be in agony, even I, surely among the best prepared of all men. . . . But I will lie down. I will replicate that silence." ("White Monkey Man")

Garber's visionary explorers succumb to the labyrinthine lure of consciousness itself. (And the labyrinth—the Borgesian paradigm of the imagination's convolutions—is an apt image for these tales.) They resist detachment; they refuse to honor those "places where we must not send ourselves"; they enter into profane and dazzling rites, offering themselves to cannibals (like the stoic captain in "The Melon-eaters"), or to pagan gods (like the woman artist in "The Black Prince"), or to someone so obvious—and so miraculous—as their own mothers, wives, and daughters (like the lyric penitent of "The Women"). Their ceremonial dramas are enacted "in evergreen country at winter's threshold, awaiting the zero hour of the solstice";

in a Spanish mosque suddenly defiled by a noisy horde of German tourists; in a sequence of brilliant, despairing letters exchanged by a gifted young woman poet and her uncle over three decades. The elderly millionaire of one of the most compelling stories, "The Host," succumbs to a mythologizing impulse in which the evolutionary mysticism of Teilhard de Chardin (the story is written in homage to Teilhard) is strangely wed with the "devolutionary" yogic disciplines of a beautiful young woman who has learned to be (again) an animal. The powerful eroticism evoked by the young woman is both physical and spiritual, and even prophetic: it becomes a catalyst for the elderly hero's self-revelation, his communings with lost and denied selves. ("His confidence was so great that he knew he could start his meditation anywhere, because when a pattern of ideas and images begins to tessellate its mosaic, the tiniest piece, placed correctly, by a kind of supra-aesthetic necessity, adumbrates all the rest. . . . What he . . . had experienced was, as it were, a living fossil of feeling. It was the remembered moment when man first saw in another, perhaps a woman, the promise of divinity.")

Garber freely acknowledges his debts to such fabulists as Kafka, Dinesen, and Borges; there is an echo of Beckett here too, and Joyce, and the Nabokov of the monomaniacal rhapsodies of those works (*Lolita* and *Ada* above all) in which language of a frequently clotted and self-referential intensity achieves its own redemption—its problematic liberation from content, story, and "plot." To say that Garber is audacious in some of his experimental pieces is to say the most immediate—and the most obvious—thing about his prose. To say that he is always "successful" is perhaps to mislead. He is generous in his enthusiasms, which have a great deal to do with the numinous and ineffable moments of which Joyce (that is, Stephen Dedalus) spoke so passionately, and in which Proust (that is, the Marcel of the great novel) immersed himself with such astonishing faith. (The luxuriant novella "Malagueña" is an attempt to hold in suspension, in a sense, three melodramatically disparate images experienced by the scholar-hero, now a middle-aged man, over a period of many years.)

Garber is also stubborn, eccentric, self-conscious, and so willfully dazzling—to be a virtuoso, or to be nothing!—that readers must be enjoined not to attempt to read this volume straight through, or even to read more than one story at a time. (For one thing, the music, the idiosyncratic voices, of the stories differ from one another and can thus only distract—which is not the case with lean, spare, underwritten, or underimagined prose.) Begin with the memorable "The Poets," or with the highly entertaining "The Host," or "Malagueña." Leave for last the parables "The Prisoner" and "The Child" or that peculiar homage to at least two goddesses (Mnemosyne and Aphrodite), "The Gamblers." Like all gifted writers, Eugene K. Garber is not to be understood—or loved—too quickly.

Joyce Carol Oates

Contents

The Poets

Her name was Sarah and she had performed many girlhood feats—ridden her jumper Jack to victory at the Windome Stakes against a field of fine male riders, won the senior mixed doubles at Salt Springs with Albert Hough, swum the Black Warrior, written the prize-winning poem for the university literary annual, which even her Uncle Carlton had conceded showed promise. This was the final stanza:

> *Now among the porcelain cats,*
> *Purple hum of listless chatter.*
> *Bend I to your chatoyant eye*
> *And supplicate your charity.*

"Nice, Essie," he wrote, "even if decadent ennui is as far from your character as gnats are to eagles." But she sent him no more poems.

A week after she was graduated from the university, the hottest June on record, 1934, she wrote from her hometown of Tumwah.

My dear bachelor barrister uncle, how are you faring in these lean times in the big city? Here the weekly is down to two pages. Even the Episcopalians can't afford to have the Sunday Bulletin printed any more. Miss Kendall's recital will not have a program this year, and the grocery store handy-bill business is defunct. So Daddy sits around the shop nipping with Tom, whom he will not let go. The county contracts go to Coggins in Melba again because, of course, old man Pelly tipped him off and he underbid Daddy by a fraction. Mama is waiting for me to accept Albert and save the family with "the only bank stocks that held up this side of Montgomery, honey." Your older sister of high ideals. Hope, *my* sister, whom I dearly love (won't you believe that, uncle dear, despite our horrendous fights?), must go to Mount Morris College for Women in North Carolina next year. (Mama judges that, unlike me, Hope would not be able to protect herself from certain undesirable elements at the university.) And where is the money to come from? My tan and exquisitely trained body, uncle dear, to fill Hope's empty head? Better that I should come to New Orleans and dance in Curly's infamous speakeasy. Can you get me on? . . .

Uncle Carlton wrote back, "Do not marry against your feelings,

1

Essie. No good can come of it." But Sarah did marry Albert. Then, in early 1937, she wrote:

Dear uncle, let me be the first to bring you the joyous news, Mama's injunctions notwithstanding. (Is the phrase juridically correct?) Your niece Hope has dropped out of Mount Morris, pregnant, paternity as yet undeclared, and therefore the child may be divine. Contemporaneously I have declared to Albert that I wish to be free of the fetters of the marriage bed, requiring no settlement. Thus ends, uncle dear, my penitential years with the heaviest hands east of the Mississippi. And now what about that job at Curly's — or has repeal killed the business?

At Carlton's invitation Sarah went to New Orleans, arriving in time for Mardi Gras. She remained two months and left abruptly. Back at Tumwah she stayed only long enough to pack. She went to Atlanta and got a job as a receptionist at the Coca-Cola Company, winning out over a score of other applicants.

So, uncle dear, I have a job despite your gloomy prognostications. Even so, I apologize for failing twice to accept your avuncular counsel vis-à-vis matters of the heart. I should not have married Albert. You were certainly right about that. But I should not have dropped Maurice, you say? Dear Maurice. He was as gallant and passionate as my most romantic notions of the French. And his coffee money was certainly more fragrant than Albert's farmer-fingered bank notes. And what idealism! But I venture that he will not really, now that I am gone, hie him to Spain to fight the Falangists. No matter. The truth is I do not love him. By now you know my dark secret. I want a man like you, Carlton — strong, intelligent, and unfamilied. Probably I want you. And, alas, the shadow of that forbidden desire falls over all my suitors. Why else do the men here seem as insipid and caramel-sweet as our product?

You asked about the family. The father of Hope's firstborn (due in late July, a sweaty labor) has manfully stepped forward, Charles Moore, son of a Virginia tobacco-man. Do not consult your Dun & Bradstreet or other directories. Charles and Daddy became quickly if wordlessly reconciled by sharing an all-night bourbonic stupor. Mother continues to say that Hope and I have good blood and will eventually find ourselves. Where, Mother? Amid the quaint transformations of these southern nights, when we apple-cheeked Alabama virgins become roiling ladies in our husbands' stews? Anyway Hope and Charles have been married in a quiet (not to say secretive) ceremony at home by old Judge Lyle, without benefit of clergy, who preferred to remain aloof from the stain of this premature conception.

Shall I explain to Hope and Charles, her mental equal, how nature arranges these things in the unlikely eventuality that they wish to exercise some control over future occurrences? No. Because in the arcane recesses of my thorny heart I envy her.

Jack, my only true love, is sold and the money has gone into our Hope chest along with my works of hands and nights as the recent Mrs. Albert Hough.

Dear Essie, felicitations on the occasion of your reaching the quarter-century mark. And still alive! By what miracle of inner strength? Neither thrown to your death by the fiery stallion, nor swept away by the raging Black Warrior, nor immolated by alien tribes beyond the pale, nor lost questing for love through our torrid regions. Indomitable Essie! You are my epic. But do not imagine (do you know that I am forty?) that you suffer a fatal incestuous passion. That kind of junk only happens in bad southern novels. E.g., distraught niece succumbs to passion beyond reach of volition, confronts uncle with her towering desire, uncle's desire does not tower reciprocally because he has, alas, been emasculated by an overbearing father; finale: hopeless embrace and tears. No parts for a noble pair like us in that tawdry drama!

I have written Hope and congratulated her on the birth of Joel. The wire came yesterday. I have also bidden Sister Martha to accept all. Even in the worst of depressions, especially in the worst of depressions, nobody is going to stop smoking.

II

In 1939, when the war came to Europe, Sarah joined the Red Cross and went to England. During the Battle of Britain in 1941, she wrote from London.

. . . I have seen a terrible image in the ruins of the cathedral at Coventry, Carlton. It was my body. I was charred, laid out, crucified, ruined, not three feet of me still standing erect. All my precious chalices and flagons melted down for easy transport, thieves' goods. I tried to soothe myself, saying: "There will be a resurrection. It's only your own ravaged past you have lost in the ruins here, you shallow egocentric." But it was not so. I saw us all there, all of us in this war I mean. One body would fit that blackened bed as well as another. Because I have seen under my hands too many broken bodies, Carlton, and my body under too many hands. Write me, learned uncle, who must I read to plumb this dark relationship between sex and war? Schopenhauer? Freud?

When the war comes to America, don't you dare volunteer for anything. If I do not have you to come back to, I will die.

In 1944 Carlton wrote to Sarah, who was still in London.

Martha and Hope asked me to write you and tell you that Charles was killed in Normandy last month, several days after the invasion. Poor Charles, I saw him only the once, shortly before he went overseas. I never saw a man more certain of his death. We think that only the brave go toward the night with clairvoyant eyes. Our poets are in error. Simple Charles wore his death almost nobly, like a rare black flower on his breast. Finis.

Hope is not shattered. Martha is delighted with her role as grief-stricken mother, grateful to Charles for having the decency to get himself killed. Now her great hopes for her two beautiful daughters rise again. Do rise, Essie, like a phoenix, out of your ashes of Coventry. Come home and tell me, you my Nestor now, what the meaning was that you discovered deep down in the eyes of the suffering. Here significance is occluded by boom, profits, power, and the approaching hysteria of victory.

Your father is drinking much less and working much more. The shop has a small government contract.

In 1945 shortly after V-J Day Sarah came home, the daughter, sister, niece seven years absent. She stayed in Tumwah about a month and then visited Carlton in New Orleans for a month. But before Sarah left for New Orleans, Hope wrote Carlton.

Mama told me to write you and tell you that we are depending on you to help Sarah. None of us can because she is too smart. What it amounts to is that all the suffering she saw has unsettled her. Dr. Thomas says many have come back this way. She shouldn't have stayed so long. You must be careful that she doesn't put on a courageous act for you because we know here that she is barely holding together. She lies awake at night and smokes and does not eat. She is thin as a rail. She won't see any of her old friends and she won't tell us anything that happened. Little Joel, who is bright for nine, says she looks like somebody who has come back from the grave. Little Joel is getting smart-alecky and generally out of hand. He needs a father and I am going to give him one, John Mullens, who is in roofing here. You might remember his daddy who played on the same team with Bully Vaught. Sarah doesn't know this because she doesn't take any interest in anything. She doesn't even know about Daddy's cancer and whether it is cured or just has remission. It takes two more years to tell. That is all our news. Sarah should be there before long. You are her favorite. In fact you are the only one she ever loved, though I would not tell that to Mama or Daddy. I hope you can help her.

III

So Sarah went to New Orleans. She spent a month with Carlton and then she went to San Francisco. From there she finally wrote him in early 1946.

Dear Carlton, I am finally settled in a small apartment near a park by the beach. I can see the ocean from my kitchen window. But I'm not writing to tell you about my life here except to say that I am eating and that many hours of my sleep are at last dark and dreamless. I have not written before this because it has taken me a great while to digest that long month of talk, which I know was hell for you. Thank you. Maybe I will be able to do something for you some day, but I hope I never find you in that kind of need. You surprised me utterly. How could I have guessed that in New Orleans you were wrestling with the same thoughts that were destroying my sleep in London? And I was furious that you hadn't written to tell me, but when I saw how many nights it would take to say it all, I wasn't furious any more. That last sentence isn't quite accurate, is it? It didn't take so long to say it. Rather, it took a great while to find it there in the middle of all those words and then it took another great while to celebrate it, to dance around it. And then it took another little while to know that the dance was ended and it was time to part. I didn't share, there at the end, your exquisite sense of timing, Carlton. So you must forgive me for staying—what?—two days too long. I won't excuse myself by referring to all the old saws that establish the woman's greater passion for afterplay. And I won't apologize either for referring to our month as a sort of honeymoon. Because you will admit, Carlton, that there in the chaste and severe leather of your study, and surrounded by those great tomes of learning, we were lovers. You will admit that. Despite the perfectly unincestuous distance through which our words passed, we were lovers because our deeper bodies leapt out from us and clasped invisibly.

This is how it was. I came to you with a body so broken and bruised that I wanted to give it up, was in the process of giving it up. My Coventry cathedral, my charred ruin. And you kept asking me what I had seen. And I kept telling you about bodies wasted to the bone and about bodies hidden all in white except where the red and yellow suppurations appeared like little mouths crying out for love and about bodies with eyes in which the light slowly receded as if in a long tunnel and about how I would run down those black tunnels with my little nurse's torch of charity, but the dying light went too far and I always had to turn back. And I wondered, why is Carlton making me remember all these things? So I can die quicker? But when all the bodies were laid out in my mind's eye, you told me there is only one body. And you showed me how to see all of us as one great mole erected against the sea of death. And in that mole the bones and flesh constantly die and are born. The rote of the sea seeks out the dead, but the living cast the sea back. But in war comes death disproportionate. The mole begins to crumble and the shock of death runs through the whole body. That was what I felt, you said. But the war was over, you said, and the world's body was building. You said the sea of death would be pushed back and continents would touch like lovers. You said that for a while you, too, had wanted to die, but now you wanted to live more than ever, and I must live. At first I thought you were only a shallow optimist, for the tide of death was running hard in me. And then your words one by one began to stand up in me and staunch the flow. I felt them root in my bones and flourish in my blood until I conceived a little delta, barely a fingerlet, but I was reaching with you for another continent.

And now I don't ask myself, how did Carlton know how to save me? Because I know in that great mole of bodies our two lie contiguously, sharing, just as the old poems say, one heart in its temporary cage of ribs. And now I know that my poor little poem was to you, Carlton, my wise old cat with the deep green eyes, where all the lights that had fled me came back and glowed like verdant fire.

You said that everything that is given is restored sevenfold. It is true. Let me tell you how I feel now walking in the park. I feel like a virgin and a mother at the same time. I don't have any trouble understanding that old story. Obscenity and cynicism can never touch it. Do you see what I mean? Paradoxically your words have made me conceive. And that conception has closed all the old wounds and breaches. So, as the spring grows here, Carlton, I reach a kind of fullness. But whose hands can I trust it to?

I've read your letter dozens of times, Essie, and it has, as old Cousin Nan would say, warmed the cockles of my heart. The heat has risen up through every vein until my scalp tingles, as though your fingers were nested in my hair. But I cannot answer you in kind. Instead can we pretend that we both wrote your letter to each other? That it passes now perpetually from heart to heart like a quick-flying messenger-bird?

In my sleep the other night I saw you riding Jack by the bank of the Black Warrior. And suddenly I understood the meaning of your girlhood feats perfectly. But how could I have guessed then (when you were sometimes a beautiful girl, sometimes a sweaty raucous tomboy) that you were testing your strength, training arms, legs, lungs, and heart for that deep dive into the black waters of war. You have gone and come back, Essie. And you have brought us, my questing heroine, the only boon to be snatched from that wretched war—knowledge of the indestructible life at the center of everything.

IV

The forties passed into the fifties without striking news from Sarah. She tried several jobs with agencies specializing in the care of the poor or the mentally or physically handicapped. In her letters to Carlton she seemed to smile at herself, at this perhaps incongruous resurrection of the youthful idealism that had carried her off to England a decade before. She ended up as the receptionist in the office of a psychiatric clinic. "Here I sometimes take the disturbed by the hand, Carlton. I do not try to embrace them. I have learned the limits of my strength." But then in 1952 came news.

Dearest Carlton, this is the most difficult letter of all, bearing news of what must seem at first a defection. I thought that our invisible embrace in the russet air of your old study would be the last embrace of my life. And in a way it was. But I have found that I need to corporealize it. You will grant, Carlton, that if this is a failing it is more human than personal. I know you have the strength to go on alone. You remind me of Father Simms, the chaplain of the psychiatric ward here. He is so hirsute that the black hairs climb up above his white collar and burst from the sleeves of his cassock. He actually breathes with a sort of animal stertor, and not the strongest lotions can bury the odor of his sweat. I have to imagine that he has simian appetites. Smile if you like, but it seems to me that you two share that mysteriously ferocious celibate love of God, or whatever it is that the word of God stands for.

All of that is a kind of nervous, though true, introduction to a difficult declaration. Imagine, if my forty years will allow it, that I am a girl again sitting in your study drinking bourbon with fidgety hands and plucking smoke inexpertly from the end of one of your Chesterfields. I am trying to prepare myself to tell you that I am in love though I am particularly anxious not to use that debauched phrase. Imagine yourself bending toward me and soothing me with the wise light of your green old cat's eyes so that at last I can put away drink and cigarette, still my hands, and tell my story.

She came to our office several months ago. And though her troubles were endlessly complex, her fundamental need was simply love. I frightened her at first. My love growing six years since that month in your study must have seemed to her like some enormous and obscene yeasting. Here is how it was. I didn't recognize her when she came in, although I had seen her face on the jacket of her book, because she has to wear thick owlish glasses that discolor the flesh around her eyes and diminish the brown and black cores to tiny hollows. And yet I was not repulsed. In fact I went out strongly to those eyes. I was determined that they would not outrun me, as so many had in the war, to a place too dark for my courage. Later, when I found out who she was, the poems confirmed my intuition. But it is important that you understand that I knew her *essentially* before I knew her name, before I reread the book. Because I am not in love with a book.

There is no need to recount the small revelations and discoveries, the accidental meetings, the abrupt and embarrassed little exchanges, and then the long talks in which the words were less words than frail bridges of feeling bearing the two of us over dark waters. No courtship was more ordinary. I was the gallant and she the coy mistress. But, Carlton, I cannot describe for you our embrace. Unless every word were perfectly precise, every phrase as supple and warm as twined lovers' limbs, it would be a kind of breach of faith. And I haven't that power with words. But I address a prayer to you, Carlton, or perhaps through you, as I did in my old poem and have many times since. It is this. Because you are bigger and wiser in love, hold the two of us in your hand. Breathe upon us. Keep us warm. Because if this embrace grows cold, as in my marriage, as in the many wayward bestowals of my war-torn body, I do not think even you could snatch me from the sea again.

It is good that I have found her, Carlton, or else the new war might have cast me down, but she reaffirms for me your great thoughts of six years ago. She is my continent, all I can grasp, while you reach across the seas and perhaps across the skies to new planets. You are our loving giant, Carlton.

It is good, too, that the news from home is so bright—Daddy's cancer gone, business booming, Mama a burgeoning grandmother and pillar of the community, Hope and John breeding like rabbits for a future that needs all the life it can get. You were right, Carlton. The war that killed so many only confirmed in this curious species of ours its furious will to live, and this new war will not hurt so deeply. So you see, even a maimed war victim like me, thanks to you, can reach out for her tiny share of the new love. I send you my love's book. Write me, Carlton, reach to me across the continent, for my love is yet a little in suspense, waiting for your nod, the wise wink of your green eye.

Carlton read Sarah's lover's book of poems, which was entitled Amyster, *Amyster being an imaginary horselike animal, lover, and alter ego. He sat down immediately to write Sarah. But the letter which he began with passionate heat he did not finish. Instead he mailed another. These are the two.*

Dear Essie, your letter was never so difficult as mine, for I must tell you that I have read *Amyster* and I am in great fear. These things are not so much poems as they are plunges into chaos. And this animal of hers is not so much a Pegasus as it is a Minotaur. And so far as I can see she is lost in the labyrinth. No, my own metaphor (or is it hers?) fails me. Because sometimes it seems that she herself is the Minotaur—those passionate descriptions of smoking gobbets of human flesh. They are not the necessary purgative images of a war-torn world, they are the wild bacchantic paeans of anthropophagi. No, Essie, I do not think you can be Theseus, or Ariadne to her Theseus, or whatever in God's name she is and needs. No metaphor can hold her. How can you? Her own poem cannot give shape to her mind. Once I helped you, held you, you said, when you had fallen into the pit. But you cannot help her similarly. She *is* the pit. . . .

Dear Essie, before I express my great joy in your new love, I have to take a moment, in mid-embrace, to subject you to a most gentle avuncular chiding. Hold your love in suspense for me? You know that everything dear to you is dear to me. In fact your letter and *Amyster* shower me with such varied treasures that I cannot as yet sort them. Again, as in the war, you have run ahead of me to new vistas. Wait for me. Better yet, come back and give me your hand, by which I mean write often, keep the sky bright with our heart-to-heart messenger-birds.

But Carlton received after this only short notes which explained their brevity as a consequence of the demands of clinic and apartment. "You would laugh to see me, Carlton. I am a caricature of the mid-century husband dutifully dashing between home and work, too prosperous and optimistic to need goals, but I do need a kind word from my wise old green-eyed cat." The kind word, however, was not answered, nor a subsequent one. Instead a letter came from Hope.

Dear Carlton, I don't know how I got to be the family correspondent, but here I am again. First, we're all very proud of you. Senior Partner in the best law firm in New Orleans! And old man Carter down at the *Bugle* got us a copy of the *Times-Picayune* with the big marine-disaster case you won against Gulf, because he knew you wouldn't send it yourself. When are you going to come and see us? We want to see you and we love you, but I won't lie about it: we want to show you off, too. Daddy is retiring next fall and some are planning a little festivity to mark the occasion. You can't say no to that. Mama says I'm to be very firm. It will be in October when it cools off. It's already getting hot. It's hotter every summer if you ask me. John says it's an effect of the bomb. Anyway mark your calendar.

But the real reason I wrote, Carlton, is not the good news. We called Sarah last night to wish her happy birthday, and something is wrong. Some woman answered the phone and said that Sarah was sick and that she was taking care of her. Sarah couldn't come to the phone, she said, but she wouldn't say what was the matter with her. The woman sounded like Billy-Goat Gruff. I wouldn't want her near me if I was sick. So we're suspicious. It's not like Sarah to refuse to answer, and I know she was there because I heard her say something in the background. So she's not in the hospital. I have a nightmare of one of those crazy people she works with getting hold of her. Anyway, we think you ought to call her on the telephone. Incidentally, I tried to call you, but couldn't get through. That's why I'm sending this air-mail special-delivery. I didn't know you were that big of a shot, Carlton. Anyway, if Sarah is in trouble again, you're the only one that can help her, as always. And please let us hear right away what you find out. Mama and Daddy are worried sick, though Sarah doesn't ever seem to think about that.

John and all my boys are fine.

Carlton flew immediately to San Francisco. Two days later he

*reported to Hope by phone that he had Sarah in the hospital under
the best care available, after a nervous breakdown. A few days later
he wrote a letter.*

Dear Martha, Hope, and Colin. Tomorrow I am flying back to New
Orleans. Essie's recovery, though it will take time, is now assured.
The doctor's judgment and mine concur in this. So we can all take a
deep breath and relax. But I will confess to you that I was frightened,
because she would not talk to me for several days and was in a state
of extreme physical debilitation. The doctor, however, says that it
was probably not as close as it seemed, because Essie has vast
reserves of strength which are beginning to show themselves now in
the form of a firm new grasp on life. So she is on the way back.
Martha, you mentioned on the phone the possibility of flying out.
The doctor forbids it. I know that's painful for a mother. Perhaps my
groping explanations that follow will help.

Essie has been on a long quest for love. She did not find it with
Albert, as you know, because Albert's boorishness alienated her. She
could not find it with you at home because love of family is not
enough. And I, though we have had a few fine long visits, did not do
well by her either, busy as I have always been with my work. All of
this does not mean that we should heap our heads with ashes. In fact
at this point Essie needs our love and understanding, not our regrets.
But to go on.

In London once again Essie did not find love. I am sure she did not
expect to, there amid all the bombings, the rubble, and broken
bodies. But nevertheless she came back broken herself, as you saw.
Then in San Francisco she steadied herself and got the job at the
clinic, where everybody loves her to the point of idolatry. But that
kind of love is not enough either. So a while back she began to see a
brilliant poet somewhat younger than she. It looked as though it was
going to work out, but finally it did not. That is what cast her
down—yet one more failure of love.

There is no doubt, as I said, that Essie will recover completely. But
she will still have her old need for love. And what must we do? Here
is my advice to all of us. (Pardon me for offering it unasked.) First, of
course, not a word of reproach of any kind. Shower her with love and
good wishes. Invite her home, but do not insist on it. And I would not
put too much emphasis on Colin's retirement festivities lest she feel
compelled to attend before she has her strength back.

But you can depend on my coming, Colin, shipwrecks be damned,
to lay claim to my share of the bourbon and Brunswick stew and to
celebrate your honorable career.

On the Fourth of July 1954 Carlton wrote the following letter to Sarah.

Dear Essie, I have here in my study your fine and lucid letter of the 25th of last month written in your own firm hand at the desk in your new apartment overlooking the bay. I have called Dr. Temple to ask her permission, as you suggested, to write you the full account, which you request, of my experiences with Amyster. I have permission and now I have a holiday. So I in my turn sit to paper here at my desk, make abeyance to Mnemosyne and Justitia, and begin. Headnote: I call her Amyster whenever I have to name her as a way of reminding you that your old rationalist uncle had an encounter not with a young woman of ordinary appellations but with a mythical being, and as a way of paying tribute to the courage and strength you must have had to live with that extraordinary being for two long years.

You must begin by understanding, Essie, that I came to San Francisco with my mind absolutely closed and a plan already laid out. I had always kept from you my true feelings about Amyster's poetry. From the very first it seemed to me absolutely frenzied, and (I think I said in a letter never mailed) even cannibalistic. When the second volume, *Woeman*, appeared with its gashed pages of dismembered images, and when I could recognize your poor body strewn in that wreckage more chaotic than any war's, and when you did not send me a copy, my heart was divided between hope and terror. On the one hand I hoped that you had seen Amyster for what she was and had freed yourself. On the other I feared that she had eaten you up and was vomiting you piecemeal in her poems. Forgive the horrible pun, the horrible image, but they are necessary to convey the revulsion I felt.

So when, after your long silence, I got Hope's letter telling of your illness, I went into high gear as only a compulsive legalist can. I arrived at your apartment with writs, injunctions, law officers, and court medical observers enough to snatch you away from ten Amysters. Thus is law, in this world, superior to myth. And though I try to keep the tone light, Essie, I am serious when I say that we must thank the law, for if I had been forced to face her nakedly, divested of my legal powers, I might very well have failed you. For one thing the ambiguous look you gave me from your sick bed might have undermined my resolve. Your eyes from the deep well of your suffering welcomed me, but they also seemed to say that I had no right to intervene—moral right or psychological right—but I had my legal rights and I stood on those. So my gentlemen in white jackets whisked you away in a stretcher—hardly the right image for the rescue of the towered beauty by her prince charming. And Amyster was wise enough to retreat to higher ground. In fact she had not quite known what to do herself, she said, and was, though a bit ashamedly, glad that someone else had made a decision. She found it less agreeable that she was simultaneously being evicted from the apartment, and less agreeable still that she could not have her possessions until you returned to make division in the presence of an officer of the court. The locks, I told her, would be changed. Thus, Essie, I made her drink to the dregs my bitter legal prescriptions. She left with great dignity, promising that we would reunite under better circumstances. I thought not, having instructed hotel and hospital to reveal my whereabouts to no one. But she found me, and when you were clearly out of danger, I consented at last to meet her, agreeing on a neutral time and place, my hotel lounge at two. Our colloquy, my trial by combat with the mythical monster for the bound maiden, took almost three hours, the three longest hours of my fifty-seven years. And so desperate was the struggle that it seems to me the issue is still in doubt. You must be the final judge of that. But I am getting ahead of myself.

She came off the street in a long green gown and a white silken blouse that turned opalescent in the curious lighting of the lounge. She had pearls in her ears. And when she sat down across from me and took off her glasses, she was so extraordinarily beautiful that it almost took my breath away. To protect myself, I said inwardly: "The beauty is all my Essie's, veritably leeched from her flesh by this monstrous succubus." But what had I done except to impale myself even deeper on the paradox that already was bleeding away my courage—I mean that my love for you and your love for her were horribly entwined in her seductive person.

She began speaking in that undulant voice you have known so well—Lotus-eater, Siren, Nixie. And I thought: How utterly is this not Amyster, not Woeman. But I did not know whether it was a true alternate self or a purely theatrical concoction. I will tell you my judgment of that later. So I was desperately afraid of her, but I had wisely brought with me, as a talisman, a powerful belief. This is what it was: that whatever power of words, profession of love for you, sweet moisture of eye she might produce, her essence was the ravening void, and because of that void even I, weak and tremulous as I was without my legal armor, was ultimately stronger than she—a proposition sorely to be tested.

Essie, you know us legalists, how we mercilessly demand of our

witnesses microscopic accuracy of image, word-for-word rendering
of all that was said, etc. But here am I, unable to record verbatim
more than a small fraction of what she said to me, and mistrustful
of my recollection of all I saw. Perhaps my victory over her still
seems to me so narrow and uncertain that I cannot with equanimity
push my memory back into the rhythms of that remarkable voice.
But I will try, where I can.

She began by saying that you had let her be everything for you. She
was the child you never had, "conceived by the Word." And because
of this virgin birth she sang miraculously of things still hidden in the
bowels of earth. "I am her inner eye, her secret spelunker. All the
tunnels of the war-torn body which frightened Nurse Sarah I have
explored with unflickering candle." And then she had risen up and
was the light-handed husband you never had and the father, too,
you never had and the mother. "In the absolute dark, of unindi-
viduate being we lie twined indissolubly. In the morning we release
a butterfly of self onto the streets of the city and call it back at night
to the woven core of our love which our hearts never leave." And this
was her profound pun, that the poetry which rose from your twined
being made the universe. And she said a great deal more in this line.
Does it sound chaotic and farfetched here on my paper? You will
know how to recast it, recapture its marvelous melody. And you will
understand that when at last she finished this long paean, it seemed
to me that the words I had planned to speak would be nothing more
than a kind of floating ash blown across her beauteous vision as
from an alley fire. But speak I must. "Between the vision and its
incarnation fell the shadow of death. How do you explain that?"

She lit a cigarette, the fire orange and the paper purplish in that
silly light of the lounge. But such was the ambiance of her presence
that even that frightened me, as though she had power to skew the
spectrum. As it turned out, my single thrust had sunk deeper than I
knew. But at the moment I feared I was lost. Remember, I had
chosen the lounge as a rendezvous because it was a public place
demanding certain proprieties. But her opening speech had altered
everything. The bartender and the meager midafternoon clientele
seemed to me as removed as if they were projections, on clever
translucent screens, of personages who in reality were in other
places, perhaps other times. Thus we were utterly alone, beyond call
of ordinary mortals.

She wished to hurt no one, she said, in a vastly altered tone, much
more ordinary, to my relief; but I would soon learn that she had only
climbed down from one poetic pinnacle to ascend another even

more dizzying and terrible. She wished to hurt no one, but it was necessary to characterize the counterforces that worked against your happiness. "What was it that drove the child, like a homuncular Lear, out into thunderstorms?" (I had forgotten that curiosity of your childhood, Essie, forgotten that old Bessie once told Colin you were a changeling, a witch's child.) "Why did she ride wild Jack, embrace the swollen river, enter into combat against men, lay herself down in a loathsome marriage bed, and finally plunge into the hellfire of war? Because an older generation of child-eaters sent her on impossible missions in the hope of destroying her. But the subtlest of these conspirators, breathing on her his poisonous breath summer after slow summer, old serpent of the Mississippi, was an incestuous lover. This one wooed her with his 'messenger-birds,' birds that dipped their beaks in her heart's blood so that she could not love another." (So you had shown her my letters, Essie, as was proper—lovers should share everything.) But even the subtly amorous letters, she said, were not as wicked as my cunning sallies against other lovers. "For one poor lover he created the image of the labyrinth and set her down in the middle snorting and horned. And who but the incestuous one could play the hero of that scene, could follow the thread spun of the spittle of his own constant palaver?" In short, against such a family of death-dealers, the last one in particular, your vigilance had momentarily lapsed, a poisonous barb had pricked your heart, and you had sickened. In the hospital you were reasonably safe, but when you came out you would be vulnerable again. You would need her. Essie, I was stricken speechless. That image of the Minotaur I had once written to you but never mailed, and yet she had ferreted it out. Telepathy, divination, what? But she had thrown over me a shadow even deeper than the possibility of extrasensory powers, a shadow that cast everything beyond the table into a ghoulish gloom. All I could see was her face and beneath it the opalescent blouse like an image of unearthly light on ruffled water. The dark lips were saying: "Beware the green-eyed monster." And in my heart I was crying out to you: Essie, tell me quickly, did I imprison you in my affections? Never so unwilling a jailor, never one so anxious to give up the key. But you were not there to answer, and the dark lips were saying: "You always kill the thing you love." In another moment she would have taken you from me. I do not know what she would have done, what words would have passed. I only know I could feel you almost physically passing from me to her waiting embrace. So I had to speak. I said, "Yours is the ultimate sterility. Sweaty straining without issue. Endless naming of nothing to name, the animals in flight and the flowers rank. Words, words, words."

No, I did not ignite the air, did not exorcise that beautiful pearly face. It still hung there before me like a lamp of the moon. But my speaking gave me a little hope. I shut my eyes. I saw your hand, warm and still there on the hospital sheet where the sunlight lay boldly in a wide swath. I reached out and touched you. Then Amyster began to speak again. I opened my eyes. Her dark lunar lips eclipsed my sun. My soul, hunkering there in the shadows like a fear-frozen hare, shuddered. I can never forget those words. "You are going to instruct me in the arts of creation? Do you know who I am?" God knows I did not, Essie. Do not now. If she had said I AM THAT I AM, I could not have contradicted her. "I will tell you. I was born of earth, became a creature of the middle air, and later plumbed the bowels of my mother. In a moment I will show you the future. But, first, the past. One time when I was flying over the deserts of my childhood, I saw a black river, and beside it a beautiful rider on a white horse. I knew that someday the two of us would sit that stallion together and ford that stream." She is mad, I said to myself. But the words scraped about in my head like November leaves. "So when the time came I did my mating dance by the side of the road down which our warriors returned, because my mother told me my lover would be among the wounded. I crowed and danced such a madcap coxcomb's song as only my blackwater whitehorse rider could love — not knowing then that her left ear was stoppered with your chastely incestuous spittle." I must have winced. She reached out and touched me. I feared that hand on mine, but it seemed, to my great surprise, as warm as the one I had imagined lying on the sunny hospital sheet, and human. "That was only an aside. So when my lover came to me naked upon a white horse, we rode together across the black river and made on the other side such singing and wild whooping that the shades rose up and praised us. And we have mounted together into the sky and sung such ecstasy that the moon blushed. But all of this has only been a prelude to the time we ride into a white fire and consume each other utterly. And even that is only a prelude. We will rise again, a phoenix, flame and feather indistinguishable. And what flight could we not make after that?"

I was lost, Essie, blown on the wind of her words like dry husk toward an autumn flame. The barkeep and his trade posed motionlessly in the purple light that shone from behind the velvet valance — Amyster's Wax Museum of time past, my time, I as motionless as they. Well, twice before I had managed to speak. But this time there was not the slightest hope. I was a null. If I had opened my mouth I could not even have made that mouselike chittering which they say the souls of the dead make as they are ferried across. So I was lost, you were lost. You were hers. And then, the treasure hers for the taking, she cracked.

Maybe, paradoxically, it was the very frozenness which her words had created in me that defeated her. Maybe she thought she saw in my atrophied face stony stoicism, immovable opposition. At any rate her lips began to quiver. Her chest heaved and she began to weep. My senses came back to me. I saw the figures at the bar move and heard them make a burred noise. I smelled tobacco smoke and tasted the flat scotch on my tongue. The rug thickened under my feet and the cold slickness of the tabletop pressed itself against my fingers. So I was saved, because I was merely a ludicrous fat old man, sitting uncomfortably in a cocktail lounge beside a weeping younger woman. What tawdry images must have been in those turned heads at the bar! But Amyster began to recover herself. Her eyes crisped. I do not know what further flight she was capable of. I shudder to think, because I could not have survived it. I seized her hand and spoke to her. I said that she was an absolutely remarkable person, not remotely like any other I had ever known. But in another way, I said, I knew her of old. She was the demon lover of the old stories. In that mythic world she had her way with me. I gave her the victory without quarrel. I was the pompous avuncular adviser, fat and ineffective. But in this world the victory was mine. To wit, I was a rich man, I said, with many resources, all of which I would willingly array for the winning of your life and health. Therefore I had set people to watch. If I should learn that hereafter she ever approached you, even fleshlessly by letter or phone, I would build up around her such a legal, and if necessary extralegal, maze that she would never find her way out. In short let her keep to her haunts of the other world, where she had sway, for in this my vigilance wreathed around you a loving cordon impenetrable. I would like to think, Essie, that at that moment my leaden eyes recovered something of that green flashing which you have sometimes, perhaps only flatteringly, attributed to me. This I do know. She withdrew her hand and shrank away from me, down into that lair of the other world, where I did not dare to follow. Perhaps I only imagined it, but it seemed that she actually bared bright teeth. Amyster, I called after her, it is enough that you have invaded our dreams and stolen away our nights. It is more than enough that some ultimate day we will turn a corner, enter a door, and find ourselves again in your den, and this time without escape. But in the meantime, for whatever little time, I will have my days and my Essie will have hers. That is what I said and struck the table with my fist. So I was the secular judge of that day, Essie. And I will not yield to the judges of the underworld until I am forced to.

You will want to know of course, Essie, the precise facts which lie behind the threats I cast in Amyster's teeth. All were true. Private detectives in my hire watch you and watch her. Lawyers retained by me stand ready at my signal to prepare charges against her. The only falsification in my threats was one of omission, as you will already have surmised. That is, I stand ready to disband all of these adjutants when you advise me, for I have great hope that with Dr. Temple's help you are building up strength and wisdom which will stand proof against any revisitation of Amyster, whatever form it might take.

Well, Essie, I have filled much paper. My hand is cramped. Take it in your warm grasp. All of its recent deeds, well or ill performed, were lovingly done, for our old love's sake.

Dearest Carlton, now I fear the scales never can be balanced. You were always kind enough to say that I rode out to war for you and that you would have to spend a lifetime repaying me. But in truth, as I suspect you have always known, I rode out for myself, selfishly, compelled to explore that horror. But you rode out against Amyster for me. Yes, for me. I say it humbly, knowing nevertheless that nothing else could have tempted a wise one like you to challenge that darkness. So I remain eternally in your debt. I do not hope to repay you, because to do so I would have to find you in desperate need. So all I can do is say thank you.

I have read and reread your letter. Dr. Temple and I have made it the subject of several sessions. We agree that it does not matter that the Amyster I knew and the one you confronted are not quite the same. How could they be? The fact is that you saw deeply and acted correctly. However, in the heat of writing that marvelous letter, you left two questions unanswered. (Or did you, my sly old cat, leave those two little barbs, little knaps a-purpose? Dr. Temple thinks you may indeed have been so ingenious, for they are, from her point of view, *the* questions.) Was Amyster acting out real alternate selves or was she putting on pure theater? I think that I myself would have said the former. But Dr. Temple has pretty well convinced me (remember A. was once her patient too) that the truth lies some-

where in between. A. was essentially unformed. I tried to give her form, but I couldn't. So she was forever, in life and in poetry, trying new possibilities. Gide, incidentally, was a great hero of hers. But I was too weak to sustain her multiplicity. I began to lose my grip and go under. Now, you will be happy to know, I am back at work, only with a difference. Dr. Temple says that my experiences and insights are too valuable for the front office. I have become a "case recorder." I actually observe sessions and discuss results with Dr. Temple.

The other question you left hanging you will already have guessed the answer to. Did you really win the battle with A.? Of course you did. I have never seen her or heard from her again. She has not even shown up to get her clothes. Dr. Temple's prediction is that one day I will receive a letter which will tell of a new lover and a new book. It will be full of soft spite. And then a few years later, says Dr. Temple, we will read of her suicide. No one can handle so much chaos for very long. But I join you, Carlton, in your tribute to her. In fact I extend it. Not only does she possess our nights and our dreams and await us in death, she is, more than I ever was riding to war or you ever were riding against her, the ultimate rider against the night, the ultimate deep-river diver. Carlton, you remember I once wrote that I could not survive a parting from her, that if it happened you would not be able to pull me back from the sea of death. Yet I do seem to have survived. Here is how—and Dr. Temple knows it. A part of me rides with her yet, down the dark tunnels behind the bruised eyes of those who come to us too broken and loveless to go on alone.

Dr. Temple is a kind and clever old witch. Of course you can go to Tumwah next month, she says. I can get along without you for a few days. As though my own health were not in question. And perhaps it's not. But Tumwah at the moment seems to me such an alien place that it frightens me. Can I breathe the air there? Will I remember the language of my childhood? But you will be there, Carlton, to lend me your strong arm.

So in October of 1954 Carlton and Sarah joined the family and many of the townspeople of Tumwah to celebrate Colin's retirement. At Christmastime Hope sent out cards with a photograph of her four boys. On the one to Carlton she wrote a note.

Dear Carlton, what wonders you have done for Sarah. She looked like a queen. You looked like a Supreme Court judge (but not one of these new liberals) and she looked like a queen. Everyone said so. We were all so proud. Mama loved taking credit for having such a daughter who, she says, is practically running the most famous clinic in the West. But Daddy got tight and said something that made us all laugh. He said that it was clear to him that old Bessie was right. Sarah was not his and Mama's child. She was a foundling that Bessie brought in from the woods, left there by the royal witches, whatever they are. He said he wished he had made her tell the truth about it before she died. So you can see what a big thing it was the two of you coming. Out of room. All love. Hope.

V

A number of uneventful years passed. Sarah went on with her work at the clinic. Carlton in 1958 gave up his partnership and took a considerable financial loss to accept a seat as a federal judge. In a letter to Sarah he declared that he would not forget that the letter killeth and the spirit giveth life and that in court he would keep one eye on the law and the other on the future. In 1959 Carlton and Sarah returned to Tumwah for Colin's funeral. Martha, as widow, found it profoundly significant that he had died precisely at the biblical age of three score and ten in spite of having courted ruin and death at earlier ages. She herself would normally have two more years to live, but God had afflicted woman with longer life to punish her antics in the garden. The letters that Carlton, Hope, and Sarah wrote to each other were short and of settled affection. Even when in 1963 news came of the suicide of Amyster, there passed between Carlton and Sarah only gentle nods, as it were, of recognition and sad fulfillment. Then in 1965 Sarah wrote the following letter.

Dear Carlton, I have had occasion to look back over some of your letters. I'll tell you why in a minute. But first I have to ask pardon, my gentle judge, for a sin of omission. Do you remember that when you talked with A. she accused you of binding my heart with an incestuous love? You wrote in your account of the meeting that the accusation hit you so hard that you could not speak out to defend yourself. And I, unless I misremember, have never spoken of that in any letter since. Why was that? Perhaps I never wanted to deny the strength of my love for you under any circumstances, Carlton, even to exonerate us from incest. Well, I am not sure of my motives, but I am sure that you are blameless and that I ought to have said so long ago. Forgive me that omission. Before long I think I will know my motives and can report them to you. That is what I am writing to tell you, that at the age of fifty-three I discover, miraculously, that there are still two great adventures left to me. You have corrupted me with your flattering epic metaphors, Carlton. Suppose I tell you that I feel like

Lord Alfred's Ulysses. No, I am serious. After my spotted childhood, after my morbid marriage, after war, and after A., still two great adventures. One, of course, is death. The other I will already have embarked on by the time you receive this.

Some of the following is Dr. Temple's, some mine. We have talked so much that I can no longer distinguish. The surprising thing to me is that any of it (I mean aside from personal facts) is mine, that I have, as Dr. Temple constantly assures me, advanced her understanding of certain things. And now I am to be an emissary, as you said I was in the war. And I am to bring back understanding, as you also said I did from the war. I am going into my mind. But it is not only *my* mind. To begin another way. I have been dreaming again of Jack and the Black Warrior. I have been riding in the direction of the voice of someone who has gone before. It could be Daddy, or A. It is too distant to identify. And I always turn back. I lose courage. But, as Dr. Temple says, it is not only my white horse, my river, or my deceased loved one. In some peculiar way my childhood and my adventures in the war and with A. and, yes, my love of you, Carlton, have tended to sum up in my mind this whole generation of fear. Are you wondering what exactly I mean by "this whole generation of fear"? Our generation, of course. But is it possible that our generation has summed up the whole history of man as brute? In that case, maybe what Dr. Temple and I are trying to do is plunge down past this brutal history to the deep place of light which, you always said, , the center of life. So we have arrayed our unheroic powers: my reams, my old white horse, some crude potions from the phar-acopoeia of our time, and our strongest staff, Dr. Temple's wis-om and courage. Two aging and childless women in quest of othing short of the omphalos. What could be quainter, Carlton? nd I am afraid, of course. But we will attempt it. We will keep a ecord, we do not know in what form—something I will write or say r sketch, or some combination. And you will see it all. Dr. Temple agrees to that.

So this is why I have been rereading your old letters, Carlton, to ore up my courage with the beams of your optimism. You were too odest when you wrote that you vanquished A. only in this world, that in the other she was the victor. In fact you pursued her very deep. No doubt I will meet her again. And perhaps this time I can snatch her up onto Jack and ride her to where her snakes are beautiful hair again. It is clearer and clearer to me that every act of mine is an extension of my love for you, Carlton. And all of your vuncular advice, which you used modestly to offer and humorously

lament my ignoring, I have in essence taken. I take it now, searching
for light. I ride my poor old Jack, saddlebags stuffed with your letters
and love.

Immediately upon receiving this letter, Carlton sent Sarah a tele-
gram. "Good-bye and Godspeed, Essie my love, who never waits for
my valediction." He also wrote a note to Hope telling her that Sarah
had embarked on a difficult psychological experiment and that she
and Martha should not expect to hear from her for some time. But
he himself did not have to wait long for news of Sarah. She and Dr.
Temple were good to their word. In less than a week he began to
receive typed transcriptions, fragments chosen by Dr. Temple from
the various stages of Sarah's journey.

   . . . I am writing a poem again. It is a lament for the body of
my mother Martha standing naked by the little gas heater,
drying before dressing for my father's funeral. Stomach
creased, marsupial. Drooping dugs, withered bush. Broken
blue veins match the flame behind. This open gas fire, they say,
maddens. . . .
   Here is my sister Hope floating on her back like a big-bellied
island of easy entry. And here is my Uncle Carlton asleep in his
chair like a big tom. His glasses are pushed up on his forehead
where there are no eyes. Only I, the mischievous niece, know
that behind the pale and veined lids burns the green entry of an
endless tunnel. But I am not going to let old Bessie spank me,
because I did not laugh at my father's funeral and because she
stinks worse than a corpse and told stories on me. I am going to
get on Jack and ride away. . . . You can tell when a horse is
afraid of another beast. The ears quiver and the whinny is
high-pitched. But I would not let Jack shy off the day we found
the bull in old man Chrissum's second pasture. I made him
jump two stiles. And we ran that bull until he could only stand
smoking in the winter field. And I said, "Bull, if this was a
sword instead of a crop, I would get down and kill you as nice as
Manolete." And I wrote a poem, too, about the bull which
called attention to what has always been known, that a bull
steaming in a winter field looks exactly like a cloudy continent. I
gave the poem to my Uncle Carlton and he dropped it into his
deep green eye, where it lies yet. The only thing I have not
spoken of is the bodies that lie under the ground pierced by
bullets and the mad old man who drew pictures of apple trees

rotting in their hearts. I do not wish to speak of that. Let the earth have some secrets.

. . . This is one of the honey dreams. I can step slowly one two three. I can row slowly with my arms — stroke stroke stroke. But I will never get there against this tide. Is it the honey you put in my arm, doctor? I make a black shadow on the bottom, which hides all the little things. This is not going to work. I will not have a message for you when I get back. Everything down here is closed up tighter than a skin. What are the little things? Let me try to see. A path of white bones, leading to a skull, my Daddy's. A crab peeks out of the mouth. I do not know why but I am sure it is his. If I were a blind girl like that famous one I would know a face dead as well as alive. The fingers do not even have to enter the mouth. The other little things are my Uncle Carlton's green eyes. The honey does not allow me to bend over and peer down into them, but I know that they are laughing over my last poem. It is a wicked satiric poem. I got it out of my anthropology class. It is about old BM, M, M in Melanesia. About the maidens by the sea, by the sea, by the spermious sea. Rare but not unique, especially in certain foamy seasons, seasons, seasons for virgins to conceive. Do not under any circumstances show this to mother or father, say laughing Carlton's green eyes. No. But why did I, when the water was all my love, let Albert lay his pissy hands upon me, fill the sea with organ sounds, break the coral chapels? That was a poem, too, that your naughty niece wrote about second skins, Carlton, and never showed to you. . . .

. . .Two are up here I never expected to meet. One is Hope's Charles hunkered on the precipice. Sometimes he shifts his weight nervously from foot to foot and rotates his shoulders, but not the roaringest Andean wind of all our lives, Carlton, will ever bear this creature aloft. You said he could see far. Perhaps he can between the times the membranes and the fluids soup over his eyes. But what good is it to see and not be able to fly? You remember how you would not let me admire *I have slipped the surly bounds of earth on laughter-skittered wings?* I admire it still. The other is old Bessie sewing in the sun. I dance around her and tease her. You can't sew, Bessie, because you can't see to do it. Go away, child. You can't sew, Bessie, I can see the threads going ever-whichway. Go away, before I lay my

hand to your bottom. I don't need that old dress anyway, Bessie.
I'm going to fly away. No, you ain't. Not even a witch's child like
you can fly. But didn't I fly, Carlton, on my laughter-skittered
wings out of Bessie's reach? And later on Jack? And later didn't
at least one or two of my poems mount up into your eyes? And
later, didn't my letters join continents? Tell me I flew, Carlton,
in spite of that old black woman. . . . Once I flew on the back of
another, our lovely A., the longest dreaming of my life. Dark
things can be high too, Carlton, and I knew she would be here
with her great wind of words. They cannot drive her down.
From the longest falls her defiance mounts up again. I do not
even ask that she recognize me, dazzled by so many assaults on
the sun. Because she already told me once: when you were just a
little flower stalk of a girl making your slow way on Jack the first
time down the river bank, your knees quivering against his
flank and your arms trembling against the pull of the reins, I
was already in you. . . .

Be sure to tell Carlton that, as only once before, I did not tell him
quite all of the truth, that I was dying of cancer before we
began—the little sea-bottom creature that has shuttled back
and forth between Daddy and me for many years. It is fitting.
We share what we can. . . . Who could guess? Wait. Father
Simms once told me of one who believed the continuity of the
inanimate, vegetative, and animate worlds. So I ought not to be
surprised that mute stones still hold the scream and thunder of
bombs. Put your ear to a conch shell and hear the roar of ocean.
Put your ear to a stone of Coventry and hear the clangor of war.
And do not tell me, my green-eyed uncle, that the sound is really
behind my capped ear, that the war trills in my blood and
clamors in my heart. I will write you a posthumous poem that
you must publish to all, that the stones of graves must be chosen
with the greatest care, examined by poets and paleontologists
or we know not to what hells of din, from trumpeting mam-
moths to keening shells, we damn the dead. But how will I
explain, Carlton, why the touch of all my doomed soldier-lovers
hissed with a fire so beyond passion, even beyond love? Because
some did think they loved me. The war had ignited them. Some,
even before they were dead, floated around London like fox fires
sporting the green glow of their putrescence. . . . Some cities
lean against the sea, last projection of westering or eastering.
Others, like mine, hold it in a mild embrace, calm its clamor,

and nest with it. That is the beginning of another posthumous poem which tells how a girl was raped by wild horsemen and thus had preview of the making of flesh. I already told who my child was, doomed in her green years like my consumed soldiers. This is the hardest way to follow, doctor, down into the fire, where she waits for me. I do not think I can tell it. I can tell you that the comical islanders and my sister at bridge tell it true, that the first one is a searing fire and the rest come teeming easily from the broken horn. But I do not want to lie to you. At first I did not have even an intimation that my lover was my child. I only knew the ecstasy of body when she came over me like a fiery-feathered thing. Here is where we ought to have been practicing those tricks of free drawing. I would choose a stylus varying in width according to the pitch of the hand. I would dip it in red ink and make such beautiful calligraphy and flourish that it would be the red-letter poem of all poems of love. You could read in it curling ecstasy, laced limbs, lovers' sighs like woven fires, and all else pertaining thereunto. . . . I am near the end, doctor, most fortunate in my double death. Drowning, see all past pass before me in an instant. Consumed by fire, know that the stars curve inward to consummate a second gathering. Tell Carlton, my green fire, that in my embrace I reconcile him to my red fire, that we three make a blanched and beautiful noon.

Once more Carlton used his legal powers in Sarah's behalf. Cowing courthouse, morticians, and family with complex claims of executorship, he had Sarah buried in a plain pine box in a stoneless grave, unbled and unembalmed, by the bank of the Black Warrior. In deference to the memory of Colin and to the feelings of Martha and Hope, friends of the family, brooking Carlton's eccentricity, walked the overgrown path to the grave in the mounting June heat to watch the clergyless noon burial and to hear the last words, of Carlton's own composing. "Here lies the body of Sarah, whose love for us we still see but through a glass darkly."

The Lover

Here is a beginning. I am a tow-headed boy in the depression South, walking a dusty road by a creek. I am with two other boys, brothers. The older and taller is Abner Ellis, Junior. The one my age and height is Frank. Abner is seventeen. Frank and I are fifteen. Their mother is thousand-eyed. In my dreams I see her beautiful ocellated face fan out and cover the stars. She knows me, knows that I desire Frank. Abner has no inkling. Frank himself does not understand it. But she knows.

If she had been of a higher caste she undoubtedly would have had a significant history. Maybe she forfeited celebrity when she married Dr. Ellis upon his graduation from Tulane medical school, but I don't think so. Marie Crevet. There are no socially prominent Crevets in New Orleans, not even a marginal family who might marry an extraordinarily beautiful daughter upward into the ruling classes.

Anyway, she came as a bride to Laurelie in south Alabama, melon capital of the world, a patchwork of loamy fields and red clay hillocks, rank with the sweat of blacks and raucous with the hymns of Baptist farmers. No apparent destiny here for her beauty. The doctor liked seclusion. Probably he didn't trust the gentlemen of larger towns. Who could blame him? He was an unlikely husband for such a bride—gangly, big-eared, deformed by an Adam's apple that rode under his collar like a thieved melon in the toils of a creek, and crack-voiced, as though his glottis were arrested in perpetual adolescence. Everyone knows the type, "raw-boned, Lincolnesque." Everyone has read dozens of such biographical sketches. He made the archetypal sacrifices of the poor country boy to secure his degree in medicine: scrimped to save his tuition while still helping to support a widowed mother, studied blear-eyed by midnight oil for his entrance examinations, etc. By the time I knew him he'd already had one heart attack. There was good reason for it, other than his youthful sacrifices—an exhausting practice among blacks bloated by fatback and cornmeal, among gnarled fundamentalist dirt farmers too guilt- and God-ridden to come in time with their ripe tumors. So I despised him from the first for the constant outpouring of his charity, which left us in his home only the rind of his love.

I was his nephew, sent down in the summers from a motherless home in the great city of steel, Birmingham, by a sodden coal-blackened father. And it was I finally who provided the occasion for the heroism which such beauty as my aunt's inevitably has exacted of it.

Marie Crevet Ellis bore to her husband two sons, Abner and Frank. Abner was his father's son—blue-eyed, willowy, an effortless charmer of girls. Frank was his mother's son, dark and beautiful. He was marvelously hirsute, his nostrils dark and densely tendriled, his face shadowed below high cheekbones. His chest and limbs and even his back bristled with hairs that made beautiful black rivulets when he rose like a young sea god from our creek. But such dark beauty was uncouth in those parts, and so he was lonely.

So was my aunt lonely, in constancy to her faith. She attended mass every Sunday afternoon. It was celebrated for her and two old women by a circuiting priest at a side altar of the Episcopal church, rented no doubt for the occasion through an uneasy alliance of prelacies in that benighted stronghold of fundamentalism. In the dead heat of July and August she still put on her black dress, covered her head with a black mantilla, and walked through the downtown streets to her devotions. The ice-cream eaters in front of the drugstore and the old men on the hotel verandah stared, but they said nothing. I myself would have liked to ask: why this penitential black in the seasonless summer, Lent past and Advent yet to come? What was she guilty of? Failing to rear her sons as Catholics? Later she had more to confess.

I began to succeed in my advances toward Frank. But I can say this for myself: as unthinkable as were my desires in that time and place, I always kept in view his good. When his gentle loneliness began to unfold to me, I touched it always with delicate love. If he wanted to tell me that I was beginning to trespass on his feelings, he only had to speak my name with a hint of admonition and I would stop. Still, I confess, my yearning outstripped the slow melting of his reserve. I found it more and more difficult to guard my feelings, even in the presence of others. Once at supper my uncle, noting our silence, suddenly said, "All right, Frank and Joe, what's the big secret?" Caught completely off guard, I blushed hotly. "What are they up to, Marie?"

My aunt's dark eyes looked straight into mine. "Oh, I think they've found something at the creek."

"They spend enough time down there," said Abner. "It must be a mermaid." His own wit surprised him and he guffawed.

"We don't have any secret, Father," said Frank with a voice as clear as a bell.

"Good. Then let's talk to each other instead of acting like we're at a wake."

I don't know where the conversation went from there, but I do remember that when my frightening embarrassment had passed, I was suddenly suffused with great pity—for the man with the youthfully cracked voice and the dying body; for my beautiful aunt, whose dark eyes pleaded with me to spare her son; for Frank, who was forced now for the first time to lie to his father; and even for Abner in his innocent ignorance. I should have leaped up and cried that I was the serpent in their bosom, that they must scotch me or be ruined. Instead, I excused myself on pretense of nausea. And after that I made ready a face to meet any comment that might touch my relationship with Frank.

For a while I kept my distance from Frank, sensing his revulsion toward the lie he had told his father, though it was not a deep lie. After all, we had only feasted eyes, touched hesitatingly. So, a few days later I resumed my courtship, and I was overjoyed to discover that the lie had left no taint, that the warm promise of his slow yielding was still there. One day when we had swum a while nude in the Blue Hole, we lay together on a flat rock at the lip of the deep pool. We embraced. I felt the hairs of his back, exposed to the motley sun in the trees, dry and grow erect. But after a few moments he disengaged himself and rolled over on his back. I leaned beside him, my body intensely hot. He looked up through half-closed eyes. "What is this thing, Joe?"

Then I knew that he felt, as I did, a palpable presence embracing us. I might have called it the god of love. I actually thought of that, but I only said, "I don't know. I don't have to know." I leaned forward and kissed his teat in its nest of black hair and it hardened against my lips.

"I do need to know," Frank said.

"Tell me when you find out."

Do I make it sound as though there were only these episodes of pursuit? Not at all. We played American Legion baseball. Abner was a star pitcher. We flew model airplanes. Frank's, the most delicately balanced, stayed up longest. My aunt caught us and made us mow, weed, shell peas. My forte was frogging. Many nights we waded the creek. Frank carried the gunny sack. Abner hypnotized the frogs with the flashlight, and I snared them in the long net that I myself had woven, hooped, and secured to an oak sapling. My uncle loved the legs breaded and fried, but he had to cook them himself because my aunt could not bear to watch the final contractions in the pan. Of course, we boys one night saved out a hapless creature for the classic experiment. When it was newly dead, we passed through it a small battery current. The twitching of legs bewitched us. We tumbled over each other and gyrated splay-legged about our bunk room— three adolescents having a saurian orgy. But even in that crude prank, as in the chores and play of every day, the current of my love for Frank never for one moment ceased to galvanize my heart.

Besides my aunt's vigilance, there was one other threat to my love for Frank—a series of monologues that Abner delivered in the bunk room when he got home from dates. He would lie on his back in his bunk and light up cigarettes that he had stolen at the drugstore. In the morning the room would have a dreadful smell, but Abner's nicotine crimes were never detected because my aunt was forbidden by my uncle ever to set foot in the bunk room. His motives were twofold, he explained. No lady should have the offensive job of cleaning up after boys. Conversely, boys must have their sanctuary. Every Saturday afternoon my uncle himself inspected our quarters. For this we carefully spruced up, or titivated, as the doctor was fond of saying. Otherwise, the room remained a congeries of clothes, balls, bats, string, balsam scraps, etc. So Abner would light up one cigarette after another. He didn't inhale and probably didn't even like the taste. But he obviously liked the big white plumes of smoke that rose up into the moonlight at the window, bequeathing his words a ghostly presence and wreathing about them the wraith of eroticism and nocturnal mystery. Here was the essence of his story repeated over and over with little variation. He had two girl friends, Betty and Harriet. Betty, the hotel manager's daughter, was only a decoy, Abner said. Harriet, a rich farmer's daughter, was his true love. Frank and I had seen them often, of course, and they were true in appearance to the character that Abner assigned them in his midnight monologues. Betty was a saucy little thing with black hair and dark eyes. Harriet, on the other hand, was blond, the perfect Aryan match for Abner. Betty must have absorbed what little there was to learn of vice in Laurelie, living in a hotel suite and helping with the travelers, because a great number of Abner's narratives dealt with her innovations in kissing—frenching, the love-bite, the lobe-lolly, etc.

I found all this repulsive, but I wondered what Frank thought. He made no signs in the dark, no response until one night he pressed Abner for details of a rare kiss from Harriet. "It was a soul kiss,

Frank. Our tongues never touched, but it was a soul kiss, better than all of Betty's kisses put together."

"What do you mean, a soul kiss?"

"I mean the kind of kiss that makes you feel like you aren't there any more. You feel like you left your old self behind, like snake slough."

"Where did you go, into Harriet?" A dense fountain of smoke shot up toward the ceiling. "It's hard to tell, Frank. I did sort of feel like I was dropping down into her mouth if you can think of a mouth as big as night. But I wasn't thinking *this is Harriet*. I was just . . . going out of myself."

The halting of Abner's ending was more eloquent than his words. Silence descended on us. But I lay awake thinking: what has Frank learned from this? That one kiss from a true love is infinitely better than all the inventions of promiscuity? That the only true love for a man is a woman? But I found that I could not imagine for myself Frank's thoughts or desires, probably because my own were so simple: I wanted him.

That night's exchange with Abner had a profound effect on Frank. The next afternoon, when we were alone at the Blue Hole lying in shoaling water on the lip of the pool, I caressed his thigh, but he set my hand aside. "Don't touch me, Joe, and don't talk to me about it for a while." I feared he meant forever. I feared it with a wintry contraction of the heart that numbed all my senses. And I felt helpless, forbidden to plead my case with the one I loved. He was determined to work things out alone. My uncle noticed Frank's abstraction and joshed him. "Any chance of you getting out of the dog days of August, boy?" Yes, the summer was almost over, and I knew in my bones that it was this summer or never. I knew that if I could possess Frank even once, I could go back to my smoky city and my sodden father and sing in my heart despite their sooty faces. But if I went back with my desire all locked up, I could not live until another summer.

My aunt watched. One night I overheard her say, "I know what it is, my Frank. I know you will choose the good way." They were in her sewing room. I couldn't see them, but I imagined her taking his hand, stroking his hair, speaking dark eyes to dark eyes, excluding me forever. My heart raged against her. But I made no sign. I knew that if anything caused Frank to suspect I did not love her he would shut me out of his heart forever. So I was the serpent under the flower, waiting for something to come my way. And just when my patience was wearing dangerously thin, I was rewarded. The one who had almost ruined me gave me new hope—dear crude Abner.

My good fortune came on a Tuesday night. Abner was eating with Betty at the hotel and then they were going to the movie. Later, Frank and I learned that her parents were out of town for the night. From Abner's excitement I might have guessed as much, but there was something else on my mind. At supper my uncle had revealed that a much loved fellow doctor over in Minnville was hopelessly ill.

"Physician, heal thyself," I said. The moment the words were out I was horrified. It was as though a demon had spoken through my mouth. My uncle lay down his knife and fork. "The reason he is dying, Joe, is that he has worked himself to the bone for the people of Minnville. He couldn't turn away a sick nigger on Christmas morning." He spoke sharply.

"That's what I meant, Uncle Ab, about small-town doctors. Their patients take everything."

"Joe's right, Abner. You all work too hard." Pity and love streamed out of my aunt's eyes: for the husband with the slightly ashen face whose death would not lag far behind his friend's, for the son in whose dark eyes toiled warring images of awakening sex, and, yes, even for the perverse nephew whose thwarted love tipped his tongue with involuntary malice. She was our *mater dolorosa*. But I couldn't love her, not even for redeeming in Frank's eyes my wayward remark.

After supper the house seemed full of gloom. Halfheartedly I suggested frogging. To my surprise Frank agreed. Down at the creek we waited for the deepening dark to bring the sound of the big croakers. I had one of Abner's cigarettes, which I lit as soon as we had settled ourselves on a rock. Frank must have been surprised because I had never smoked before, but he said nothing. The smoke made a pale image against the moonless sheen of the creek. "Want a drag?" Maybe I hoped that mixing spit on the cigarette paper would seal our lips.

"No."

A moment later I threw the cigarette into the creek and spat after it. "I don't know what Abner sees in those things."

We waded into the creek. Frank went ahead with the flashlight. I followed him closely with my net. The croaker sack was tied over my shoulder. One by one I dropped the big frogs into it. But when we had maybe a half-dozen, I began to be invaded by a curious feeling of deep kinship with the frogs—slimy singers of unmelodious love

songs flung into a hairy darkness to writhe hopelessly until a ham-
mer delivered them from confusion. So strong became this projec-
tion that it grew almost hallucinatory. The flashlight beam did not
hypnotize them more than their glistening eyes fixated me.

"Are you going to get this one or not, Joe?"

"No. It's a mama full of eggs. We got enough. Let's quit."

Back at the house I pretended to knot the neck of the sack before I
dropped it outside the bunk-room door. But I didn't. I knew the frogs
would wriggle free. But could they find the creek a half-mile away?
Could they follow its sound or smell? Or would the sun catch them
struggling lost in the crab grass and thickets? It was do or die for
them once more, just as it had been the moment before I netted
them, when they made that last jump. Some had cleared the hoop
and won freedom, but these had landed in my net. That's what I
determined to do now, make my leap. In just a moment, when we
were both naked, I would take Frank into my arms as gently but as
strongly as I could—my fatal leap of love.

Abner saved me at the last possible moment, bursting in on our
nakedness. We had been undressing in the near dark, by the small
nightlight—like white-bellied frogs, I was thinking, when the edge
of the flashlight beam first touches them. Abner's bunk was closest
to the door. He went straight to his bed light, turned it on, and
looked at us with an expression of wild triumph. I shook fearfully.
Somehow, I thought, his dull eye had spied me out, detected the
truth in our surprised nakedness. But it was quickly obvious that I
had misunderstood. The wild triumph was something he brought
from the hotel, where he had been in Betty's bed. He quickly flung off
his clothes and stood before our tall mirror inspecting himself
minutely.

"What's going on?" said Frank, his voice already touched with
disapproval.

"I was in her, in her." I looked at Frank. Disgust narrowed his eyes
and turned down the corners of his mouth. So I pressed Abner with
pretended innocence.

"Who?"

"Betty." He was still admiring himself in the mirror.

"In the car?"

"In her room at the hotel." He turned around suddenly and threw
himself with a groan face down on his bed as though onto some
palpable afterimage of Betty's body. Frank turned away. I followed
his lead. A moment later we sat simultaneously on our beds.

"You won't believe it when you finally get some," he said. A tone of coarse tutelage crept into his voice, but when he turned and looked at us, that changed radically. "What the hell's the matter with you two?" Neither of us answered. "You, Frank," he said, "what are you looking like that for?"

"Why don't you go take a shower?" I had never heard Frank's voice so hard.

"Take a shower!" He sat up suddenly. "Take a shower when I saved the perfume for you boys?" I would not have guessed that Abner could be so sardonic. But he had obviously seen the utter disgust in Frank's face, and it infuriated him. He leaped from his bed and threw himself on Frank. I saw the naked limbs of the two brothers writhing together strenuously as Abner deliberately smeared on his brother the secretions of love. Then there was suddenly a cry. Frank had driven his knee into Abner's groin. Abner fell to the floor with a groan and lay there doubled up. Frank hurried into the bathroom. I heard the instant hiss of the shower. After a while he came back and put on his pajamas. Abner was now lying supine on his bunk with the back of his hand over his eyes. "Don't touch me," he said. I had been wondering which of them would say it first.

The next afternoon, as the two of us lay naked in the shallows at the edge of the Blue Hole, Frank allowed me to lave him with cool water. I touched him everywhere, chastely. I was consoling him, of course, and washing away Abner's bestiality. But I was also making him ready for my embrace. All my intuition assured me that on the next afternoon would come the full consummation of our love. Yet it was not to be. When we returned to the house we found my aunt and uncle making arrangements necessitated by the death of the doctor's colleague in Minnville. My aunt, who lay in bed, was saying, "I don't feel well enough to go, but you go, and take the boys. They ought to be there. Jep has been like an uncle to them."

"I can't leave you alone, Marie," said the doctor.

"It's nothing serious, Abner, and besides, I've got Joe."

I had even then an inkling of the truth about my aunt's illness, but I did not reflect on it because I was so upset by the prospect of being separated from Frank.

At last, at my aunt's insistence, my uncle agreed. They would have to spend one night away, no more. And before they drove off, my uncle laid upon me the usual charge: I was the man of the house in his place and must see that nothing happened to my aunt. I promised and then watched them leave. Abner assumed the older brother's prerogative and sat in the front seat beside his father.

Frank sat alone in the back, keeping his eyes constantly on me as a kind of promise until the car turned out of the driveway.

I sat in the living room that afternoon as my uncle had instructed me. I was also to sleep in the guest room that night with the door open so that I would never be out of earshot of my aunt's voice. About three, an old black woman came to the kitchen door. A half-dozen sacks hung from her shoulders. "Field peas, crowders, black-eyed peas, snaps, butter beans," she sang through the screen.

I hurried out to the kitchen. "Be quiet," I said. "Mrs. Ellis is sick."

"Lemme see her then."

I had run into this old black before and she had always looked at me curiously out of her rheumy brown eyes. She was either addled or preternaturally wise. She made me nervous. "Didn't you hear what I said? Go away. If you wake her up, I'll tell the doctor when he gets back." Too late. I heard my aunt's bare feet on the floor behind me. "It's all right, Joe. I'll speak to her." I went off into the dining room but I hid behind the door and listened.

"Hello, Granny. What do you have today?"

"That one say you sick." Why did she say *that one*? It gave me a start. Was she pointing at the dining room doorway, knowing I was there? Or did she say *that one* because she considered me a creature unnameable? I listened.

"You want me to send Seth with some of the black pot?"

I almost burst out laughing. Obviously the hag regularly sent this concoction to my aunt, a doctor's wife and a Catholic still clinging to some old Creole superstition. But if I had known then what I know now, I would not have been tempted to laugh. I listened. My aunt said something in a hushed voice. All I caught was the insistent concluding phrase, "You remember."

"I remember, Miss Marie, if you sho' that's what you want." My aunt apparently was sure, because the old woman left. I retreated quickly to the living room, where my aunt now came instead of returning directly to her room. "I'm sorry," I said. "I tried to keep her from waking you up."

"I wasn't asleep. It's too hot." Her cheeks had a hectic flush, and pinpoints of perspiration moistened her upper lip. She stood before me as if dazed. The light from the window shone through her sheer nightgown except where the cloth folded upon itself, so that I saw the outline of her body broken only here and there by thin streaks of shadow. It was beautiful in silhouette. In the flesh it would have the same delicate ivory as the skin of her arms. But I didn't go far with this imagining. Something in her manner put me on guard. For the first time I got a definite intimation that she had contrived for the two of us to be alone so she could separate me from Frank permanently. She must have guessed the day after Abner's midnight abominations that our relationship had resumed with a passion. After a few moments, saying nothing further, she walked slowly and not quite steadily down the hall to her room.

Now my mind began to work with a fierce heat, assembling a jumble of possibilities. Yet even in those first stages of thought, chaotic as they were, I had no doubt that I could pierce my aunt's intentions. If that seems too precociously self-confident for a boy of fifteen, remember: I had a mother who had been beaten to death by poverty and abuse, a father who was a villainous drunk with the strength of an ox, and wretched schoolmates who watched for every opportunity to humiliate me because I learned fast and whetted my tongue on their stupidity. It was only quick perceptions that enabled me to escape the fate of my mother, the sister whom the doctor had not saved. So I sat in the chair in my uncle's living room with an unread book in my lap. Here is what I had to think about. What was it that my aunt had ordered from the old black? Was it more of the same potion that already was causing her to change—some vial of it left from a much earlier episode which the old black had to fetch up from memory? I thought it must be. But why? Why make herself woozy and strange? It must relate to Frank and me, but how?

I let the questions tumble about in my head. Meanwhile I listened carefully for any noise which would signal a secret delivery by Granny's Seth. I asked myself more questions. If behind the potion and the mysterious behavior was the intention of separating Frank and me, why hadn't she gone about it more directly? Why not plead with my uncle to send me home? He wouldn't refuse her. Or why not call Frank in and tell him that he must break off from me? There was such a strong bond between them that she would inevitably be persuasive. But even as I considered these possibilities, I understood why she wouldn't accept either. The separation must come from us somehow. Otherwise, Frank would be left with crudely detached emotions which later might attach themselves, even more tenaciously, to a similar partner. Perhaps she was also concerned in this way for me. That settled that. But if severance was her goal, how did the potion-induced change fit? Was she going to tell me that my perverse love of Frank was driving her to addiction? That would explain why she ordered from the hag not curative black pot but some potion of different effect. On the other hand, she would know that it would be very difficult to convince me that she was so suddenly and deeply stricken. And even if she could convince me, was that likely to separate me from Frank? She must have known that my passion was strong beyond virtually any compunction. Here I came to the end of my thinking. I was confronted by possibilities none of which seemed quite right. So there was nothing to do now but listen and watch. I would find the answer. I was confident.

For supper, at her request, I brought my aunt a dish of chilled consommé and a glass of iced tea. I tasted both before taking them to her. The dark consommé surprised my tongue. I had never tasted it before. Its rich saltiness suffused my mouth, startling me, bringing back a dim memory of the taste of blood.

"What are you having, Joe?" my aunt said, sitting up, setting the tray carefully on her lap. She seemed more alert, more herself, except that her solicitude for once sounded a false note.

"I already had a double-decker sandwich."

"Then you can sit with me."

I took a chair by the window. The sun was down, but the yard was still full of the gentle gray light of the long August dusk. I looked at my aunt, lovely in the failing light, her thin blue nightgown darker now against the white sheet and the pale ivory of her throat. But it was her eating that arrested me. She spooned up the consommé very slowly, allowing each globule to melt on her tongue before she took the next, hand and mouth moving as if in the slow rhythm of a trance. But the uncanny thing was that my own mouth began to salivate, to fill up with salty flavor. So powerful was the taste that I feared I was being hypnotized. All my other senses were dimmed by the rich sensation in my mouth. Then a bizarre thought came to me: the consommé contained the potion. Seth had somehow slipped it by me.

"I'm not much company, am I, Joe?" She smiled. "But the consommé was so good." She put the glass of iced tea on the table by the bed. "You can take the tray now please."

When I approached the bed, she sat forward. "Here. Give me a kiss, poor boy, left to take care of an ailing aunt." I bent down and took the tray, offering her my cheek. But she turned my chin gently with her fingers and kissed me lightly on the lips. I went away to the kitchen careful not to lick the trace of salty saliva her kiss had left on my lips. At the sink I washed my mouth out and scrubbed my lips roughly with the back of my hand. Then I went to the back door and breathed deeply, but the air was not cool yet though dark was descending rapidly.

I was just beginning to work again at unraveling my aunt's intentions, which were growing clearer now, when Seth suddenly appeared around the corner of the house and stopped at the foot of the steps. I looked down at him. "What took you so long? Mrs. Ellis needs the medicine." I held out my hand.

Seth shuffled. "My granny say give it to Miss Marie herself."

"All right then. You'll have to come back to her bedroom." Seth shook his head. "One way or the other," I insisted, continuing to hold out my hand but at the same time making room for him on the steps if he chose to enter the house. After a long pause he finally handed me the potion. It was a small glass vial about as big as my thumb. "I'll see that she gets it," I said. But he just stood there. "I said I'll see that she gets it." He left then. The fast-falling dark swallowed him up—head, torso, and limbs first, then the colorless cotton of his short pants.

By the kitchen light I examined the potion. It was about the color and consistency of molasses. In fact I suspected that it really was mostly molasses. I unscrewed the cap and smelled it—saccharine and bitter at the same time. I smiled—ground bone of bird's leg, frog's eye, drop of woman's blood. You don't catch me, Aunt. I hurried to her bedroom, anxious to see her reaction to my knowledge of this folly.

"What is it, Joe?"

"Seth brought you something." I walked to the side of the bed and handed the vial to her. Then I stepped to the window and called, "You can go now, Seth. She has it." I had heard him rustle in the bushes. Now he burst out with a great thrashing and raced across the yard. I laughed and turned back to my aunt. She was smiling. I could barely see her face now. "You won't tell on me, will you, Joe?"

"What is it?"

She made a high girlish laugh that I had never heard from her before. She was holding the vial in both hands next to her bosom as though it were some tiny creature, a bird or a mouse. "It's a magic potion."

"What's it supposed to do?" I spoke harshly, feeling that I had a definite advantage now.

"It's dream medicine. It makes me dream wonderful dreams and wake up all new."

"Let's turn the light on and look at it," I said, dropping my words as heavily as I could on the songlike lilt of her voice. If the bed lamp were on, the light would reveal the lines in her face, the neck and arms beginning to go sinewy. It would show those simple hands with the unpainted nails foolishly clutching the old black's worthless concoction. It would be the end of her plot against Frank and me.

"No. The light would hurt my eyes." She spoke absently as though she had to fetch her mind back from distant imaginings. Then she sat forward a little on the bed, held the vial out, and unscrewed the cap.

"Molasses," I said disdainfully.

She put a little of the viscid fluid on her finger and touched it to her tongue. "Yes," she said. "Yes." Not, of course, assenting to me but affirming that the formula was correct according to taste. She took several more drops from finger to mouth.

"Molasses," I said.

"Take some, Joe. Taste it."

"Why? I'm not sick."

"It doesn't hurt anybody to dream, especially if things are out of tune."

"Nothing is out of tune with me."

"Yes there is, Joe. We know that, don't we?"

"No."

"What a bad trait in one so young." She tossed herself back and made a little bumping noise on the headboard.

"What?"

"Holding on to something you ought to let go of, especially when there's so much else."

"I never had much, Aunt Marie. So I hold on to anything I get."

"And being foolishly afraid of something nice, something different from anything you've ever had."

"I'm not afraid."

"Yes you are. You're afraid of me. You're afraid of my dream medicine. You say it's molasses, but you think it's a love potion."

That made me swallow hard because it showed that she already knew what I was thinking. So she was ahead of me. She had the advantage. "I'm not afraid," I repeated doggedly.

"Here then." She sat forward and streaked the end of a finger thickly with the black liquid. I hesitated. She licked it off herself, but quickly made a new smear. "If you're going to take him away from me, Joe—in a room that I can't even enter—don't be a common thief in the night, a low miner's son. You're better than that. Win your love. Have courage. Here." I stepped over, took her wrist, and licked the viscid fluid off her finger. It tasted like molasses. "Am I supposed to take more?" She shook her head, sadly I thought. I didn't feel any effect. Of course. It was just an old hag's silly concoction. I began to be a little sorry for my aunt, having to put on this stupid act with dim lights and sheer nightgown. And suddenly the wrist I held felt as brittle as a bird's wing. I dropped it.

"Kiss me goodnight, Joe." I bent and kissed her lightly on the lips. "Now go to sleep. You will dream of me and I will dream of you. In our dreams we will settle with each other."

"I always dream of Frank," I said.

"If you dream of him tonight, then you have won, Joe." She spoke very simply.

I left then. I went straight to the back steps and sat down. This was my fixed resolve: if the potion did begin to work on me, I would run to the creek and throw myself in. But nothing happened. A high breeze in the moonless sky stirred the tops of the pines. The crickets made great bursts of chirruping and then sank into silence, on and off as they sometimes will, I don't know why. When I was sure that the potion was a fake, I went into the guest room. I undressed and put on my pajamas and then opened the door as my uncle had instructed. Down the hall my aunt's door was closed and no light shone underneath. I lay in bed listening to the crickets and the passing of an occasional car along the road at the end of the long front walk. For a while I was too uneasy to sleep. But it was not fear. It was this—my aunt, self-hypnotized by her own curious behavior and by her irrational belief in the potion, might do something horribly embarrassing for us both. But the house remained quiet, and after a while I fell into a light and dreamless sleep.

Sometime much later I awoke to the sound of my aunt's crooning. It was like nothing I had ever heard before—high, piercing, unearthly, coming from no particular direction, and burring my head as though a fatal earwig were boring into my brain. It unnerved me badly. I got out of bed and stepped into the hall. My aunt's door was still shut and dark. The crooning was almost constant, but in the short silences I heard the stillness of the night. The crickets were quiet. I went out into the kitchen and shut the door behind me. There was a moment during which I heard the comfortable low rattle of the refrigerator. But the crooning quickly resumed. I went out on the landing of the back steps and shut the kitchen door behind me. At last I heard only the mild susurrus of the pines. She wouldn't follow me there and I could doze until morning leaning safely against the door. As I grew drowsy, I began to fill my mind with sweet images of Frank lying naked in the creek, his penis wavering under the light current and the hair of his body slanting downstream like deep green water grasses. But soon I went into a black sleep where even my unconscious marked no time so that when I awoke, or thought I awoke, it was into the body of a borderless night. I was lying on my back looking up. The wind in the pines had become water among dark tresses. Frank was gone. My aunt was bending over me. Her mouth, even in the black night, was red. It came down on my lips hot and salty. I began to throb. I felt the creamy essence of my desire rise for her as she stroked me with hands as gentle as the water winds of my dream. So she had been right. Why cling to Frank when there was this? I slipped out of my pajamas, entered the kitchen, crossed it, and opened the hall door. The house was full of warm breath. I felt my desire quicken as I stepped down the hall to the door of my aunt's room, where I did not pause but immediately turned the knob. She was waiting for me there in the dark, I was sure, because the moist heat of her breathing was suddenly denser. I started to make a sound, her name or merely a moan, to show that I had come from my dream to answer her call. But at that moment, I will never know exactly why, my mouth filled up. I do not say with saliva because the liquid was saltier and denser even than my aunt's consommé. And when I swallowed it down, it almost made me gag, for I suddenly knew what it was like—the terrifying richness of a tongue-bitten mouth full of blood. So the door I had just opened was not into my aunt's bedroom but into the heart of a night three years before. It was the summer after my mother's death, the eve of my first visit to my uncle's house, the only time my father had driven me down. That day he came home from work and drank nothing. He bathed himself violently, sputtering and fuming. Then he put on the suit he had not worn since my mother was buried. We left a little before dark. For a while he drove in silence, then he began to talk almost as furiously as when he was drunk, stitching his words together in angry patches. "They'll talk about me like I was coal dust. That's all right. They'll say I'm a God-forsaken drunk and a demon. That's all right too. But if they come down on you, boy, if they start to give you chicken gizzards and nigger's work, you write me. I'll visit them." He laughed wickedly. "I'll have a set with that sawbones and his Cajun beauty." He ranted on. "Glorified vets and bayou belles don't lord it over me or mine." I had heard all this before. I stopped listening and went to sleep.

I woke up to the sound of my father's curses. At first I thought he must have had some whiskey in the glove compartment and had drunk himself into a black fury. Even in in the pale dash light I could see the sweat standing on his forehead and the jaws tight around his clenched teeth. "Goddamned son-of-a-bitching suck-egg frogs," he hissed.

"What is it?" I cried out in alarm.

"Sucking frogs."

I sat up and looked out over the hood of the car. Frogs by the hundreds were making white arches in the headlights, thumping against the car and bursting under the tires. In the glare above the highway I saw their mad glazed eyes, saw the flat bodies and pallorous underbellies gliding toward death. "Stop!" I cried.

"Shut up! These suckers have been crossing ever since we left Harlow County." He beat on the horn. "No end to the sons-of-bitches, goddam 'em."

"Stop!" I hollered again.

"Shut up, you little peckerhead. I'll mash you same as I mash these sucking frogs." He stepped on the accelerator and howled out his execrations. The tempo of the thumping and popping of the frogs rose until I couldn't bear it. "Stop! Stop!" He hit me with the back of his hand and made me bite my tongue. My mouth filled with blood. I swallowed it. A moment later I threw up. "Stick you head out of the window, goddamit!"

When we got to my uncle's house, I was white and rank with the smell of vomit. "We passed through a frog migration twenty miles long," my father said grinning. "He'll live, though he is of the delicate kind."

Standing there in the door of my aunt's room, I saw again the doomed white frogs, heard the drum and hiss of their innumerable deaths, felt the weight of my father's blows, and smelled the acid odor of my own vomit. My aunt stirred. "Joe? Joe, is that you?" I ran. Wriggled out of the sack. Ran through the grass toward the creek. Ran for my life from the angry glaring light that raced across the gray morning toward the horizon.

I thought I would not make it. In my frenzy I missed the path. Blackberries snared me and bled me pitilessly. And soon the sun would blaze forth and cook me down to a dry parchment of brittle bones. I could feel its great heat poised behind the pines, ready to beat me down. But when I had fallen a dozen times and a dozen times been turned back by thickets, I at last heard the murmur of the creek. That gave me courage. I burst through the last barrier of underbrush and plunged into the shallow water. I cried out because the cold water at first burned my wounds. Even the creek, I thought,

had betrayed me. But after a while the current became more sooth-
ing. So, sunrise did not catch me in the open after all. Even so, moved
by a lingering fear of the heat, I made my way downstream to the
Blue Hole. There I dove down into the dark water and for a while
hung by roots in the shadow of the high cut bank. Underneath me
wavered the image of my splayed, foreshortened body, the little frog
that had miraculously made it across the sun's wide way.

After a time I paddled over to the lip of the Blue Hole and lay in the
shoals looking at my body, which was lengthened and human again,
though badly scratched. As I lay there, hope and fear divided my
heart, but neither finally imaged itself beside me in the water—the
black-haired body of Frank or the ivory body of his mother. I tried to
think about that, but I couldn't just then. I got up and walked around
to the sand bar and looked down at my image in the quiet backwa-
ter. My face was so scratched and puffy that it hardly seemed me. I'll
tell you what it did look like though. It looked like the face of my
father the morning after a particularly bad night, one in which he'd
lost a fight. The thought made me smile. The smile was crooked like
his because my bottom lip was torn. "Well, Father," I said to the
image, "you were almost right. They didn't give me gizzards and
nigger's work, but the Cajun beauty gave me nigger's medicine and it
almost made me crazy and killed me." Then I spat on the image.

About that time Seth came down to the creek calling out my name
in a quavering voice as if it were the name of a demon that might
start up after him at any moment. "Here I am, Seth."

"Miss Marie say come back to the house." He kept his distance.

"Go get me some clothes."

When he came back with them, I put them on and went up to the
bunk room and began to pack. My aunt came and stood in the door
in her housecoat. "What are you doing, Joe?" I looked at her careful-
ly. She seemed entirely herself. "I'm going now, Aunt Marie. The
medicine worked."

"That's backward, Joe. It means it's safe for you to stay here now,
as long as you want to."

"Yes, it's safe," I said. I kept packing.

"Come in the house and let me put some salve on those cuts."

"No. I don't need any, Aunt Marie. But I'll tell you what I could use
is some money, for bus fare."

"Your uncle Ab would never forgive me if I let you go this way."

"You couldn't explain to Uncle Ab what way I went if you wanted
to, Aunt Marie. So just tell him I ran off. I'll never tell him different.
In fact, it's the truth. I am running off."

"Where are you going?" That surprised me a little, how obviously she knew I was not going home. When I didn't answer, she shook her head. "They'll take you back to him."

"Maybe once or twice, Aunt Marie. But I'm a smart boy. Everybody says so. I'll learn pretty quick how to get away for good."

"From us, too, Joe?" I nodded. "I never wanted that, Joe."

"I believe you, Aunt Marie, but you knew it had to be, even if you didn't want it."

She went off and got some money and brought it back to me, almost a hundred dollars. I gave half of it back to her. "It's too much, Aunt Marie. I have to start learning right away how to get it myself."

My aunt looked at me with a face so drawn in upon itself that I thought she would begin to weep. But all I wanted then was to get away from her. Before many years, though, I would pity her. This is how it must have been with her. There I stood destitute, having lost mother and cousin lover, having renounced father, uncle, and aunt. All I had was an old grip, forty-odd dollars, and a scarred face and body. But I was free. And there she was, twenty-five years older, with a dying husband, one son no more like her than day is to night, and another son separated from her by the perpetual secret of what she had just done for him. All she had left was her God. Or had she even traded God for son that night?

"Tell Frank I said good-bye."

My Aunt Marie was wrong. They never did take me back to my father even once. I went straight from Laurelie to New Orleans. I changed buses three times, traveled mostly at night, and never talked to anybody.

My aunt laid upon me either a great blessing or a terrible curse. Here is how it has been with me. For over thirty years I have been absolutely free of desire. Remember? At the lip of the Blue Hole that last day no image appeared, neither Frank's nor hers. None has appeared since. Of all the beds I have slept in, I have shared not one—all as clear as the limpid water of the imageless creek. From what I have seen I would count this a blessing. But I don't press the point. Each must be his own judge.

The Host

Homage à Teilhard de Chardin

1

So Stedford House was to be occupied again. For a month John Gannett had thought that he would keep it empty until his death. That would seem selfish to some, but he would not live much longer, and then he would leave the house as well as his own quarters to the foundation along with several millions. His maiden sister had died three years ago. There was nothing now to divide the fortune which his father had seeded and he had nurtured. That was the consolation for being the last of an atrophied plant. The division of stem and flower ceased. The whole blossom fell intact into hands not consanguineous and therefore grateful.

His decision not to offer the house again to the foundation, but to rest on past and posthumous generosities, held firm for the month during which he wandered the rooms day after day taking in the redolence of the great priest. But at last the saner side of his mind warned him that he was engaged in a diseased parasitism — especially diseased in view of the fact that the host was entirely absent. Indeed the great priest, with a scrupulousness that he could have wished less precise, had taken away everything: books, personal effects, every scrap of paper, and even — with the aid of an air freshener — the pungence of his pipe. Would that the penultimate occupant, a dour classicist, had been as meticulous, but that one had broadcast into every corner the evil odors of his decaying person. Yet, ironically, the priest was the older of the two by far, but his flesh at the edges of his cassock had always seemed to Gannett a brilliant bone white, stripped clean by the leopards of the spirit.

So Gannett determined to relinquish the house again to the foundation, but he could not deny that those bright first days after the priest's departure had been filled with a marvelous vicarious delight. He had, of course, during the year of the great man's residency read the master work, and so he brought with him to the unoccupied house many images. Here, for instance, the priest had sat at the desk beneath the window looking out past the garden to the broken stones of the sea wall. Perhaps he had seen against the horizon

Australopithecus dancing hand in hand with other little hominids in the first circle, the first intuition of the wholeness from which they sprang and toward which in the long arch of evolution they returned. Here he had eaten his spare suppers watching the ancient oak rustle in the sea breeze. Surely it was the image for him of the great tree of life which took root in the confused sea of giant molecules and branched upward season by season in growing companionship with the Son. Here he slept under the blessedly blank high ceiling, resting from process, revisiting the primeval darkness where consciousness is a black vibration, unseen, unheard, felt only as a rumbling disturbance of earth in a distant millennium.

But not long after Gannett began to wander the house, his own sleep was disturbed by a massive and obsessive yeasting of biotic forms, crowded and confused at first, full of a deafening gabble, but emerging finally into a prehistoric tropical ambiance. Within several nights a jungle emerged more brilliant than any imagined by "Le Douanier" Rousseau. Animal life stirred, at first shyly, behind the fronds of huge ferns. Then the beasts appeared more boldy— opossums, kangaroos, wombats, Tasmanian wolves, all marsupials. Presently a whole phylum of marsupials passed before him— long-snouted insectivores, semiaquatic herbivores, lumbersome pachyderms munching rich bouquets of greenery, and finally fierce carnivores including even a bloody-eyed saber-toothed predator of immense speed. At first each bore in its pouch its young, which assured a domestic distance between the dreamer and his dream animals. But then they began to come empty. They transgressed his dreamer's distance and bore down on him with hungry eye and empty pouch. As though maddened in some evolutionary cul-de-sac, they attacked him. He woke up rolling in sweat. He locked Stedford House, left his own quarters across the bramble in the care of his keeper Haig, called the foundation, and booked passage to London with a good supply of tranquilizers. Blessedly the dreams ceased. The stay in London was deliberately literary and historical.

It was four months now since the departure of the great priest, and Gannett was returning home from London to meet the new occupant of Stedford House. The foundation had forwarded the usual dossier, but he had not looked at it. Though he had broken the diseased element in his relationship with the priest, still he kept within him the golden kernel of the presence and the master work. He was not ready to learn details of the person who had supplanted the great man. He would meet his new beneficiary cold. He would read the dossier later—or never, if the man was dull. He did not expect to be very interested ever again in the occupant of Stedford House. Linguist, historian, political scientist, classicist — let them all fade quickly in the shadow of the great paleontologist and man of God.

Even so, his interest was piqued when he learned from Haig, the old Scotch keeper, that the foundation had sent a menage of four, a young literary scholar Peter Stern, his wife Ruth, his son David, and his wife's younger sister, Abbey Kristol. They all came to the garden gate when he rang the bell, but not before he had overheard Stern say, "I tell you, Abbey, his God is more arbitrary than Job's." So Gannett had sighed even before he saw them — how easy it would be to keep distant this time. Stern was a thin man with dark eyes coiling upon themselves, upon that exquisite and elaborate intellectualism which has no referent but words — words upon words. His wife, a heavy woman, was the vanguard. "This grant of yours is a lifesaver for Peter, Mr. Gannett. Everybody and his brother has written about Kafka, a lot of psychoanalytic garbage, but you have to read it all before you can write a word. At school the students hang on him like flies."

"An agony and a glory. The young know instinctively where to find intellectual nourishment," said Gannett, nodding, almost bowing, money to mind, but with a touch of ironical exaggeration caught by the husband, not the wife.

It was the two youngsters who threatened Gannett's detachment. David was shy and pubescent, his feelings glowing near the surface like a constant blush. He stood silently, peering out from eyes even more deeply tunneled than his father's. Gannett's sympathy went out. Abbey Kristol said, "I love your wall by the sea, Mr. Gannett." What teeth she had, like an apparition from Poe, huge, perfectly ranked, and glistening with a pearly polish as though wetted by perpetual hunger.

"I hope you will all be comfortable."

"We're already comfortable," said Ruth. "Come in and have tea or a beer."

Gannett shook his head. "Rule of the estate: the visiting scholar is to suffer no disturbance." The eyes of the man who studied the arbitrariness of God showed gratitude, but Gannett did not stop to seal his beneficence. He summoned a blush. He was frightened in his celibate millionaire's soul, let them think, by offers of domestic propinquity. He rushed away. At home he shook his head. It was quite impossible: study the sad Jew of Prague on the majestic cliffs of this coast and with such company — a wife with feelings as approximate as her body, a boy entering the fever age, and a girl with the dripping teeth of a carnivore.

Gannett put out of mind the Kafkan and his curious retinue. He was absorbed again by the pleasures of paleontology, reading more about the recent discoveries of the coelacanths and the like. Left to these enthusiasms, he might have passed the entire year without revisiting Stedford House. But Haig, serving breakfast one morning, muttered something about odd disturbances.

"What is it, Andrew?"

"The boy, running everywhere."

"What did you expect of a boy of fourteen?"

"Nay, I don't mean kids' skitterings."

"What do you mean then?"

"Sneaking about, spying."

"Must be exciting for him — catching me with a book, you working in the garden."

"Not us, his own people."

"What would he be doing spying on his own people?"

Haig shook his head. "I don't know, but he's at it like a demon, behind stones and sea wall, in trees, and amongst bushes — darting and panting like to be caught was his death."

Gannett smiled wistfully. "It must be the game of a lonely boy, Andrew. He is the scout and they are the fell enemy."

Haig grunted. Gannett's mind leaped backwards to his own boyhood. He was in a velvet jacket by the sea wall, there was an old sailor beside him with a string in his hand, the sea rose in the distance — or was that only a painting? He shook his head sadly. Easier to see the great awkward coelacanth clambering at the water's edge than to see himself as a boy on the cliff by the big house. The great priest was right. We are more deeply rooted in the tree of life than in our own histories.

So the image of the spying boy did not leave much of an impression and might have faded altogether had Gannett not in the course of an unusual morning walk surprised young David spying with an old long glass from a covert of blanched stone. It was bright September, sea and sky blue and windless. Gannett chuckled. The boy jumped up into the sunlight as though to run, but settled again on a rock and challenged Gannett with his dark eyes.

"Well, David, how is the enemy deployed this morning? Man-of-war in the offing? A long boat with a landing party in the bay? Or have the devious devils crawled ashore by night to rustle among the trees?" But the boy had been spying on the house. Gannett knew that. The boy knew he knew. Gannett held out his hand. "May I see your long glass?"

David handed it over without hesitation. Gannett put it to his eye, screwed out the lens to correct for his myopia, and said, "My father got this from a Dutchman. Each evening before dinner he would stand at the window 'sweeping the bay,' as he said."

"Was he worried about keeping his treasure from pirates?"

"No, the treasure was already safe in the vaults of New York banks. 'Sweeping the bay' was a sort of daily tribute to the origin of the treasure." Gannett handed the glass back to the boy. "Tell me, David, what are you looking for?" The boy was silent, but not defiantly so. Gannett extemporized. "You notice, when you look, that spot on the edge which is shiny like mica?" The boy nodded. "I suspect the lens threads are producing some tiny flakes of rust. Try a little oil."

"My father," said the boy suddenly.

"Your father?"

"I'm looking for my father."

"He's in the house. I saw just now through the long glass, at the study window, typing." Immediately Gannett regretted this second disingenuousness, because the boy obviously thought it shabby. "I'm sorry, David. I know that's not what you mean. What do you mean?"

"He's disappearing."

"Into his books?"

"No. It's my aunt, Abbey."

"She's making him disappear?"

"She's doing something to him. I'm positive."

"And you're spying to find out what it is?"

"Yes, then I can stop it."

Gannett shook his head. "That's a tough assignment, David. Even if you're right about your aunt, it may not be something you can see with a long glass."

"I don't believe in the invisible."

"You don't believe people can do invisible things to each other?"

"Oh yes, but it always starts visible, smiles or a look in the eye, before it turns into the invisible, like bone into cartilage."

Gannett admired that hardheaded precocity. "All right. What have you seen so far?"

Instead of answering, the boy handed Gannett the glass. Gannett focused again on the window. Stern's hunched concentration was unchanged, so Gannett ranged back and forth over the low hedgerow with the small field of the telescope, but he saw only faceless old stones and wide veins of mortar. These familiar textures, exposed mercilessly to the morning light, inclined him toward pity and arrested his search. But then Abbey Kristol appeared in the field of vision, strolling casually, reading a book, virtually naked in a white sunning brief. Her flesh was resplendent bronze, her limbs and torso strong and perfectly formed, her hair brilliantly red. Had the bush of her pubes been exposed, it would have burned red, too, and ignited his desert heart. Desire, or the memory of desire, stirred in him, but only briefly. There was something else in that slowly moving body that was prodigiously more important than mere sex. What it was he would discover with later reflection. At the moment David was speaking. "It's not sex."

Gannett focused on Stern's face. The scholar followed Abbey's passing, but there was not in his eyes the faintest glimmer of lust. On the contrary, they showed a kind of dark and dolorous wonderment. Gannett handed the glass back. "I'm sure you're right about that, David."

"Do you know what it is?" The boy gave him a sharp look that mixed hope and skepticism.

"No. No, David."

"But you think you will know."

Gannett sighed. "You are asking me to enter with you into two rather strange stipulations, David—first, that your father is suffering from some malicious influence; secondly, that this influence emanates from your aunt, Abbey."

"That's just what I already know."

"You know it, but I don't know it. I would have to learn it for myself."

"No," said the boy vehemently. In fact, he struck the stone with his fist. "Take my word for it. It was not until she moved in with us that my father started to disappear. And my mother is changed too. She was pretty and strong, but since Abbey came she's gotten tired."

She could never have been pretty, Gannett thought, but she obviously did have a considerable if crude strength. "What about you? What happened to you after Abbey came?"

For some moments the boy did not answer, but his eyes never flinched. "What happened to me is normal. I'm not worried about that. I'm worried about my father and mother."

This was remarkable. It made Gannett aware of just how far they had come in a few minutes. "Quite proper, David. I can see that you are a person of great character. On the other hand, you know nothing of me. You must decide whether you should have me for a confidant on such brief acquaintance."

"You or nobody," said the boy. "Besides: you see. I could've told if you didn't see."

"I will try to see, David. Let's part now and think about things for awhile, then meet again."

"All right."

Gannett stood and walked away, but the boy stayed at his station. From the last vantage at a turn in the path Gannett looked back to see him raise the long glass to his eye, turn the lens carefully, and resume his vigil.

Not until long after supper, when Haig's rattlings in the kitchen finally ceased, did Gannett allow his mind to return to David. The first thing that he remarked was the enormous courage and candor of the boy. How clearly he saw what it would mean to be entering adolescence in the same house with Abbey—the forbidden images, the sweaty autoeroticism, and the little guilts clinging like leeches to his swelling manhood. In fact, one needed to consider whether it was this that transformed itself into irrational fear for the father's well-being. Gannett didn't think so. There was the clear ring of the boy's "it's not sex." Besides, there was Gannett's own observation, which supported the boy's, that Stern was not terribly substantial. He was intellectually substantial of course—Gannet had read the dossier that afternoon. But he had no presence. In the brief exchange at the garden gate Gannett had perceived that he floated precariously on his wife's solicitude, on the attentiveness, entirely mysterious then, of his son and his sister-in-law. Indeed he was, as David said, vulnerable to vanishment. The careful typing there at the study window prosing its deliberate way into the Kafkan arcanum was not proof against that.

Suddenly and surprisingly Gannett found himself more than mildly angry. His experience with the foundation, coalescing now with the character of Stern, discovered for him a whole subspecies of such men, a huge solipsistic biological backwash which in the conditions of nature would be happily doomed. In the society of men, however, these pale parasites with their great lobes and convolutions of useless learning were fed the affections of countless women and children. Incapable, of course, of making loving return to the human ground of their being, they leached their soil soullessly. Such a one was Stern most certainly, and Stedford House now the bleak terrarium of his rank bloom. The man sickened Gannett, and he could find no consolation in the fact that he was only a temporary and distant host, whereas Ruth and David must constantly give blood to Stern's necrotic stem. Presently, with the energy of anger, Gannett banished Stern from his mind, but not until he had the strong premonition that this pallorous creature would, before his departure, force him to some painful and perpetually regrettable decision.

Gannett turned his mind to Abbey, to the discovery he had promised himself of what it was that was not sex. But he discovered nothing, nothing at all, despite the fact that there by the rocks with David he had been perfectly sure he could uncover it at will. He was acutely irritated. No doubt the problem was that Stern had created in his mind an afterimage so inimical to Abbey's that they could not coexist in the same mental space. He tried reading, but the further accounts of coelacanths failed to provide the distraction which will sometimes surprise the unsuspecting conception that has eluded alertness. A generous brandy nightcap only fuzzed his brain. He prepared for bed.

It was after midnight that a vision of Abbey came, not to Gannett's dreams nor to his wakefulness. It was not a possession of his mind—he would always insist on that. It was a revelation in the form of her passing again, not necessarily below Stern's window, but simply passing, out there in the moonlight. Her appearance might have been shared by David or Haig or anyone. There was nothing proprietary in his seeing her. Her gait was what first struck him. You have seen herons, giraffes, stalking cats moving with such deliberate grace that it seems an exhibition of the anatomy of movement, the precise compaction of huge energies barely concealed. So Abbey's legs, even in her careless walk, suggested the capacity for incredible quickness. She was holding something before her, just as she had that morning. But it was not a book this time. What was it? Gannett thought it was something she would eat—not a slab of flesh merely, but some kind of dense and luminous aliment. It lighted her face. It commanded her rapt attention. But the legs continued autonomously that long rhythmic step. Suddenly Gannett had a wild intuition—Abbey came from a future where food was condensed and sacramental and where a richly elaborated biogram provided in the human body for new coordinations. It followed, then, that this gliding walk was only a fraction of an immense choreographic repertoire. Gannett's eye sought other newness in movement. But suddenly she was gone. He leaped out of bed and ran to his window, but he felt foolish before he reached it, because he knew that her passing was in a middle distance unrelated to the window's vantage or to the wall and the sea beyond.

The next day he met David against the rocks. "Anything unusual, David?"

"No. Did you see anything?"

"I saw Abbey walking last night." He watched David carefully, but the boy only shrugged. "So did I, but that's nothing new. She's walked every night since she came to our house."

"How long was that?"

"June."

"Where had she been before she came?"

"She was in college and then she was in Tibet, and India."

"Studying?"

The boy smiled wryly. "You should hear my mother on the subject of hippies in Asia. But now she thinks Abbey is gaining some stability—reading, eating regularly . . ." He stopped abruptly.

"But what?"

"That's not what she's doing."

"What's she doing?"

"She is trying out on my father the power she learned from gurus."

"But you don't know what the power is?"

The boy's dark eyes narrowed. "No. And I don't have much time to find out."

"You mean before your father disappears altogether?"

"That won't happen. Because I'll stop her even if I don't know what she's doing."

"Be careful, David." Gannett paused to give his injunction weight, then he said, "You say you see her walk often at night. Does there seem to you anything peculiar about her walking?"

"My mother says it's excess of youthful energy, but it's not. She paces like a wolf."

"Does she usually carry anything when she walks?"

"She eats. She says walking makes her ravenous, and she eats like crazy, anything in the house." At that moment the boy slapped the long glass in the palm of his hand, a sort of punctuation. "I've told you all I know, Mr. Gannett. What are you thinking? You must be thinking something, to ask all those questions."

"All right, David. I want to make a hypothesis. Then I want you to watch and think and tell me your conclusion in a day or so. Suppose your aunt is not actually doing anything. Suppose it's simply the power of her presence that is diminishing all of you. I'm sure it's not rare for a person to come into a situation and draw everything to herself so that the other persons no longer nourish each other as they are accustomed to. You don't need to posit some power derived from gurus. All you need to have is a very compelling person, a special kind of person who dominates everyone else's interest. You think about that."

The boy shook his head. "That's group psychology or something. This is freakier. It has to do with her nightwalking and chants and exercises."

But Gannett did not take that up. He was firm. "You can't test a hypothesis, David, if you close your mind to it. Give it a fair trial. And remember, certain disturbances in groups *can* be very freaky, as you say. Historically they have produced witches and all manner of arcane phenomena."

That seemed to impress the boy. He nodded slowly. "OK, I'll give it a chance."

"Good."

Gannett considered when he returned to his house whether he should have been more candid with David. But he absolved himself. How could he tell the boy at this point that his father was an evolutionary dead end, that he was probably, even as they talked, playing his deadly end game with the mad Jew of Prague? And how could he convey his futuristic vision of Abbey? He was not yet prepared to try to explain to David Abbey's power, to try to supplant the boy's sexually suffused speculations about exotic transcendences and the other claptrap of youth cult. He had to work out the meaning of the vision more thoroughly for himself. He was confident he could. Then he would let it burst upon the boy with all the brilliance of the great priest's thought.

By suppertime his confidence was so buoyant and his spirits so high that he could accept with unusual good humor Haig's inimitable mixture of indirection and crudeness.

"Well, sir," said the old Scot, "won't they send the boy on to school? Surely they won't leave him to gallivant on the property the year through."

"A note attached to Stern's dossier says that David is very advanced and is to be allowed a year of independent study."

"He needs a stick to his skittishness." The old man bore down with louring brows. Gannett drew back amused. "I didn't make the arrangement, Andrew. But I am in consultation with David about a matter which is the chief cause of what you call his skittishness. The problem concerns his aunt."

"The naked one?"

"Yes."

"I don't wonder."

Gannett decided not to attempt to refine the crude assumption which obviously lay behind Haig's remark. He was surprised when the old Scot himself carried the matter a step further. "And you, sir, are giving the lad counsel?" The wonderment was so wide-eyed that Gannett laughed almost boisterously. "Well, Andrew, I have after all passed the seven ages of man, including that one. And I do think that I can help the boy cut through some of the foggy romance of youth."

"Good for you, sir." That was sincere, if clipped. But Haig went on. "I wish it would take hold better, though. I still see him lurking about most darkly with that old long glass of you da's."

"True. But give me a bit more time. We've only had two short conferences."

Gannett went off to his study assured that this evening's self-communings would achieve what they had so miserably failed of the previous night. In fact, his confidence was so great that he knew he could start his meditation anywhere, because when a pattern of ideas and images begins to tessellate its mosaic, the tiniest piece placed correctly, by a kind of supra-aesthetic necessity, adumbrates all the rest. Mozart, of all men perhaps, had the keenest intuition of this. The great priest, his recent guest, knew it most cosmically. Begin, then, with the humble coelacanth, a living fossil. What he, John Magan Gannett, had experienced was, as it were, a living fossil of feeling. It was the remembered moment when man first saw in another, perhaps a woman, the promise of divinity. All is fire. Her flesh burns with a bronze fire. Her luxuriant hair in that primordial moment is a mantle of sun fire. Her eyes and her teeth are scintillant. *Silex scintillans*, says the old poet and mystic. But that was not all. Follow the pattern outward from the center of the mosaic, out to the most distant verge, where the eye strains to encompass the whole. Here is the same pattern only in a different figure. Here you do not begin with the coelacanth. You begin at time's other end, the dream of the fictionist of the future: the extraordinary creature whose being is so nearly pure energy that its flesh flows translucently in a sea of prismatic light. Is this not the same fierce fire arching across the eons? Yes. Our living fossil of feeling, that first clambering up from the dark sea into the sunlight of distant divinity, begets our prescience of the final fire, the bodiless light, alpha and omega rejoined.

Haig came with the snifter of warm brandy and left it at his master's elbow without speaking, sensing no doubt something of Gannett's transport. Gannett took up the glass with an almost ritual movement and for a moment held it high like a chalice. How immense was his gratitude at that moment. With what an utterly unique concatenation he had been gifted: the visit of the great priest as a kind of novitiate, the keen pubescent boy, and the woman of extraordinary beauty—all conspiring to bestow on him the moment in which evolution and devolution folded upon each other in the rosy fire of the ultimate mosaic. He drank. His eyes moistened. And some minutes later he descended into the kind of sleep which he had always imagined the great priest knew—a darkness so perfectly void that one seems to hear the first warm procreative suspiration of God. And each morning's awakening is like the first awakening.

2

When Gannett awoke to that rare dawning, the most significant perhaps of his life, he lay for a long while in the afterglow of his great vision. If he never saw further, and probably he would not, he knew enough now to give him an equanimous proof against the pangs of his own mortality. Death had not yet mounted to his casement. There in the offing, though, just beyond the morning mists of the bay, he rowed a black bier over smooth water trailing a garland of lilies. Gannett knew that, though younger, he would precede Andrew because the old Scot, he fancied, had the strengths of both ancient branches—chordate and arthropod, backbone and shell. What an angry snap would signal the parting of that life. But none of this troubled him. In fact, the warmth of his body, though he knew it was fading inchmeal down the evening of his life, was sufficient presentiment of the eternal fire he would join.

Thus Gannett might have whiled away the whole mild morning under his eiderdown, feeling not the slightest pang of hunger or any other lack. Andrew had given up on him, left something in the warmer, and gone out to the garden. Was it time already to mulch the roses? He heard the blade of the hoe strike the soil in a slow but powerful measure. But it was not the disapprobation in the old puritan's stirrings that finally roused him from his sublime torpor. It was the thought of David. It ran through him like a sudden chill. How on earth could he hope to convey to the boy the meaning of Abbey, knowledge that, for all he knew, required sixty years' cooling of the blood and the deep study of a great mentor. How could he tell him that his aunt, against whom all his being was set, was the way of life; that the father could not ultimately be saved from the trammels of his own deadly devotion to the mad Jew of Prague, who hungered for but never tasted his awful God? Yet tell something he must, because the boy's agitation inclined him already toward dangerous acts.

Gannett arose, dressed quickly, and hurried out to the rocks without eating. David was not there, though it was only a few minutes later than the time of their previous rendezvous. Gannett waited with mixed feelings — on the one hand reluctance to undertake the extraordinarily difficult explanations, on the other an anxiousness to have the job done so that he could bask freely in the last of the September sun and in the naked heat of Abbey's beauty. But the bright rocks spread upon his agitation such a warm mollification that he drifted in his waiting toward drowsiness. When a few moments later a noise commenced, he thought, with a twinge of guilt, that it was the buzzing of his own idle head. That turned out not to be true. It was a human humming all right, but it was not merely mental. It filled the space between the rocks and Stedford House. Gannett stood up and looked across that space. A head was visible at the study window, Stern. Another head showed below the window and just above the hedge, brazen in the sun, Abbey. And the voice certainly was Abbey's, in an endless chant without need of respiration, the Hindu AUM perhaps, or something even less formulated. Gannett walked cautiously closer, keeping a veil of bush and bramble between himself and the house, following more with ear than eye — not the song of the Sirens or the Lotus-eaters, but the song the maiden sings at the world's center, the omphalos. It is not the song of the singer, it is the song of the place. All sounds are gathered into the one rotundity, AAHM. All songs are the same song.

Gannett mounted a bushy hillock near the hedge. From this vantage Abbey was wholly visible. She was leaning back on both hands, facing the sun blindly, making her chant in two distinct pulses, inhalation and exhalation. When she sang in, her stomach swelled toward a promise of immense fecundity and her legs pressed sensuously into the grass. When she sang out, her stomach retracted into a concavity so deep that it seemed to recede even to the spine, and her legs withered. Watching this remarkable systole and diastole, Gannett felt the pulses of the song now fill him, now draw everything out of him. His own breathing conformed to the long measure. The wind of his lungs and the salt tide of his blood ebbed and flowed with the song. He almost fell into a trance. But at a certain moment he raised his eyes lazily to Stern's face. Here was a shocking image of inner strife. The face begged to be loosed to follow the delicious song, but the cruel knots of its own self-discipline held tight. The intensity of the conflict jolted Gannett out of the hypnotic rhythm of the song so that something above caught his alerted eye. He looked up to see David crouching in the shadow of the chimney. His eyes, like a hawk's, burned amber in that midday dark. And like a hawk, too, he seemed to ruffle his wings tentatively and rise on his feet as though to test the wind. And constantly the fierce avidity of eye flinted brightly against the dark stone. Gannett half-expected the young hawk to stoop, bury beak and claw in that bronze flesh, and fill the wind with the bloody scream that would revive the father. This tableau momentarily froze Gannett's stare—the unpenetrated mystery of the song of the center, the king dying of a bloodless heart, and the prince in the imagination of vengeance caressing the wind, already airborne.

Then with a careless slam Ruth emerged from the kitchen door. She descended the steps from the stoop with an awkward angry bustle. "Abbey, for the love of God, who can write with the Taj Mahal echoing in their ear? Shut it off." The girl rolled her head slowly forward without opening her eyes until it almost touched her knees. And there was another tableau for Gannett to store in his mind's eye: the fat goddess of the hearth standing arms akimbo above the offending maid whose fiery hair was just now beginning to fall forward coil by coil like stricken serpents. But still the king's crossed face was an emblem of agony in the uncurtained window and still the fire in the prince's eye fed on the prospect of murderous saving.

Presently the boy crawled back up over the ridge of the roof, rising for a brief moment against the incongruous blue benignity of the sky. Gannett avoided the rendezvous at the rocks and took the sinuous path out along the wall at the edge of the cliff. Below him the bay reflected the placidity of the sky. For this he was grateful, because his great vision of the night before was badly jostled. The central image and significance of Abbey was not disturbed. No, if anything, her marvelous flexing chant had strengthened that. It was the vortex of destructive emotions swirling around her that had shaken him—repulsion, fear, hatred. So he was in no mood to talk to David. But as it turned out he was forced to. The boy intercepted him just as he was turning up from the wall. Here a stand of low dry pines, trained by the frequent wind off the bay, leaned hungrily toward the garden. Gannett led the boy a few steps farther, forestalling conversation until he was seated on a rustic bench in the shade. His failure to eat breakfast coupled with the emotions of the last hours had left him weak. David sat on the grass at his feet. "I saw you watching. You still think Abbey is just a special kind of person who's not really doing anything?"

Gannett shook his head slowly, searching his mind for the right image and idiom to convey his complex intuition to the boy. "No, David, the proposition I left with you yesterday did not go nearly far enough. Abbey is not just a special kind of person. She is a messenger of time." That interested the boy, but he was on guard. He cocked his eye skeptically. "Do messengers of time always destroy people?"

"As in the case of your father, you mean?"

"Right. And maybe my mother, too, if it goes on much longer, which it won't."

"Just for a few moments let's put aside the effect Abbey may have on any given person and concentrate on what she represents. All right?"

David nodded. "OK. She's a messenger of time. What's the message?"

"Two messages, one from the past and one from the future, but both mean the same thing."

"Go ahead."

Gannett leaned back and shut his eyes. When at length he spoke, it was very slowly, in a tone almost incantatory. "Message number one, from the past. A great forest of the early Pleistocene. A lake. I, a little hominid, a little would-be man, saw rise from the water the dawn woman with hair of fire. She flew into the sky and left me behind with seared eyes. I and my kind will lapse on this shore, but when you discover my bones they will all be pointing like little arrows in the direction of her flight." Gannett stopped, but he did not open his eyes. David did not speak. All that could be heard was the light brushing of the wind among the pines.

"Message number two, from the future. A dark sky swirling with bright stars. I, a man of luminous flesh, am a galactic sentinel. I circle the lake of fire. A star crossed my last round, a rare and radiant being that pulled me into the wake of her red hair. But I could not follow her though the speed of my desire contracted my bones into little nodes of quivering song. Still, I do not sorrow greatly. My galaxy whirls closer upon itself and others upon it. We will all meet at the center." A few moments later Gannett, still without moving and without opening his eyes, said, "I'm sorry, David. It's not very good, but it's the best I can do." David did not speak, but presently Gannett heard a soft rustling. He sat forward and opened his eyes. The boy, with what seemed a kind of sorrowful reluctance, was unfolding a crumpled sheet of paper. He handed it up to Gannett, who read silently.

Each morning the man wakes up at a different window and leans on the ledge angrily. He does not acknowledge the constant sweeping which scratches along the floor outside the door of his room. One day a woman passes under the window. "Say," he demands, "who is changing the grass and the sky every day?" But the woman, despite her proximity and his reiterations, does not appear to hear him. She seems to be practicing a theatrical walk with exaggerated insouciance. All her mind is in the balls of her feet, her hips, and her shoulders. The man lifts himself over the window ledge, hangs for a moment by his fingers, and drops.

"Your father wrote this?"

David nodded.

"It's an excellent imitation of Kafka."

"I think it's a suicide note."

Gannett sighed. "All imitations of Kafka are suicide notes if you ask me, David."

"I can't read those books."

"Neither can I."

"All right," the boy said abruptly, "if Abbey brings messages about the great destiny of man, why does it kill my father?"

"Light to eyes which have long been in darkness is blinding."

David stood up. "My father is a well-known scholar with a brilliant career. Abbey is a crackpot hippie."

Gannett sighed and nodded slowly. "Your father is absolutely brilliant, David. I've read his books," he lied. "But you know, I've never had a chance to talk to Abbey at all. Do you suppose she would be willing to talk to me?"

"She would be willing to do any crazy thing. But it won't do any good. She always talks in stupid riddles—no messages from the past or the future."

Gannett shrugged. "Then maybe I will change my mind about her."

'When do you want to talk to her?"

"I'll be at the rocks around this time tomorrow. If that's not satisfactory, she can send you with other directions."

"OK."

"David, before you leave, tell me, have you lost faith in me altogether?"

The boy shook his head. "She might be a messenger, Mr. Gannett, but I think she's a phoney." He hesitated. Gannett helped him. "But if she's only a phoney, your father would see through her and remain unaffected. Is that it?"

David nodded. Gannett stood up and put his hand lightly on the boy's shoulder. "We'll work this out, David, you and I. But in the meantime you must only watch. Do nothing drastic. Is that a promise?"

"For a couple of days, Mr. Gannett."

"A bit longer perhaps."

The boy shook his head.

"All right then, a couple of days will have to do."

Gannett had not set his rendezvous with Abbey earlier because he needed the evening in his study to prepare for it. Even so, it was several hours after supper and several sips into his second brandy before he had worked out steps which seemed to have some likelihood of success. The problem, of course, was to authenticate for the Sterns the message which Abbey bore so that they could acknowledge it, let them value it as they would. Knowledge would at least diminish the disturbance. Here was the plan that Gannett devised. At his meeting with Abbey the next day he would advise her of present dangers and press the point that she must make her representations to the family less exotic, more understandable. To this end he would help her, first by attempting again to enlist the confidence of David, secondly by arranging a family dinner at his home. The dinner would provide an opportunity for the four of them, on neutral ground and under the kindly auspices of a reverend and perceptive benefactor, to harmonize their differences. Gannett believed that if he once got them under his roof he could embrace all in at least a loose alliance. For surely David, once freed of fears for his father, could reach a tolerant understanding of Abbey. And hadn't the father's face, almost rapt by Abbey's song, revealed an intuition that might eventually light his way out of the Kafkan obscurity? And even the mother, hadn't she conjured within her obtuse corpulence, the surprisingly appropriate image of the Taj Mahal? Yes, Gannett's hopeful heart sprang up. There are none, even among those evolution seems to have discarded, who cannot get a glimpse of Abbey's portentous brilliance.

Gannett set aside his brandy and shortly sank into the great priest's profound and imageless sleep where just at the verge of the total eclipse of consciousness one hears the rising suspiration of the Fecundator. He lay in that blackness until well after midnight. Then his sleep was disturbed by the same images of primeval forest which he had dreamed shortly after the priest's departure. But this time, his dreaming mind knew, the issue would be vastly accelerated and it would be something far different from that earlier teeming phylum of minatory marsupials which had sent him in flight to London. This time there was less of the ambiance of steamy abundant life and more a feeling of precision. He felt almost as though he might reach out and pluck the air and thus bring about instantly the crystallization of a form which waited for its moment in the luminous jungle atmosphere. But there was yet a period of tense musical silence before the fronds at last parted and she stepped forth — not in newborn wonderment into a green world but purposefully, making her way across a middle distance of indefinite undergrowth to his side. He accepted her. The silence was broken by the gasp of his own passion. He awoke.

Almost immediately he leaped out of bed, took off his pajamas, wiped himself briskly with them. The harshly infolded silk shot blue scintillances into the crisp autumn air. He then made his way through the dark without misstep to the dining room, where a fire was laid ready against the morning chill. He threw the pajamas on the logs and lit the fire. Precisely arranged by Haig, kindling and logs flared brightly. Gannett watched the flames rise up to the silk. At first they only scorched it, highlighting briefly by some curious process the tiny weave of the fabric. Then the flames burst out. The silk twisted upon itself, making an image of human agony and turning up to Gannett's eyes his embroidered initials, J. M. G.

"Master?"

Gannett turned. There was Haig loosely robed and wide-eyed in the fire light. Gannett's mind was not so inflamed that he could not imagine the impression he made naked against the fire, an incongruity perhaps unbearable to the eye — the poor forked creature on the last verge of his mortality set against the perpetual fire, as La Tour makes the candle flame show mercilessly the hint of green in the dead god's flesh.

"Go to bed, Andrew. I'm all right." But the old man did not move. "I only had a very bad dream, Andrew, which frightened me into a kind of fit, but I'm all right now. Go to bed."

"It's them." Haig flicked his head with surprising alacrity. "And the witch amongst them."

For a moment Gannett wondered if perhaps the old Scot's sleep had been disturbed, too, but he dismissed the idea. "Andrew, I have asked you twice now to leave me. You will do that."

"Shall I get you some fresh night clothes, sir?"

"No. Are you taking pleasure in my embarrassment?"

"You can't believe it, sir."

"Then leave me."

At that the old man did finally turn and retreat with heavy step. Gannett remained a moment longer, but he was deeply chilled. The fire seemed all light and no heat.

At the rocks the following morning David reported that Abbey would meet Gannett that night when she began her usual walk at ten o'clock. She preferred to talk to him at night. The delay was frustrating and unfruitful for Gannett. He had already decided his course in the early hours of the morning, as he lay naked in his bed watching the first light of the sun slowly gray the black of the ceiling. He saw how foolish was his dream of harmonizing the Sterns to Abbey Kristol. They were no more ready for her than Haig was. The intuitions which he had imagined them capable of were only the fair seemings of fond hope. For the father responded to Abbey against his will and, knowing only the God of the dark pages, could never follow. And the mother could hear only the rebellious chant of nonconformity, never the divine harmony within. And the boy? Perhaps someday, when free of the toils of flesh. Which reminded him painfully that he was not ready himself, proven unworthy by his dreams. So perhaps the only one was the great priest who could lie looking at the black ceiling until he fell into pure and dreamless sleep. Or was his sleep, too, vulnerable to wicked visitations? No, it was not. Gannett believed that. If the word was to be made flesh, however little the world cared to acknowledge it, there must be one, at least one who understood. But Abbey must go. That was the true widsom which his cowardice and his corruption bestowed. To protect Stern and Ruth, to protect Abbey herself from David, and, yes, to protect his own old man's sanity and celibacy, she must go. A thousand regrets, a universe of regrets, but she must go.

So, later, in the early dark of the evening he waited without trepidation. His purpose was fixed.

"Mr. Gannett?"

"Yes. I'm here."

She wore a white dress with shoulder straps that set off in the moonlight the deep bronze of her arms and neck. She came to him with a smile that revealed her large white teeth. And she brought a distinct aura—soft warmth and the mild perfume of washed flesh. Gannett had wondered, after his dream, about the effect of her near presence. Everything stirred in him as before, but only as a distant echo. He was safe on that score. Thank age for relegating its madness to dreams.

"Thank you for coming."

"I am only passing, Mr. Gannett, on my way to the wall by the cliff."

"Won't you stop here for a moment?"

"No, but I will stop at the wall."

"What's the distinction?"

"I know that you are going to say something very blue, Mr. Gannett, and I want to be where I can see the moon on the bay."

So Gannett followed her around the garden and down through the sloping pines to the wall. There she sat almost primly with her legs crossed and her dress pulled modestly over the knees. Gannett stood safely behind the wall. She laughed. It was a marvelous musical laugh. "Oh Mr. Gannett, did you think I was the demon who would cast you over the cliff onto the rocks below?"

"Yes, Miss Kristol, and then you would unfold your hidden wings and fly down to feast on by broken flesh."

She laughed again. "Oh my! Well, the truth is I'm afraid of *you*, Mr. Gannett."

"Why?"

"Because you're so rich. The rich always get what they want. I know I will have to do whatever you say."

"You surprise me, Miss Kristol."

"Why? Because David told you I was a hippie and you thought I would talk strangely?"

"Partly that." She did not inquire about the other parts, so Gannett took up another line. "Tell me, Miss Kristol, what you learned in India and Tibet."

"Devolution."

"Devolution?"

"Yes, devolution. I learned the way of the animals."

"I'm not sure I know what you mean."

"I mean, Mr. Gannett, I met a wise man who taught me how to be an animal."

"Is this a yoga exercise or something of the sort?"

"No. My teacher had his own unique system. But don't think he was one of those cynical gurus who sets up for profit. He was very learned. During the day he was a librarian in Bragat."

"In the evening he taught devolution?"

"Yes. He said that only two Americans, both writers, had ever understood the necessity of the return."

"Who were these?" Gannett never got an answer to that question, for just then Abbey Kristol began to howl like a wolf. It startled Gannett badly, but only for a moment. When he had recovered himself and was able to listen attentively, he found the long lugubrious baying quite remarkable and indeed so convincing that he fancied the warm sea shining below them in the moonlight was a frozen expanse of the arctic north. Then periodically came a high rapid barking, no doubt some important communication in what the great priest had described as the intensely social and monogamous milieu of the wolf. The cry went on for some time. She seemed altogether caught up in it. Gannett watched her bosom expand and contract, her neck quiver, and her lips curl back to expose bright teeth. Presently the crying began to fade brokenly as though her wolf were running away now into a dense forest. So delicate was the ending that even the silence of the bay seemed to return to them cautiously.

"Beautiful," Gannett said.

"Then you don't think it's crazy?"

"Not in the least."

"I have been the whole wolf, Mr. Gannett."

"I was sure you had, Miss Kristol, or you never could have made that cry."

"And now you want me to go away."

"Yes. You understand that, don't you?"

"But poor Peter needs me, Mr. Gannett."

"He needs you, but he cannot receive you at this time."

"Are you going to talk bourgeois morality, Mr. Gannett?"

"I certainly hope not, Miss Kristol. The point I make is that far from helping the man, you are destroying him—and not because of ethical conflicts but because of much deeper ones."

"I know the darkness that Peter is in with those mad books, Mr. Gannett, and Ruth's common sense can't help him out."

"But neither can your crying and your chanting and your beauty, Miss Kristol. They will only drive him to further despair, and young David will come down on you like a hawk."

She nodded slowly. "Yes, you're right."

"And you are not altogether wrong, Miss Kristol. But you have seen much further than Peter and so he is not ready for you. And David is too young and Ruth is of a very different cast of mind. So you must leave them."

"Where will I go, Mr. Gannett? Is one of the beneficiaries of your foundation studying lycanthropy?"

"Don't be cynical, Miss Kristol. I don't know much about things out there. The world has gotten beyond me, but I have the distinct impression that it is much wider and more tolerant than it was when I was your age."

"Oh tolerant, yes, Mr. Gannett. I can find plenty who will tolerate a person who bays at the moon, but can I find someone who will go any further than tolerance?"

"Someone, if you search relentlessly, who will go a great deal further."

"How can you be so sure?"

"Because I myself would have, Miss Kristol, if I were younger."

She looked down at him intently. "I believe you would, Mr. Gannett."

"It's one of the questionable privileges of age, Miss Kristol, to pass pleasantries which need never be followed by deeds. You honor me by seeing that I was serious. Another questionable prerogative of age is the making of valedictions. Will you take one of mine seriously?"

"I will."

"This is purely speculative, Miss Kristol, so please do not be offended. You say you have learned devolution. And indeed you have, marvelously well. You can visit your deepest roots. Maybe this was the task of your generation. I admire your courage. But have you learned evolution? Your generation seems to want to protract its innocence indefinitely, as though it thought it was perpetually in the garden. You might consider that."

"Do you think it's harder to be a woman than a wolf, Mr. Gannett?"

"Perhaps. And certainly harder to be what comes after woman."

Abbey Kristol's eyes shone down at him with a special intensity. "What comes after woman, Mr. Gannett?"

Gannett threw up his hands. "The wisdom is in the asking." Then he drew back a step from the wall. "Now I must be going, Miss Kristol. I am very weary. You have disturbed my old age mightily and I can't thank you enough for it."

She looked back at him, but almost distractedly, her eyes inward. "I think I'll stay a while longer."

"All right. But before I go, may I know your resolve?"

"You think I need to leave immediately?"

"For the sake of the others, instantly, I'm afraid."

"Then I'll go tomorrow."

"Do you need any funds, Miss Kristol?"

"No, Mr. Gannett."

"Good-bye, Miss Kristol."

"Good-bye, Mr. Gannett. Thanks for your lovely wall."

"Good-bye."

In the parlor Haig was robed and fretting fiercely. "Where have you been, sir? I thought I heard a wolf."

"You did, Andrew, but it was a she-wolf that is now domesticated and harmless."

"Have the Sterns brought a wolf, sir?"

"They are losing her tomorrow. Do you follow my meaning, Andrew?"

"Do you mean, sir, she made that howling?"

"Yes, but she's leaving tomorrow, I told you. There is nothing more to fear."

"Thank God."

Gannett tumbled into bed totally enervated. At the last moment all of his energies failed. He could not even finish his brandy. At the verge of the great priest's profound darkness he heard the call of the wolf, but he could not tell from which side.

3

Three days later Gannett and David sat in the sun on the rocks. Each seemed lost in thoughts which, judging from their faces, were mildly sad. Gannett was the first to speak. "Now that I don't have anything to worry about, David, I hardly know what to do with myself."

"I didn't think you were ever that worried."

"Oh yes. The worst time was the morning Abbey left. I woke up thinking that she had thrown herself over the cliff. I had told her she must depart instantly and she had jumped. It was a foolish fear, but I was sure of it. That's why I rushed over to Stedford House in such a sweat and was so relieved to learn that your mother had driven her to the station."

David shrugged, "It would have been better for her to jump than to stay here."

"Well . . ." Gannett did not make his disagreement any plainer. "Then I began to worry about your father. I feared that she had left too late after all."

"I knew he would be OK."

The two of them simultaneously turned to the window where Stern's head could be seen above the hedge. The distant tapping and tinkling of the typewriter was almost merry. Presently Ruth came into the yard and draped some damp linen over the lawn chairs. Stern looked up briefly, frowned, and then resumed his tapping away at K's arbitrary God.

"So what shall I worry about now, David? Shall I worry about you?"

"No, don't worry about me, Mr. Gannett."

"All right, then I'll worry about myself, David."

The boy looked up quickly. "Why?"

"I'll worry about why I couldn't explain to you and arrange things so that we could have Abbey with us."

David shook his head. "Nobody could've done that, Mr. Gannett. She had to go."

Gannett shook his head in firm disagreement. "I know a man who could."

"Who?"

"A man who once stayed in Stedford House, like your father, a very holy man whose flesh is translucent and whose bones are tunnels of light. He is probably the only man alive who could teach us how not to tangle Abbey in our desires."

The translucent flesh and the bones of light started David shaking his head gently even before Gannett finished. "I never know whether you're talking about anything real or not, Mr. Gannett. But you *do* the right thing. You helped me save my father. That's all I care about."

Malagueña

I

When I was a boy in New Orleans I attended Jesuit High School, the only Protestant in my class — an Episcopalian, however, and therefore in the eyes of the priests not entirely beyond the pale. Perhaps there were a half-dozen of us non-Catholics in the whole school of some six hundred. I knew only one other, the most improbable of all, a curly-headed Jew named Ely Da Silva, an accomplished clarinetist, admired and beloved by all. Perhaps not improbable. In fact, sometimes I think that the Catholics and the Jews, without knowing it themselves, have stood for centuries side by side against the innumerable excesses of us Protestants — antinomianism, latitudinarianism, enthusiasm, et cetera. Who could blame them?

I was a docile and hardworking student, come with my family during the summer from Alabama. New Orleans was a great romance for me. The very names of my classmates seemed exotic if not downright epic. Giraldo Tuminello. Marcel LaNasa. Felix Pennyworth. Sean Boylan. Raymond Rodrigo. Bernard Bouvier. Caffery St. John. Andre Orlando. Earl Ponce. The scholastic who taught my section of the freshman class was Mr. Leary, Thomas Leary, a red-haired Irishman, cleft-chinned and as lean as a whippet. We all loved him to distraction for his wit and learning and for his great vitality. He made us names and epithets and thus constellated us in the bright sky of his imagination. George Terrance he called Georgicus Agricola, Man of Earth. Giraldo was Il Giorno, The Dayspring. Felix the Unculpable Cat. Diminutive Marcel was La Narizita lisped in pure Castilian. Bouvier was Bubulus the Ox-Hearted. And so on. I was Ocellus Luminosus, Little Bright Eye, "because," said Mr. Leary, "at the same time the thick lens of his spectacles contracts the cornea, it causes it to burn like a gem in the night." Sometimes he called me Myriad-eyed or the Paycock, the latter with a wide Irish brogue. I gloried in all these names, my obvious defect transformed into pure gold. We scoured our *Beginner's Homeric Greek Reader* for a name for Mr. Leary. After long debate we decided on Doctor Rhododactylos. We would have preferred rosy-cheeked to rosy-fingered, but it was not in our vocabulary. No matter. Mr. Leary savored it. "It has the true Homeric ring, lads. Listen to the rotund assonance of the o's. Doctor Rhododactylos. Listen to the sturdy alliteration of the dentals. Doctor Rhododactylos. But these two effects are counterpointed by the sweetly falling cadence—the two lapsing trochees followed by a dactyl. Doctor Rhododactylos. I accept it, lads, with deep gratitude and humility. May I rise each day to the auroral brightness of your epithet." He bowed deeply to us. We cheered like crazy. Which of us could have guessed that we had been so learned and ingenious?

In those days, shortly after World War II, all us Jesuit boys wore the wool olive drab uniform of the U.S. Marines, including jackets that flared out from the waist and snappy little overseas caps. "The skirts," the boys of Holy Cross and St. Aloysius called us. "Yeah?" we said. "Who do the convent girls from St. Anne's and Sacred Heart look at on the streetcar?" The uniforms were free, war surplus. "A deal between the Commandant of the Corps and the Black Pope," said Earl Ponce, quoting his father, a cynic.

"Really, Pontificus?" said Mr. Leary. "Do you foresee our great amphibians evangelized, General Puller the Savonarola of a new theocracy?"

"Hypocrisy," said Earl Ponce firing blindly from the cul-de-sac where Mr. Leary's irony had driven him.

"Spell it."

"H-i-p-p-o-c-r-a-c-y."

"Just as I suspected. Government by horses, Houyhnhnm-like." We all laughed at Earl Ponce's discomfiture though of course we were as dazzled as he. "Since you laugh, I take it you have all visited Houyhnhnmland." Sudden silence. "Who knows the Houyhnhnms?" Pause. "Nay, not a mother's son. Why this is the very hypocrisy of which Pontificus lamely speaks. It may, in fact, have been a prefiguration of this doleful ignorance that sent the poor dean nodding into madness."

You can be sure that by the next day all of us had managed to scratch up some fractional knowledge of Swift and his fabulous horses. Some, like me, had even begun a desperate reading of the great satire. That was Mr. Leary's genius, to cast before us adumbrations of the great shapes of wisdom so that we all tried to struggle up from the cave of ignorance, and struggle mightily we did, for we were too innocent then to be daunted by the deepness and darkness of the place.

Well, not only were the uniforms free, but also the inevitable alterations. Three black seamsters came out to the school from the famous tailor's establishment which had its quarters in a great buzzing loft on Carondelet Street, Barry and Juden. Did I say the conspiracy between the Catholics and the Jews was unconscious? When they had fitted all us freshmen, the work of several days, Mr. Leary said, "Have all you lads been measured by the Fates?"

Felix Pennyworth said, "Atropos, Clotho, and Lachesis were women in ancient antiquity, Doctor Rhododactylos, and not to my knowledge black." We gave Felix a great cheer. In fact, he was the only champion we had that could sometimes tilt with Mr. Leary, who said on this occasion, "Well mewed, Unculpable Cat, except for a glaring redundancy. Can you stalk it and pounce on it?"

"Ancient antiquity."

"Splendid. Splendid." We gave murmurous approval. "And one last point, Felix Felicitatus. If we are to see the great figures of antiquity in our time, we must watch out for certain clever diminutions and protean transformations. Know ye Proteus, Crafty Cat?"

"No sir."

"Find him. Pounce on him. Pin him. Make him reveal to you the true nature of all appearances. And when you have done so, out of old regard, whisper in his ear that I, Thomas Leary, send him felicitations."

"I will do so, doctor." We all gave a great cheer. And now we must run to the classical dictionary and learn of wily Proteus.

Bernard Bouvier's reaction to the black seamsters was different. For several days he went around grabbing at our cullions. "Which side does you dress on, young massuh?"

"On the side sinister, Bubulus, son of Ham," said Felix.

The prefect of discipline was Father Durr, an awesome man with bushy black brows which were wild and tangled as though a tempest of anger was always on the verge of erupting from his forehead. "Stay out of his clutches, my young scholars," said Mr. Leary, "for if he snares you transgressing the most minor injunction, I can do nothing for you. Though I fall on my knees and make the heavens weep, I am powerless to change one jot of his fell penance."

It was Father Durr who addressed us freshmen on the first day we wore the olive drab. "Men have died in this uniform defending us from Hitler and from the so-called Imperial Majesty of Japan. See that you keep it sacred. In other words, if I find any of you in a uniform that is dirty, torn, or marred by any mark of neglect whatsoever, I will have you in my Penance Hall—in Dis, the ninth and ultimate circle, among the traitors, which you students of the medieval epic will remember." Later, Mr. Leary told us whom we would encounter there—Judas Iscariot, Brutus, and Cassius. So we all learned something about the Inferno.

That night I discovered the name tag sewn on the inside of the waist of my marine pants. "A. M. Graham," it said. "528-4907-63." What was the fate of A. M. Graham, I wondered. Had he died in action, washed up on the coral reef of Tarawa? Or had he survived and was now a college boy with a beautiful steady? I inclined toward the former because it did not pain me to think of being washed to bare bone in the tropic waters of the Pacific. But when I thought of A. M. Graham in college, I thought of the old car he bought with his mustering-out pay and of the nights in it with his girl, and then I would go through a terrifying bout of masturbatory temptations. ("Lads, when Onan spilled his seed upon the ground, it displeased the Lord, and He slew him.") When I look back now on those sweaty nights I can see the irony of that whole sexual abstention business as clear as a bell. The good Jesuits, through their vows of chastity, romanticizing of Mary, stories of ardent saints self-flung among brambles, and so forth, made lust for us boys so luscious that it never for a minute in our waking or in our dreams entirely left our consciousness. I sometimes wonder why the father confessors in their boxes did not raise a great prayer of petition: "O Holy Pope, we must cut the hands off these lads or else change the law. Otherwise they are all doomed to the eternal bonfire, for their contrition is hollow and their resolution is as straws in the wind."

These labels that revealed the previous owners of our uniforms were the subject of many bizarre speculations and jokes, of course. Some claimed to have inherited the garments of great heroes. Caffery St. John, whose precursor, he claimed, was Eugene Knight, said that he could feel a magic power creeping into his muscles, and to prove it he threw Marcel down on the schoolyard and then apologized because he had not realized his Herculean strength. But Bouvier the Ox-man won the prize of our most raucous laughter. His tag, he said, showed the name B. J. Biggers—69696969—a stud from Houston, Texas, half-black, half-Indian, and half-Mexican.

"Three halves?" said Felix.

"Right," said Bouvier. "That's how come he's got three nuts, like Al Rothe." Rothe was a fabled senior on the football team. "Biggers plugged the whole female population of the Fiji Islands during the war in the Pacific."

"And what benefits have you derived?" asked Felix.

"I shot a load into the air.

It fell to earth I know not where . . ."

"That'll do!" said Felix, but already Earl Ponce and Caffery St. John were bearing Bouvier down into the grass of the schoolyard, and a moment later Andre Orlando located his cullions shrinking behind the thick wool. "Renounce again the world, the flesh, and the devil, Bubulus, or else Father Orlando must perform the castigare for your own good." Bouvier laughed and struggled.

"Do you renounce, Bubulus?"

"I renounce, Father!"

"Let him up."

He stood panting. "You bastards! What if Father Durr catches me with all this shit on my uniform!" So we beat the dust and the dry October grasses off his olive drabs and straightened his tie. "Inspect him, Ocellus!" I squinted at him minutely and pronounced him clean. "Bubulus Immaculatus," I said, and we all began to mumble in mock adoration until laughter overtook us.

Who could have predicted that the two in our class to fall into the hands of Father Durr would be Giraldo Tuminello and I? For I was the most docile of all, and Tuminello, lapped in centuries of Sicilian fat, was the most affable and benign. And yet it happened. One April morning before first class we were jousting in the hallway, like young bullocks high-spirited in spring, for the love of each other—and a good match too, he as awkward as I was nearsighted. And then by luck I got my shoulder squarely into his ribs and he went careening away with a gust of plump laughter. And did not see the trophy case—the golden batsmen and golden bowlers, the glinting quarterbacks with arms cocked, the silver basketballs which glowed in the April light like the pates of old philosophers dreaming microcosms, the runners with torches, the Victoire of Samothrace. Luckily he fell against a wooden corner post and did not break the glass. But inside, a golden cup toppled down and lay rolling to and fro on its lip like a living thing in pain. And there on the glass materialized the image of the genius of high conduct and probity, Father Durr. "Stand up, lad," he said. "Stand there by the window if you please." Tuminello did as he was told. And let it be said for me that I did not desert our Giorno, our Dayspring. I stood by. Father Durr noticed me. "Is this he who delivered the Herculean blow?"

Tuminello tried to shake his head, get me off the hook, but his need for a friend in woe was too great. He could not. Besides, I was already saying, "Yes, Father."

"Then stand by your fellow." This I did while Father Durr fished from the pocket of his cassock a great ring of keys. He opened the trophy case and set the golden cup back on the little pedestal that was covered with pearly cloth. "Just so. That's much better, isn't it, lads?" We knew we were not expected to answer and so waited for him to lock the case again and continue. Meanwhile first bell rang and the hall emptied of all except us three.

"Will it be the gloves at recess, lads?" That was the standard punishment for those caught fighting. At recess they were stripped to the waist, fitted with heavy boxing gloves and mouthpieces, and forced to fight until one or both could not go on.

"No, Father," I said. "We weren't fighting."

He tsked regretfully. "It's a great lesson for the other lads. These contentions always begin heroically, with great flurries, Meleager and Ajax, and then slog down to the base blood and sweat of all disrupters of the peace. Like a little parable in action. You see, lads?"

"Yes, Father," I said, "but we're friends."

"We couldn't hit each other," added Tuminello. The horrible prospect of a bloody boxing match between the two of us gave his usually high voice a manful huskiness.

"Very well. Then we will make do with Penance Hall. I perceive several offenses. I will enumerate them slowly and you may offer defense if you choose. Misconduct in the hall. Damage to school property. Disrespect to the athletic glories of the past. Conduct unbecoming the uniform of the United States Marines. Tardiness to class." He paused. Both of us knew better than to note that our tardiness was the result of his holding us. He continued. "Then we are in agreement. Now. As you know, my practice is to assign three days in Penance Hall for every offense. Five offenses. Fifteen days." Undoubtedly both of us winced. He looked at us closely. "I believe I have not had either of you lads before. Is that correct?"

"Yes, Father," we said simultaneously.

"Good. Consider, lads. There was only the one shove, was there not?"

"Yes, Father."

"And from that sprang evils like a Hydra-headed monster. Is that not so?"

"Yes, Father."

"Let that be your lesson, lads. One small transgression, one lapse in vigilance is all the Evil One needs to plant the weeds that snuff out the soul's garden. Do you understand?"

"Yes, Father."

"I assign you three days in Penance Hall. God forgive me if my leniency is to your detriment." He looked at us sharply. "Have you nothing to say?"

"Thank you, Father."

"Three o'clock. Bring pencil and paper."

"Yes, Father."

When we arrived in class, the morning prayers were already recited. Mr. Leary received the account of our transgressions with doleful countenance, but could not keep out of his eye a sparkle of amusement. "Oh what a fall is here! What lamentations and Jeremiads, lads, can express our sorrow today?"

"Perhaps, Doctor Rhododactylos," said Felix, "Ely the musical Jew can come and play us a threnody."

"No, let us work," said Mr. Leary with comic sternness, "work on. Less stir, less suffering."

But something had occurred to me. I raised my hand and was recognized. "Do you think, Mr. Leary, that Jews are naturally more musical than we are?"

"Not necessarily more, Ocellus. Remember Bach and Mozart and Beethoven. But Jews are indeed deeply musical. Ely is of the great Sephardic branch of Jewry, which has roamed homeless half a millennium. And long before that I do not doubt that some distant ancestor of Ely's blew the shofar, the ram's horn, in the courts of the pharaohs. Exile, dispersion, wandering—a man must sing or die. And perhaps, Ocellus, when you and Il Giorno have come back to us from your suffering you will sing for us, too, as sweetly as the misfortunate nightingale, 'Tereu! Tereu!' "

So Tuminello and I went to Penance Hall for three long afternoons—three o'clock to six. The penitential task we were set was the copying of pages from the instruction manual for the M-1 rifle. I wondered briefly if Father Durr saw this as an extension of the training which we received from Sergeant Moore during Friday drills, but I quickly discovered that he did not. The pages were torn from the manual and deliberately shuffled so that the unfortunate copier could get no sense of sequence—all a jumble of bolts, latches, springs, slides, etc. So we copied diligently but dazedly. Three close-packed pages was the minimum acceptable for each hour. And while we copied—ten miserable miscreants in all—Father Durr's minion patrolled the aisles continuously. He was a veteran who had enlisted before graduation, back now for his last year. Instead of a surplus marine uniform he wore army khakis. He was a sergeant in the reserves. Over his breast pocket were three rows of ribbons—one, we knew, for the Purple Heart, because he had been wounded at El Alamein. The wound was not visible, but another ghastly memento of the desert war was. He had no hair of any kind on his head—not an eyebrow, not an eyelash, not a hair in his nostrils—all burned away, the story was, by the pitiless African sun, which had also destroyed the natural pigment of his skin leaving only a gray pallor. To Tuminello and me he was the ghastliest remnant of war imaginable, a living dead man. He rarely spoke but the one word, "Faster," accompanied by a rap with a ruler on the knuckles of the penitent caught lagging. I myself received a rap on the knuckles. It happened like this.

Every afternoon I copied diligently, though my fingers cramped and the pain crept into the palm of my hand and even up to the wrist. But there was a consolation. From the windows of the opposite wing of the school came the sound of the band practicing for the spring concert—mostly marches, fanfares for brass, and such stirring stuff. There was, however, one somewhat slower piece, to me lovely and exotic, whose title, I learned, was *Malagueña*. For many years I would not know what a Malagueña was, but as those afternoons wore on and the band practiced, the word and the music began to have for me an indescribable sweetness. I cannot specify precisely the ingredients of my feelings. Sublimated sexual longing no doubt twined itself around the melodious strains of the song. The Spanish word and my knowledge that Ely the Sephardic Jew was among the performers lent to the music a great sweep of time and space and even of race. Perhaps, too, the pain in my hand and, paradoxically, the waning of my penitential time tinged the melody with a gentle melancholy. At any rate I began to be more and more deeply moved until I had something very close to a vision.

A little after five o'clock of my third and final day in Penance Hall, the ninth of nine hours, I suddenly stopped copying. I had glimpsed out of the corner of my eye, through the open window that looked down on the schoolyard, a figure in black—Mr. Leary. Probably it was the bobbing of his red head that caught my attention. He was walking slowly across the trampled ground toward the small outbuilding which held the chapel and the quarters of the priests and scholastics. To his left, near the end of the long yard, the baseball team had stopped practicing and was gathered around the coach—a motionless tableau of perpetual camaraderie. But Mr. Leary was not motionless. He continued across the yard away from me, which made me reflect that in less than two months we would part and I would never see him again. For he was just completing his three-year teaching obligation and, after another year in seminary, would be ordained. Tears sprang to my eyes, selfish tears. I wept for my own deprivation. Who would ever again call me Ocellus Luminosus, Myriad-eyed, the Paycock? Then came the curious moment that was like a vision. Three things happened at once: a small breeze swirled into the yard and made whirligigs of dust at Mr. Leary's feet, the invisible band in the opposite wing floated out upon the afternoon air the sensuous opening of *Malagueña,* and I flew out of the window and hovered over the yard like one of the scavenger gulls that were always coming over from the river. "Doctor Rhododactylos, Doctor Rhododactylos!" I called. My mewing cry gave the words a high, unearthly sound. And with my bright eye I made a thick honey of time. I kept the baseball team motionless. I stopped Mr. Leary's feet. I folded the wind and tucked it under my wings so that the little whirligigs of dust failed and the beautiful *Malagueña* lay still upon the air like a gentle fluting, like the wimpling of the hood of a nun at prayer. But this beautiful arrest lasted only a moment. Something descended on me from the sky. My wings buckled and I fell down.

It was the hairless veteran striking my knuckles with his sharp ruler. "Copy," he said. I don't know how many times he had to hit me to retrieve me from my vision, more than once, I know, because my knuckles were ringing with pain. And then suddenly Tuminello growled, "Leave him alone." Growled it like a dangerous dog, hackles up. Who knows what intuition that fat and usually fearful soul had of my state? Probably he, too, had seen Mr. Leary cross the yard and knew the source of my anguish. At any rate, at the sound of this disturbance, Father Durr rose from the desk in the front of the room where he had been working and came back to us. "What is it?"

"He's crying, Father," said the vet, in an utterly flat voice, as though the sun had burned away not only hair and skin but even the cords of his throat and all other instruments of resonance and timbre. And at that moment, I swear it, the band ceased to play, a sharp gust of afternoon breeze rattled the window pane, and Mr. Leary entered the chapel.

"You have less than an hour, lad. Buckle down and copy, or you shall have to come back."

So I bent again to the long litany of linch pin, coil, and breech. I copied.

II

And have for many years been a sort of copyist and at the same time a faithful disciple of Mr. Leary—a four-eyed librarian, a lover of words, and an amateur Latinist. Curiously, though, the word *Malagueña* for many years lay in shadow down in the bottom of my mind like a bright thing unglimpsed on the ocean floor. I will relate how I caught sight of it again three years ago and how just last April I fished it up from the bottom, an old doubloon, the golden coin of my youth, turned it in the sun, and saw whose face it bore.

The first incident involved a black poet and another of my rare flights of the imagination. The poet came to the city where I live to give a reading. When I told my wife and my daughter Sarah that I planned to attend the reading, they were both surprised, because I virtually never go to such things. My daughter, who was eighteen then and who has always fancied herself a master of irony, said, "Why, father, this man has not been dead the two thousand years requisite to warrant your attention."

"Yes he has," I said. And I showed the two of them the newspaper publicity photo. The black poet was standing alone in a small unkempt garden. He wore a white sweater. A big black tau cross hung from his neck, and on his shoulder lay a tendriled shadow in the shape of a cross, thrown by a trellis somewhere off to the photographer's right. "See?" I said. "No dear." My wife shook her head, and my daughter said, "I don't get it."

"What a disappointment you two sibyls are."

My wife smiled at that. "If there's one thing I never pretended to be, dear, it's sibylline." She patted my head and went about her business there in the kitchen. Meanwhile my daughter continued to study the picture and the caption underneath. "Dig this, mother. 'Mr. So-and-so—' who can pronounce the names blacks invent nowadays?—'has recently vaulted into the poetic limelight with the publication of his second volume, *The Obsidian Osiris*, widely acclaimed as a mythic work of the highest order of the imagination.' " She whooped. "Oh wow, father. What do you think this guy is? A reincarnation of some old Egyptian god?"

"What else?"

"Oh boy! Have you checked out the archaeological accuracy of these Osiris poems, father? I'll bet the guy is an absolute charlatan."

I silently agreed. But we were both wrong. He was no charlatan. In fact, he read with as melodious a voice as I have ever heard. I don't know that his poems were actually very much above the ordinary— I'm no judge—but they seemed so to me. There was one long poem in particular in which he likened his Mississippi grandmother to the grief-stricken Isis rowing about the crocodile-infested marshes of the Nile calling the name of her dead brother, gathering what she

could find of his dear dismembered body into her lap. Only for the
poet's grandmother it was all her brothers and sons and grandsons,
and of course it was not the villainous Seth they were victims of but
the fratricidal white man. Yet the poem was not bitter, nor even
unrelieved in its melancholy, for in the end the dark keening of the
old woman split the gates of the underworld and plunged down like
a root of song and wreathed itself about the hearts of her sons. This
poem was so moving that it actually brought the tears to my eyes. I
was glad that my cynical daughter was not with me. My wife's
presence I didn't regret. She patted my hand, as if to say, "It's all
right, dear, weep if you want to, and no matter why." And she would
never ask why. She would simply guess that the poem had dipped
deep into some old well of feeling, and if I never revealed the springs
of my weeping, she would not care, because she willingly took to her
breast all of my foolish mysteries with myself and held us in equal
love. As one interested in archaeology, I note that earth treats man's
mysteries the same, is gently incurious about our ruins, softens
them with grasses, tints them with lichen, and takes them to her lap.

Actually, it would have done my wife no good to probe the sources
of my feelings of that moment anyway, because I have never under-
stood them myself. On the other hand, the curious transformation
that took place a few minutes later and that produced a copious
freshet from my eyes I think I understand pretty well.

After the Osiris poem the black poet read a number of more
recent poems, all spoken by a comic persona from Houston named
Garbanzo Negro who used a curious patois that mixed black street
talk and what the poet called "Mex-Tex Spanish." Full of jibes aimed
at the white man's penchant for cleanliness, sexual prudery, and
war, these poems kept the mostly white audience in stitches. Then
he put his books and papers aside, stepped out away from the
lectern, and smiled a broad white smile. He was wearing precisely
the clothes of the photograph, as though the white sweater, the
black tau cross, and the black pants were his poet's equivalent of
clerical garb. And I was thinking that he was indeed a miracle man.
In a time when it was virtually obligatory for black intellectuals and
artists to take the hard line against whites, it seemed to me that he
had resolved in his soul all white prejudice and folly and tran-
substantiated it into love. And apparently most of the audience
shared something of my feelings, for several of the young people
shouted, "More! More!"

The black poet bowed and smiled. "Thank you. I hadn't planned
to stop just yet. In fact, I was just going to warm up my guitar and as

my last offering recite for you a ballad, not as short as it ought to be I'm afraid, entitled 'La Señora Negra del Inferno.' " That brought from us a rally of applause. He took up the guitar that had been leaning against the lectern and removed it from its case. Then he sat down and after a moment's tuning began to play a lovely soft piece—by Fernando Ser, I think. When that was done we applauded him warmly. Then came the first image of several which, causing in my mind a curious transformation, produced the tears that I have spoken of.

The black poet lay his guitar across his knees and opened his hands. He was a black black man. Consequently, the pink of his palms and of the undersides of his fingers was especially striking. And of course what came to me immediately was the word *rhododactylos*. It rose up from the floor of my mind like one of those phosphorescent, bejeweled creatures of the ocean trenches, brightening fabulously as it rose, bearing with it all of my old love of Mr. Leary. But I kept control of myself, kept the tears out of my eyes while the black poet said, "Now 'La Señora Negra del Inferno.' As I recite this ballad for you I'm going to play on my guitar the melody of a song called "La Malagueña" which, as you may know, begins 'Qué bonitos ojos tienes.' "

This was not my *Malagueña* of many years before. It was a softer, lighter thing, but I couldn't today hum or whistle a bar of it. The word *Malagueña* and that opening line, "What beautiful eyes you have," immediately so amplified the feelings which the black grandmother and the rosy fingers already had released that my memory of those minutes during which he recited remains a curious blend of fact and vision. No doubt I could sort out the two elements fairly accurately, but I prefer to recount them as I experienced them.

The poem was about a black madonna who went to a dark penitential place and redeemed many whites, the persecuters of her race, and many blacks, its betrayers. She excited in them a towering lust, and then by the operation of her eyes, which were glowing coals, transformed their lust to love. The black poet did not merely speak the words of his poem but rendered them recitativo to the melody of the guitar. The black madonna looked to me like a mestiza. I saw her slip into the chapel of my boyhood and kiss the white cheek of the weeping Mary that the boys of the Sodality adored, and kiss old Father Palma, too, the holiest of all and the priest of the Sodality. In that wide niche of the chapel the white madonna of the pieta turned black, and held in her lap not the broken body of Jesus but a guitar—and plucked it with rosy fingers and sang I know not what, for then I was not there. I was in my classroom on the other side of the schoolyard and the song was broken by the wind. I was naked and ashamed. In front of me was Mr. Leary sitting in a chair. In his lap he held my marine uniform and slowly stitched it with a huge needle, as long as a sword. And what he stitched it to was his black cassock. Then there came a frightful sound in my ear, as of an ancient musketry. I burst into tears. My wife patted my hand, saying, "Don't you want to applaud, dear?" And I did. We both did.

But I was warned by my vision that night that the agents of my youth had not yet redeemed me and that I was still in a dark penitential place, where Father Durr continually described the rank unweeded garden of my soul and the hairless vet struck my knuckles with his ruler to the insistent measure of Lecuona's *Malagueña*. Therefore it was no surprise to me when my daughter Sarah made her announcement several weeks later. She broke the news to me in the kitchen on a cold Sunday afternoon in January. I was sitting at the old butcher block which my wife had converted into a table. My wife already knew what Sarah was going to say. They had discussed it. I could tell that, but I wasn't angry. Mothers and daughters should confide. And besides, I myself knew in essence what it was going to be though I had never allowed myself to put it into words. "I'm going to move in with Hannah," my daughter said. She looked at me very steadily. "You understand, don't you, father? Because I don't want there to be any falseness between us."

"I understand," I said. "I'm sorry to see you go. I'll miss you."

"All children must fly from the nest sooner or later," said my wife. That was not really the issue, of course. But I could hardly charge my wife with being too sweetly oblique. After all, that was the only thing I myself had spoken of—Sarah's leaving, my missing her, and nothing at all about where she was going.

Sarah smiled. "Don't worry, father. I'll come to town and call you up often and say ironic things just to keep you up to the mark."

"I hope you will," I said.

"See you later," she said. She came over and kissed me on the forehead, and I squeezed her hand. I should have gotten up and hugged her, but I didn't. I should have helped her out with her bags, but I didn't want to see Hannah standing there beside her car, perched rather, like a hawk, bending on us her bright gaze of pure appetency.

My wife went with Sarah out to the car—and embraced her, I'm sure. Her eyes when she came back to the kitchen were red and mildly accusatory. I said, "If I had more than one child it would matter less."

My wife, her lips trembling, said nothing.

"Maybe," I said, "it would matter less if it weren't Hannah. Not because she's a Jewess, but because she's so dark and fierce." I looked at my wife. She was leaning against the stove, still too moved to trust herself to speak. I said, "But it's that first thing that really hurts. If you have only one child, you don't want her to be sterile. You don't want the lesbians to have her."

My wife began to weep openly, which restored her voice. "I couldn't give you but one child," she said.

"That's right. And it was a close call at that. We have to be grateful for what we have." I thought that I was giving her the reassurance she needed, but she hardly seemed to pay any attention to what I said. "They say," she said, in a bitterly melancholic tone, "this happens when the mother fails to provide an acceptable pattern of femininity."

"Or," I said, "when the father fails to demonstrate that heterosexuality can be warm and rewarding."

That was the moment in which we should have come together, of course, in our mutual need, but we couldn't. I only sat staring at the scarifications of the old butcher block and pitying myself. And my wife, this once, the only time of our long life together, was frozen in her bitterness and couldn't comfort me.

That silence was almost disastrous. Our marriage bed grew cold. Our meals went silent into our mouths. January invaded the house and held it through May, through most of the summer. And then, inexplicably, with a perversity that made us smile at each other, we came together again in August, in the dog days, when the rest of the city, like a dispirited ship, lay becalmed through the breathless nights.

III

The memory of which hot nights was perhaps an indirect cause of the trip my wife and I made to Spain last spring. For it was exactly a year ago, in cold January, that we decided to go. We were sitting together in the kitchen by the old butcher block with our cups of tea. No doubt we were remembering separately that it was the anniversary of Sarah's departure, and remembering the half-year of sterile grief and guilt that followed. Fortunately nothing like that period had ever recurred. Still, neither of us had completely ceased to grieve. Enlightened and liberal people, I think, we nevertheless found it hard, having experienced an ecstasy which warms the very core of one's being, to face the fact that our child, a pretty girl child, would never know it.

"What are you thinking, professor?" said my wife, patting my hand. It's true, I was a professor. Just that fall the university in our city, in recognition of some Latin lexicographical work I had published, appointed me adjunct professor of classics, and one of their graduate students was consulting with me about his thesis. "I was just thinking," I lied, "that I haven't professed my love for you recently."

"Profess it."

"I love you."

"Very good." She kissed my lips.

"Qué bonitos ojos tienes," I said.

"No, my dear, you're the paycock." She took off my glasses and kissed the lids of my eyes.

"Are they a beautiful silvery blue?"

"Yes. Come with me." She set my glasses aside and led me out of the kitchen.

"Where are you taking me, wicked woman?" I cried blindly.

It was a lovely lovemaking, but afterwards my wife wept.

"Sarah?"

"Always Sarah."

"Don't weep, dear," I said, "because I'm going to take you on a fabulous voyage."

"Where?"

"To Spain."

"What is it? A filmstrip from the library?"

I laughed. "No. I'm serious. I'm going to take a leave of absence this spring. And my great lexicographical masterpiece is going to earn me four hundred dollars."

She sat up in bed. "Are you really serious?"

"Yes. I decided a half-hour ago."

So I arranged it—the charter flight and the apartment in Málaga, which I found through the house-exchange service our library subscribes to. And what a marvel the apartment was. The building was at the end of a cul-de-sac just off the section of Calle Granada restricted to pedestrian traffic. The entryway was guarded by a wrought-iron gate. The patio within was a little paradise. All around the edges ran a bright green creeper with fluffy yellow blossoms, similar to our St. John's wort. On the white walls climbed bougainvillea, red and purple, except for the west wall against which grew an espalier of thorn, a little like a hawthorn, but flowerless, tiny-leaved, with five branches perfectly even in length and perfectly parallel on each side of the trunk. There were two tiny lemon trees with hard green fruit, two rosebushes with red velvet roses, several hanging pots of fuchsia, and in the middle of all a thin curling jasmine so sweet that it perfumed all our nights.

The keeper of this paradise was La Señorita Emilia Cerezo Galvez, a tiny hunchbacked woman of perhaps sixty with the crispest black eyes I have ever seen, the eyes of an ecclesiastical examiner. They peeled us to the skin—no, deeper, to the very vestibule of the soul— and peered in. All in the first half-minute of our short acquaintance while we stood by her side door introducing ourselves, presenting the owner's letter, and requesting the key, as instructed. The eyes inspected us, found us safe, dull even perhaps—which was just as well, given the hordes of altogether too colorful German, Belgian, and American tourists that poured through Avenida Generalísimo Franco and up and down Calle Larios. She only glanced at the letter. "No puedo leer," she said, without the slightest embarrassment. But if she could not read, she nevertheless took the paper in minutely in that single glance—the signature, the letterhead, and perhaps other marks of authenticity.

I remarked the beauty and freshness of the little side street. All the balconies had flowers. "Una calle bonita," I said.

"No es una calle, señor. Es una callejuela."

And she was right. It was indeed a little lane. The voices and the footsteps of the passersby out on Calle Granada flowed in to us softened and sweetened by their passage through the little throat into our cul-de-sac—garganta dulce, I was tempted to say, but my Spanish is marginal and "sweet throat" might have been judged objectionable by our stern little virgin, keeper of the door. A moment later she gave me two keys, one for the wrought-iron patio gate and another for the apartment door. She pressed them into my palm and gave me precise instructions. The head of each key was a trifoil with the three centers bored out, cross or clover. I felt suddenly like the possessor of the means of entry into a royal cloister where beautiful ladies and holy monks strolled intermittently.

The señorita accompanied us through the iron door and the door to our apartment, making sure at each that I mastered the art of tripping the lock. Pleasant stay, she wished us, unsmiling. The apartment would be cleaned daily at ten. The city was full of shops, markets, and *buenas restaurantes*. Nevertheless, we were to inform her of any needs. A cook, for instance, could be procured if we wished. We thought not, but thanked her profusely, and watched her turn and walk, hunched, back toward her quarters.

The apartment was splendid—white walls, dark lacquered tile floors, hanging plants, mysterious little alcoves, bright kitchen, high-ceilinged bedroom, jalousies on the windows—air and light, everywhere air and light and precise shadow. In our city, except for a few crystal winter days, the sun embraces objects in a loose companionship. But in that apartment in Málaga light and shadow maintained severe and chaste proprieties.

"Everything is clear," said my wife. She looked at her face in the bedroom mirror, then turned and looked at mine. I laughed aloud. "Don't be afraid, dear. The light cannot destroy your beauty." But she remained pensive. "We will see," she said. "We'll see."

"Yes, we'll see," I said. "But first we must celebrate." I rushed out of the apartment and onto Calle Granada. Within ten steps of the entry to our cul-de-sac I found a shop that sold wines and liqueurs. Overhead hung the famous serrano hams tagged with cards that showed their vintage as it were. One was dated 1961. I bought a bottle of amontillado, handling it carefully, declining to let the shopkeeper wrap it in white paper, so that when I got back to the apartment I could hold the bottle up to the afternoon sunlight, give it a tiny shake, and point out to my wife the cloud of sediment that rose up from the bottom. "You know what that is?"

"No. What is it, dear?"

"A vestige of the sweet white winds that sweep the great vineyards over against Jerez and Montilla and dust the grapes."

She smiled. "Tu eres un aficionado de amontillado."

"More than an aficionado, my love—the very priest of Bacchus himself." I found small glasses in the kitchen, uncorked the bottle, poured, made several cabalistic gestures over the table, and said, "Drink this and preserve your body unto everlasting life, like a serrano ham."

My wife sipped with mock reverence, then she smiled and licked her lips. "It's salty."

"Salt is in the lips of the bibbler," I said. "For if the salt lose its flavor, whereof will it be salted?"

We took up our glasses and the bottle and wandered around the apartment, inspecting everything minutely, drinking in many places, getting tipsy. I spotted a lizard on the ceiling above the bed. It had little round suction cups on each of its toes. "Look," I said, pointing, "one of our prehistoric ancestors, among the first to crawl up out of the ur-slime."

"You would think he would get tired of hanging upside down."

"Saurian little incubus," I said. "He's just waiting for you to go to sleep."

"You will protect me, dear."

Back in the kitchen I poured the last of the sherry. "The lovely salty dregs." The light at the window was gray, all color bled away, everything chiaroscuro. Even so, a jar on the window sill caught my attention. I got up and brought it back to the table. "Look at this," I said.

"Juden," my wife said. "What does that mean?"

"Jews or beans. Which do you think is in there?"

"You're drunk."

I laughed. "We're going to see." I waved my hands over the mouth of the jar. "Abracadabraca. Abracadabraca. Answer my summons, Hannah!"

"Dear."

"Come!" I snatched the jar up by the neck and emptied its contents out onto the table—one brown bean which I scooped up instantly and skinned with my thumbs. "Too late. She slipped away."

"Dear."

We went to bed, but I'd had too much wine and the specter of Hannah rustled in the dark room—or was it the tiny footpad of the lizard as he inched his way toward an unwary insect?

Ironically there came within the week a letter from our Sarah. Hannah had had a little windfall—dead uncle. They planned to come to Spain, would like to do Córdoba with us, glance in on our little bower of bliss, three days at the most, for they didn't want to ruin our *miel de luna*, our honeymoon.

So we rented a car and made reservations for four at the Hotel Maimonides. "Don't say anything," I told my wife. "It's an excellent hotel, right across the street from the mosque. If Hannah chooses to detect ironies, it's not my fault."

"I don't know what you're talking about, dear. I trust your judgment entirely."

I told Señorita Galvez that we would be gone to Córdoba for two days and a night, to meet my daughter and a friend, who would return with us to the apartment for a visit of two days or so. The dueña had not spoken of guests, said the señorita. Nevertheless, they would be coming, I said. Consequently, the beds in the other room would have to be made. If there was an extra charge, I would pay the señorita directly, or the dueña, whom I would write to in any case. I spoke precisely and coldly. Nevertheless, I feared the virgin of the door might summon a priestly master-at-arms to demand the surrender of the holy trifoil keys. Who is the friend of the daughter? inquired the señorita. Another girl somewhat older I said, una compañera de la universidad. She nodded and went her slow hunched way. My lie sickened me, for I knew the virgin's black eyes would impale in a trice the nature of my daughter's compañera.

The four of us met, as agreed, in the lobby of the Maimonides. Our daughter Sarah looked well—no, I must be honest, she looked radiant. Her cheeks were as pink as a Goya picnicker's, kissed by the Castilian sun. She gave my wife and me great hugs and then stood back and examined us, which caused her to say in a gusty voice that rang off the marble, "I can see that the *miel de luna* is going great, guys." My wife laughed and blushed. I suppose I blushed too. Meanwhile Hannah stood aside, absenting herself graciously from our familial intimacies. Intimacies? Hardly, with Sarah trumpeting them to the tourists of every nation that thronged the lobby. Nevertheless there was a different quality to Hannah's presence. If Sarah was radiant, Hannah was darkly liquescent, as though the sun which had pinked Sarah's cheeks had softened at last those hard limbs and those hungry hawk's eyes. Even her Jewishness and her sex she wore lightly now, gone the great single earring, the cat's-eye that used to shine from her index finger, the boots, and the tight britches. She wore a long severe dress of dark blue and an amber toquilla on her shoulders. Her black hair was pulled back in a bun. We called to her to come to us. My wife kissed her cheek.

But amid these gay greetings and happy transformations I wore a serpent in my heart. I hated Hannah, because it galled me that Sarah should shine in her presence so much more brightly than she ever had in our house. The truth was that ever since Sarah's departure that bitter January, I had hoped she would be suddenly repelled by Hannah and come back to us. Nothing now seemed less likely. Nevertheless I smiled to hide my venomous sentiments. Away we went to the bar to hear of the great cities of Castile, which rolled off Hannah's tongue with such a perfect intonation of harsh Spanish music that I was actually startled, wondering half-seriously if she were an avatar of some old medieval Jew living learnedly among celtiberians in the shadow of the caliphate—Salamanca, Avila, Segovia, El Escorial, Madrid, Toledo, Aranjuez.

We drank amontillado. At a certain point, as the afternoon drew to a close, our daughter said, "Guess what we saw in Toledo."

"I can't," said my wife.

"I will," I said. "The great El Greco, the Burial of Count Orgaz, and among the heavenly hosts Mary, with a face much like Hannah's."

"Gracias, señor," said Hannah with a perfect Castilian lisp and a slight bow of her head. I had been careful to keep any hint of irony out of my voice. She was equally careful.

"Oh sure. Everybody sees that," said Sarah. "But what I had in mind was the synagogue of Santa Maria la Blanca."

"The synagogue of Santa Maria la Blanca!" I snorted. "No doubt here they have a Blessed Chapel of Santo Maimonides." I laughed. Sarah laughed. And even Hannah made a throaty noise of dark mirth. But my wife refused to see any incongruity. "Well, there's a cathedral within the mosque."

"Yes," I said, "we'll see that in the morning."

My wife pressed on. "So, why shouldn't they name a synagogue for Mary? It was in synagogues she prayed all her life." And she continued, almost musingly, "But why la blanca, Sarah?"

Sarah turned to Hannah and gave her the question as it were—perhaps because the effect of the synagogue had been greater on Hannah and so it was hers to describe. "Because," she said, "all the lower walls are white, also the columns and the arches, the high frieze, the windows, and the light in the windows." She paused. "The rest is brown—the carved ceiling, the bima, the upper walls, the capitals and the pediments, and even the floor tiles, the azulejos, which aren't so much azure as brown."

"How lovely!" exclaimed my wife softly. Did she see in her mind's eye those whites and browns mingled, like the limbs of miscegenous lovers? Or was she responding to the slow cadence of Hannah's voice much deeper here than at home, as though it had assumed something of the sinuous rhythm of the Guadalquivir, which even then, just south of us, was making its slow brown passage through the sunset.

"Yes, it was," said our daughter. I looked into her eyes, poor little ojos azules, almost eclipsed in this brown, brown land. "What's the matter, father?"

"One sip too many of old Jerez, daughter." I turned to my wife. "We must go to our room, dear, rest and freshen up before dinner. We'll meet you in the lobby at eight, ladies."

We ate at El Caballo Rojo. I mention the elevation and sequestration of this marvelous restaurant—through a long patio and up a wide flight of stairs. I mention its inexhaustible courtesy—the tulips of sherry that came gratis, the saucers of chanquetes (tiny crisp anchovies with huge black eyes), and the gay rosy pitchers of sangría. I mention the zarzuela, which came with a shiny red langostino in the center like the boss of a great shield, and all around the edge the purple shells of the mussels, opened to reveal orange flesh, and the shells themselves glazed with olive oil, brushed by an army of cook's boys, little Zubarins of the kitchen. I mention all of this only to say, alas, that even in the radiance of culinary grace the serpent still wreathed my heart. I wanted my daughter free of Hannah, and I didn't care if it meant the destruction of Hannah. Perhaps I preferred that it did. Meanwhile, I said, "What other Latinist and librarian of this world is eating such beautiful food in such beautiful company?"

"Gracias, señor," said my ladies, my graces, in chorus.

I shined my eyes at them. "It is true, then, the meek shall inherit the earth."

So we were up early the next day strolling in the mist toward the mosque, through El Patio de los Naranjos, pretending that the shy fragrance of the shiny leaves—for there were no oranges upon the trees then—was perfuming our morning. Hannah led the way, reading to us, impatiently I thought, from her Michelin. The early light fell down through the trees and onto the book with something less than radiance. She looked to me, in her long dress sashed at the waist, like a novitiate with his breviary, struggling for illumination. Presently we arrived at the wall the foolish Christians put up—the mosque, Hannah read us, having been originally open on all sides. The door was closed. So we stood waiting in the mist, still, silent, and a little chilly—except for Hannah. The impatience which had shortened our stroll through the orange trees continued to manifest itself as an almost febrile quickness of the eyes, which darted against the closed wicket of the ticket window.

"A las nueve." I read the sign on the door, unnecessarily, uncharitably. "Forty more minutes."

But at that moment a small door within the large door opened inward and out stepped a bustling little priest clutching a thick sheaf of music. "Señores," he said, not unamiably, and rushed through our party, leaving behind a small storm of morning vapors. Hannah stepped to the little door, tried the handle, and opened it. She turned to us with a wicked little smile and said, "Pasen, se-ñores." So we entered the great mosque free.

The first thing we experienced was the imperious rotundity of the organ playing off to our left in the cathedral. But the sound was broken, striated if you will, by the forest of columns before us and by

the interwoven arches that rose above them. From high up, through
apertures we could not see, fell an intermittent slant light, the same
light, of course, that had shone down through the orange trees onto
Hannah's book. And it retained, curiously I thought, the grainy image
of the morning mist. Well, the mosque is a magical place at any hour,
I'm sure, but the conditions under which we entered it made it even
more so—mist and music and the absence of all people but ourselves.
By a silent mutual agreement we all went our separate ways. I went
off to the right, it being my intention to gain some sense of the
extension of the mosque by tracing its boundaries. I thought of myself
as a blind man. Since there was no hope of *seeing* the whole of the thing
through the shifting enfillade of columns and arches, I would let my
feet and my inner sense of space inform me of its dimensions.
Presently the organ stopped. A moment later the sound of my feet
went out and came back in multiple echoes. I wondered: could even a
man blind from birth sort those laminous sounds into a sightless
image of the columns? I paused. The sound and echoes of the feet of
the women came to me—now two or three mingled, now one
alone—but at last absolute silence. I could see no one of them. For a
long while we all stood silent, aware of each other, waiting for the first
step. It was thrilling, like a child's game. When a footstep finally
came, I moved too, cautiously, keeping to the edge. Who would I see, I
wondered, in this curious child's game? Whoever I saw first, there
would be a terrific significance to it, a fatality. So I stepped slowly
through the dim morning light, pausing now and again to listen to the
footpads of the others. They seemed to me very distant. "In another
part of the forest," I said to myself, smiling, but I was incredibly
titillated, I confess. The back of my neck tingled. Which of my lovely
distant echoes, in essence some mysterious resonance of myself,
would I finally come upon, tapping with my feet, trailing, like one of
those miraculous vines, over the old stone toward my soulmate.

It was Hannah, of course. She was standing in the Kebla, the
golden-domed vestibule to the mirhab, the niche of the Koran. Her
head was tilted back. She was looking up into the gilded tracery of
the dome. She had undone her hair. It fell down her back like a
talismanic hanging, an animal pelt, luxuriant and barbaric. Her
dark upturned face was dusted by a fine aureate light from the dome
above. She did not see me. And I, at once thrilled and fearful,
declined the gambit, slipping away among the rosy fingers of the
temple, excusing myself with cynical reflections—dulcet damozel,
lapsing lady, spurious exoticism not worthy even of Beardsley or
Burne-Jones.

Presently the large door swung open and the paying customers swarmed through with a great rattle of feet upon the stones and with exclamations of wonder. Safe again, I rounded up my ladies and shepherded them from the mosque. Under the orange trees Sarah said, "Who would have guessed?" My wife shook her head. Neither Hannah nor I spoke. Sarah sighed, distressed by our silence, until my wife patted her arm and said, "No one can say anything, dear." And then she accepted our reticence, which nevertheless continued a bit heavy, I thought. So we visited the innumerable shops across from the mosque, pawing through postcards and trinkets and finding our voices again at last, to laugh and joke about the tastelessness of it all.

After lunch we strolled into the Juderia and found the house of Moses Maimonides with its lovely high ceilings and balconies and with its cool interior patio which that afternoon the sunlight, catching only the russet walls above, never touched. And all the while, ever since we left the mosque, I was in a curious state. Inside of me coiled a small dense mass of strong feeling, the nature of which was a mystery to me. It centered on Hannah, of course. But I didn't know what it was. I knew what it was not. It was not merely an intensification of my old antipathy toward the one who had stolen my daughter. And it was not an exotic eroticism born there in the burnished light of the Kebla, though for some moments I had imagined that it was. I shrugged and said to myself, "You are unbalanced, man, by too many sights and sounds, because there's no such thing as a strong feeling which is neither repulsion nor attraction."

My wife, noticing that I was preoccupied, tried to draw me out by pointing to the garish artifacts and doleful memorabilia of the great Manolete, all melodramatically arranged in sequence. "Well, dear," I said, "it's very stirring, but how do you suppose hygenic old Maimonides would feel about having in his house these mementos of blood, sand, excrement, and eros?"

Hannah laughed, showing her white teeth, but it was not the ironic bravura laugh I might have expected. It was more restrained. It betrayed, in fact, a hint of something very close to shyness. Probably from this it was that I derived the strong intuition that Hannah was aware of the powerful hidden feeling in me. I wondered if there was also such a feeling in her, wondered if she already understood it and was waiting for me to come to the same knowledge. At any rate, I was sure of the one thing—we were circling, like two dancers, and soon we would have to touch. Yet I felt I had been right to step back from that meeting in the mosque. The time was not ripe. In fact, I was sure that we would not join in Córdoba at all, but later, when we returned to

Málaga. I was right. But there came a moment, shortly after we left the house of Maimonides, when our tryst almost transpired.

We were in the synagogue, having stumbled upon it almost by accident. We knew it was near, of course, from the guidebook, but we hadn't planned to visit it because we knew it was vastly inferior to the two in Toledo, especially the synagogue of Maria la Blanca. We would have passed it by, but an old woman stationed outside the door looked up from her knitting and said, "¿Quieren visitar el synagogue, señores?"

"We might as well, dear," said my wife. I suspected that she was moved by the sight of the little dish with its pathetic sprinkling of small coins, there being no set entry fee—a suspicion confirmed when she said, "Give her a bill, dear."

"Yes." I laid a hundred-peseta note in the dish. "And as soon as we're out of sight she'll slip the bill into her apron pocket with the others and look as dolefully pauperous as before."

We went in. There wasn't much to it. A pale light in the high windows illuminated the white tracery of the walls sufficiently for us to see that the craftsmen had emulated, almost slavishly, their Moorish masters. Perhaps I shouldn't say that. I think there were Hebrew words woven into the design and stars of David, though my memory is indistinct. Nevertheless, my impression was that the art of the Moorish masters was insufficiently Judaized. Even so, there was something touching about this tiny little temple. Though built in the high days of Jewish prosperity under the tolerant caliphate, it must from the very first have seemed tenuous, ephemeral, as though the hands of the stone masons and sculptors already were shaken by chill harbingers of the cold wind of Christianity from the north. I don't know how I undertook to divine all this—pure romantic imagination probably, though I may have had a genuine insight based on the fatal powdering of the crude stones that were exposed in a number of places. And I should add that Hannah accentuated somehow the vulnerability of the temple, standing forlornly in the far corner, the floor going to rubble at her feet, the stones gaping behind, and the rich sheen of her black hair at once vibrantly quick and poignantly mortal—she, too, obviously moved by the mild melancholy of the place.

I was just on the verge of suggesting that we wend our way hotelward—which was precisely the foolish word I intended to use to lift from us the sad weight of the ancient expulsion—when suddenly there came a noise at the door and a dramatic entrance.

A tall woman burst through the narrow entryway holding aloft a black umbrella to which was tied a long red streamer. She herself wore a handsome black pelerine which, as she made a military about-face in the center of the synagogue, swirled around her revealing a red lining. "Hier ist es!" she shouted. I wanted to say to my companions that we were now in the presence of a female Mephistopheles, who might transport us seven centuries back, fill our little temple with the black-capped Sephardim of the caliphate, show us the great unraveler himself pricking the fineness of the law from the Torah, and many other wonders. But we were scattered around the synagogue, and besides, the woman's charges—a great swarm of middle-aged Germans—soon pressed us to the wall and separated us even further. I caught a glimpse of Sarah to my right smiling and lifting her eyes to the ceiling comically, then she was gone behind the rubicund head of a beaming burgermeister, or so he seemed to me. My wife was on the opposite side of the synagogue, so I had lost her as soon as the statuesque tour guide reached the center of the room sweeping the air with her black wings as it were, a huge fledermaus. Hannah was in the corner to my left. For some moments I could still see fragments of her dark hair and dark dress behind the gay shirts and dresses which these pink-faced northerners wore in pleasance with the Spanish sun. But soon she, too, was out of sight.

Now the guide began to speak briskly. And here I must confess to a linguistic prejudice. I, though a speaker of English—a harsh and difficult Germanic tongue—love my old rotund Latin and therefore the romance languages, but cannot abide German, which starts everything just behind the teeth, on the tip of the tongue. Its words seem to jump out unrelated to the volition of the speaker, like the naughty little princess's frogs. I don't deny that there are melodious moments in German, but as soon as they begin to unfurl, a fricative or a sibilant leaps out, lances them in midair, and down they fall in shreds. Consequently, though I necessarily read much German, I never speak it, never even pronounce it to myself, and never listen to it. So, the guide's rapid-fire spiel flew past my ears as merely a mild cacaphony. I watched the point of the red-ribboned umbrella prick out all the details of major importance, watched the silent pink faces bob up and down dutifully. I don't doubt that the commentary, precise and compressed, caught the essence of the place. And the listeners, too, were properly serious, showing respect and even a mild awe. Then, upon the instant of her final word the guide, umbrella on high, cut back through her charges, who opened a corridor for her almost magically, and led them forth from that crumbling memento of the dispersion.

In a matter of moments the little temple was as still and silent as when we entered. I looked to Sarah, the ironist, to share my amusement. But the face I had expected to see bright with mirth was clouded. I followed her eye to Hannah. Hannah had begun to laugh, but it was a dark premonitory laugh which quickly began to rise toward a hysterical pitch. But actually the laugh was not as wrenching as the sudden slackness of her body. Her arms went limp, her head fell forward, her hair slipped to one side of her neck and hung awry. And I was sure that under the dress her legs were giving way, for she began to weave. So I was about to rush to her and hold her. And if I had, perhaps our inevitable rendezvous would not have waited until Málaga. But Sarah was ahead of me, took her in her arms, and held her up. A moment later my wife, too, put her arms around her—the three of them one body of grief and comfort. And that was what Hannah obviously needed, because she quickly began assuring them that she was all right. Meanwhile I was moved and at the same time jealous, because my own flesh was warmed by no embrace. At last Hannah smiled, and Sarah smiled with her, saying "It's hard enough being a Jew in Córdoba, isn't it, love?—without the Krauts."

I wondered if Sarah should have said that. But Hannah squeezed her hand and we departed the synagogue without further ado. Outside, the old knitter looked with mild interest at Hannah's red eyes, said nothing, comprehended nothing, I suspect, and so consigned the tears, with millions of others, no doubt, to Mystery.

The thing that had made me apprehensive about our return to the apartment in Málaga did not materialize. That is, Señorita Emilia Cerezo Galvez did not impale Hannah and Sarah on her eyebeams and bear witness to their perversity. On the contrary, she actually smiled at Sarah and, much taken with her long blond hair, called her La Rubia, rolling the r softly. Hannah she called la señorita, with considerable deference, more, in fact, than she had ever shown my wife, the señora. Actually I was not greatly surprised by this, given Hannah's deportment. As we had driven south, in fact from the very moment we left the synagogue in Córdoba, she began to regather her old properties—the lean erectness verging on hauteur, the upward tilt of the chin, the almost supercilious arch of the brows, and the fierce scintillance of the hawkish eyes which seemed to bespeak an ancient pride and purity. So what Señorita Emilia must have seen, what she must have heard, too, in Hannah's slow precise Spanish, was an avatar of the dark masters of a distant past. And so, what was Sarah to Hannah in the señorita's for once dazzled eye? Mistress, paramour? Hardly. Only a blonde, rosy-cheeked slave girl, worshipful La Rubia.

At least I'm pretty sure that's the way things were. Of course there was never any way to verify my interpretation. But of one thing I'm absolutely certain. This deference of Señorita Emilia toward Hannah, verging, as it did, on obeisance, paralleled the fading of my intuition that my daughter's lover and I were approaching a rendezvous. The fact was that she seemed to have set entirely behind her those exposed moments in mosque and synagogue, drawing about herself again the garments that had always served so well—reticence, austerity, and the aura of erotic mystery. The result was that I felt the prospect of our opening to each other hopelessly dimmed. And that depressed me because in Córdoba I had sensed very strongly that we were going to reveal something to each other, something which, at least in my case, would release and resolve feelings that had been for a long time pooling and shoaling, glimpsed but unacknowledged in my mind. Now the surface of that half-conscious pool silvered over and hid the treasure of golden images that I was sure lay below. So I drifted away from the women, let them go without me to the shops and to the mercado and up to the Alcázar and down to the port to see the ships come in. Presently Sarah and Hannah planned their departure. They were going to take a tour over to Tangier and Tétouan and on down to Marrakesh. They urged us to accompany them, but we declared that it would be far too exotic for us.

Thus came our last day together. We were to have a farewell lunch at a marvelous tapa bar on the Plaza Merced. The women were to do some morning shopping and I was to meet them in the plaza by the news kiosk at one—"en punto, a tiempo, a la Inglés," I said. "No dawdling." Sarah stuck her tongue out at me.

I arrived early because the warm spring sun in our patio made it impossible for me to read. It lighted the yellow-blossomed creepers and the bougainvillea with a brilliance my sunglasses could not defend me against. It filed the thorny espalier so sharp and blanched the wall so white that my scalp tingled and my flesh crawled. And all the while the lemons and roses wreathed about me their contradictory fragrances. Unable to sort these extremities of pain and pleasure, I fled to the street, bustled along with the crowd and quickly reached the plaza. There I found a number of things to interest me.

It was on this day, in the plaza, as I have already foretold, that I had the third and, I suspect, last vision of my life—a vision to go with my mewing and broken flight over the vanishing image of Mr. Leary in the schoolyard, and to go also with the strange sights which the black poet plucked for me from his guitar: the mestiza madonna kissing the white, and my nakedness while Mr. Leary stitched together cassock and olive drab. And finally it was the vision, as I have said, which fished up and revealed the full face of *Malagueña*, the golden talisman of my youth.

On the north side of the plaza, across the street, was a huge plastic canopy which had been erected to cover an Easter float under construction. I remember the lacework of heavy steel and the huge candelabra. I remember groaning inwardly at the thought of the parish men hefting that thing upon their shoulders. But what arrested my attention was the madonna. She stood about ten feet high, swaddled only in the sculptured folds of a white robe, for the precious tiara and the jeweled cape with long train would not be put on her until late in Holy Week. I gazed upon her creamy face, upon the black sorrowful eyes and the two crystal tears, one on each cheek. I remembered vividly what I had felt as a boy in the Jesuit chapel — that confusing mixture of reverence and erotic titillation. I turned abruptly away from the float to recross the street and lose myself in the pleasant shade of the tree-lined plaza. There was a sudden screech of tires. A taxi braked just in time to avoid striking me down. The driver shouted something out of the window and then, as I hastened to complete my crossing, continued on his way with an angry gunning of his motor. In the meanwhile a blue-suited policeman with white hat approached me shrilling his whistle. "Cuidado! Cuidado, señor."

"Sí, sí," I said, nodding emphatically to show that I would indeed take care. Then I added that I had been moved by the statue. "Yo estaba muy conmovido por la María."

"¿Quiere reunirse con ella en paradiso?"

I shook my head. "Todavia no. Mas tarde." Not yet, but later, I would join her in Paradise.

"Por eso, mucho ojo, mucho ojo." He pointed to his eyes. And I nodded, painfully aware, as I had not been since before Mr. Leary dubbed me Ocellus Luminosus, how beady are my eyes behind their thick lenses.

I sat down on a bench under the trees, not far from the news kiosk where the three women were soon to appear. I made up my mind to wait quietly without moving because I did not trust myself to absorb the sights that I would see if I continued to stroll about. Already powerful images of past and present were conspiring to heighten my consciousness — the madonna, the many eyes, and for some curious reason, a fleeting recollection of the glass case of gold and silver trophies where Il Giorno the Dayspring and I fell under the dark tutelage of Father Durr.

I leaned back on the bench and shut my eyes. The images moved teasingly along the edge of the round dark. I did not summon them. I wanted to know what they were grouping to convey, but I didn't have the courage to summon them by an act of will. Let them come of their own accord and stage their meaning, I thought, or I will sit here in the blind dark. But I knew it would be the former.

Presently I heard footsteps approaching. I opened my eyes. It was a member of the Guardia Civil, walking alone, which was rare, for they usually go in pairs, mutually protective. And yet there was nothing potentially very hateful in the appearance of this one. In fact, his little cap with the shiny upturned visor and his carefully pressed olive drabs gave him something of the appearance of a comic-opera soldier. At any moment, I thought, smiling to myself, he might stop and sing a light aria to the woman in the kiosk. Well, he did stop, took his cap off momentarily and ran his hand over his head which, lo!, was bald. And though it was brown and pleasantly brindled by the broken sunlight in the trees, I shuddered and fidgeted nervously for my copyist's pencil. For here was my old tormentor, the castigator of my knuckles, only this time on the obverse side of the history of fascism—or had that other one really been a true soldier of democracy? No matter. All things conspire. I looked at him. He looked at me. And what were those dark eyes telling me? *Go to work. Copy. Or you'll have a foolish vision and get your knuckles rapped again.* No, of course not. The eyes merely took in the image of an effete purblind tourist lolling decadently in the shade, unworthy even of disdain. The Guardia replaced his hat and walked on.

I leaned back again on my bench, convinced that there had begun and would continue, irreversibly, a rhythm of recurrences. I shut my eyes. It was suddenly very quiet. The dinner hour had come. Traffic around the plaza had ceased, and even out on the thoroughfare of Calle Victoria there was only the occasional passing of a car. Time passed. I don't know how much, for I was descending into sleep— no, not sleep exactly, but a kind of dark deep-breathing of the mind. That was my state when I began to hear the horn. Perhaps it was only a stuck car horn or a horn from the harbor, but in my séanced ear it seemed to wind from a high field far beyond the Alcázar. My memory scurried back twenty years and more. *Da Silva, is that you after all this time? Why are you calling me?* There was no answer of course—only the horn again, and not a tantara or a fanfare exactly, but nevertheless the sound of an annunciation. *If you, Da Silva, old Sephardic Jew, think that you are trumpeting into my mind the presence of your kinswoman Hannah, do not trouble yourself. She lies always near the surface of my consciousness.* But the horn went on making its stately announcement of a coming—a great host, perhaps, traversing a wide desert. Suddenly there was an animated chattering. I opened my eyes.

Approaching me from the other side of the plaza was a priest in a black cassock cinched at the waist by a silver chain from which depended a large cross. He was a squat powerful man who walked determinedly, head forward and cassock swirling about his legs, as though he were cutting a swath through the smirched air of the city for those behind. And those behind—who were they? I adjusted my eyes and brought into focus the priest's charges, a dozen or more barely teenaged boys all dressed in the uniform of their school—black suits, white shirts, and black ties. Where they had been I don't know—a museum, a demonstration of some sort. But whatever it was it had set them up wondrously. Every interstice in the close-knit pack of them must be filled with a celebration of laughter and words. How avidly I searched their faces to find the one wearing glasses. And there he was all right, his eyes limned by thick horn-rims, bruised by the shadow of them. But he was nothing like the fair-haired blue-eyed Paycock, Ocellus Luminosus. He was tall and dark. He was graceful and commanded the attention of his fellows. Consequently, his spectacles were not the stigma of a defect at all but rather the emblem of precocious wisdom. Also, the priest (impatient with their loitering, signaling them on now with a vigorous motion of his hands) was not Doctor Rhododactylos. No, neither rosy-fingered nor rosy-haired. All here was chiaroscuro. So, to tell the truth, I was a little disappointed. All things conspire. But sometimes, apparently, with a certain crude approximateness, and even with significant inaccuracies. Nevertheless, I leaned back again, determined to resume my trancelike reverie, though now with less confidence that the pattern of recurrences would fall into place. But I had just shut my eyes when once more I was aroused by a sudden sound. It was a bird. For a brief moment I thought it was the scream of a peacock. But it was not. It was a gull that had flown up from the harbor. Mewing plaintively, it hung there in the breeze over the plaza. But I did not think it sorrowed after the priest and the boys. Oh I saw the sharp scanning of its eye, but I knew it could not secure the present moment against time's passage anymore than I those many years ago, though gull-winged and gull-eyed, could impale the wind and the wimpling

hem of Doctor Rhododactylos's cassock. *Fly on, my feathered friend*.
What did I mean? On to some less densely populated quarter of
the city where the scavenging would be easier? Or did I mean on
across the years—to pluck up, my soul's gleaner, the more recent
scraps of this slowly accumulating feast of memory? The latter, of
course, for when I had closed my eyes again and the mewing of the
gull had faded on the breeze, there came down gently from above
the sweetly brimming voice of the black poet, accompanied by the
thrumming of his guitar. Well, this was not exactly the annunciatory
mode of Da Silva's old shofar, but its conjuring of an imminent
presence was as strong, if not stronger. For I knew, of course, what
he was singing—the black grandmother and Isis and La Señora
Negra del Inferno. And I knew who was the present avatar of all
these. So it was to come after all, what had eluded me in Córdoba,
what I had all but lost hope of here in Málaga. *Well then*, I began
bravely—and continued bravely, filling with strong invitation all the
wide chamber of memory and the long halls of hope as well—*blow
the annunciation, Da Silva. Rend the veil, obsidian poet. I am ready*.
A certain time passed in silence. Then I heard "Qué bonitas
Malagueñas!" It was the kiosk woman. I opened my eyes. But it was
not the dark lady I saw. It was the other, Maria la Blanca, La Rubia,
standing before me impudently, giggling. Then the other two came
around from behind me, giggling also, amused to find me asleep on
a park bench, or so they thought. They formed up in front of me,
arms linked like a musical-comedy trio. And then I saw why the old
woman called them *Malagueñas*. Each of them had bought a small
piece of black lace and thrown it over her shoulder. Each of them
had a red rose. My wife and Hannah wore theirs in their hair. Sarah
had hers in her teeth. The old woman laughed. Sarah took the rose
out of her mouth and said, "Guess where we have been, father."
I looked at her sternly. "Nay, I know not, you naughty child."
"To a bodega with dozens and dozens of beautiful barrels and we
drank from each of them, one after the other."
"But the amontillado was still the best, dear," said my wife,
leaning against Hannah, tipsy as a calf. Comic that she feared I
would accuse her of enological infidelity.
"Ladies do not enter bodegas," I said.
"Ladies!" My daughter made a high crowing laugh. "Oh father,
what a delicious anachronism you are!" She stepped forward and
kissed me on the forehead and then rejoined her companions. The
old woman in the kiosk laughed.
As I looked at the three of them, my eyes fastened on Hannah. And

then it happened—as it had happened that day long ago in Penance Hall and again years later at the black poet's reading. Everything changed slightly. Everything brightened. I saw that Hannah was a little apart from my wife and daughter, slightly behind them, her right hand and arm at their backs. I saw that with a delicate gesture she was presenting them to me, giving them to me, these two with light hair and rosy cheeks, whom she was nothing like. I saw tears in her eyes, tears which, because she was patrician, would never be allowed to run upon her cheeks. They were the tears of dispossession, older by far than the tears of the madonna across the street. So that was how it was. She was giving back to me the wife of my marriage bed and also my daughter, the only fruit of my loins. But what was it the falcon eyes were saying to me? *You have them now, your fair ones. But it is only because in this world I cannot hold them. In that other world beware.* Then her eyes flashed. And out of the flashing of the eyes came an image which was suspended before her—not in her hand, but in the bosom of her will as it were. *Do you remember this one from that old green world of your youth? Do you remember his red hair and his fair face?* I swallowed hard. *Yes, I remember him.* And how I longed to leap forward and embrace him. My eyes moistened. *You are the dark madonna, aren't you, that has descended into hell and lifted him up to me in this paradise of trees.* And then I did start to lean forward and open my arms. But there was a sudden high piercing laugh that shattered the image.

Hannah was laughing. Sarah had stepped forward and was holding an oblong paper in front of my eyes. "Do you know what this is, father?"

"No. What is it?"

"El Gordo! El Gordo! The fat one. A ticket for the lottery of the blind. Mama bought it. It was all Hannah and I could do to keep her from buying a ticket from every blind man on every corner of Málaga. Here, take it. She said it was for you."

I took it and looked at it through the wavering moisture that had welled up in my eyes. It must have been one of the more expensive tickets, for it was embossed with a golden seal in the form of a doubloon, which bore the head of a lovely lady, a saint. Under a halo her aureate hair glinted with heavenly grace. Elsewhere on the ticket I spied the word *Malagueña*, but I could not tell whether it referred to the holy personage or not, for the moisture in my eyes had thickened. It was time to look up. There was my wife, laughing. And so was Hannah, and Sarah. So I laughed too. "El Gordo, eh? Why then we're rich beyond the dreams of avarice."

The Women

In evergreen country at winter's threshold, awaiting the zero hour of the solstice, I, James, practice mortification. Like Teresa, who in the shadow of castellated stone pillowed on wood, I too am habited coarsely here in a cabin willed to me by a dead friend who burned flesh away with whiskey, charred innards with tobacco, and yes, I swear it, Lawrence was his name. I have climbed well beyond the last line of deciduous trees, am three layers of fir-brushed wind above the purling river. Already the deer are driven down under the hunter's bow and the bears sleep.

I have come here to compose the memory of grandmother, mother, daughter. Otherwise, some day at the gate of my most urgent desire they will howl against my entry: crone, fierce mother, and my roaring girl, in direct descent, I and my wife but the hapless vessels of ancient fury. So here I sit before a low fire burning in dead Lawrence's grate, eyes closed, the glow of the flame a pale rose under the lids. I open the gates of memory. Come to me, my women.

My Grandmother

Had a husband of torturous dreaming. All of his life, they said, though I can attest to only the latter years, my grandfather noised his sleeping to the skies: snored, bibbled, whistled, shouted in unknown tongues, and practiced the stertor of the moribund. Sometimes he opened his eyes fever-bright upon God knows what riotous scenes glowing against the dark ceiling, sometimes twisted and groaned like Laocöon in the final throes, and sometimes fell into breathless silences broken at last by a blowing like the trumpeting of a surfacing whale.

"It frightens me," said my grandmother, "to think where the devil takes that poor man night after night, never fail." It was true. Christmas to Ash Wednesday, Easter to Advent and the penitential seasons, too, the antics continued undiminished. But in the morning my grandfather professed to remember nothing, to have, as he said, "slept the sleep of the innocent."

My grandmother herself never dreamed, of course. Said my mother to her father, "There is no room left, for God's sake, Daddy, for poor Mama to dream because the house roars with your wildness every night. So all of her stuff comes out in religion. Before you are dead, mark my word, she will speak in tongues and bleed in her palms." Nor did I, the grandchild who visited every summer, ever in that house dream. Further, I believed that the whole town did not dream, that over its modest dwellings rose nightly the great rotunda of my grandfather's visions: demons with pitchforks, broom-riding hags, bristling cats, crowned serpents, falcon-eyed sun discs, clouds and coverts full of trolls and ogres, and so forth. Meanwhile the staid citizenry of Elton—merchants, farmers, and country blacks—slept peacefully. Thus, to me, was my grandfather a hero, assuming nightly the dark beings of his brothers' psyches. But my mother said, "It's unthinkable that we have to lie awake half the night listening to the gabble and the death rattle and the banshee scream and then be told in the morning that he remembers nothing, absolutely nothing. I can't bear it!"

When I told all of this to my daughter, my roaring girl, she said, "He was lying nobly when he said he didn't remember." No, I don't think so. In the morning his eyes were as clear and blue as my beloved river is now in winter, his hand that held the steaming coffee cup as steady as the great fir trunks outside the cabin widow. He scooped out his soft-boiled egg with great precision and left us, off to the hardware store, with his unvarying valediction: "Happy day, boys and girls!"

One day when he was at work my mother said, "Mama, there is a hypnotist over in Upela that can direct the will of a subject against a trouble spot."

"No, daughter, 'direct the will' is the way you learned at the university to say 'put in the hands of the Devil.' You can't expel one evil spirit by another though the Pharisees were hardhearted enough to believe it of Lord Jesus when he sent the demons wailing out into the desert. No. If you want to help, get down on your knees with me and pray for him."

Then came the night of the vines, the night of my grandmother's vision. Across the top of the high headboard of her mahogany bed crept ivy which grew from a planter that I had helped her nail to the wall behind. By the summer of my grandmother's one dream the ivy had reached the bed posts and was climbing toward the canopy. My grandmother said, "When it reaches the top, daughter, I will tear down that dead worm-spit silk of my mother, who was not a believer. I will have a roof of rising green, my mark of eternal life." But my grandfather tore it down. In his sleep he reared up with a roar and tore loose old vines and tender new tendrils alike. He uprooted all from the planter, soiling summer sheets with earth and crushed leaves. When he had done this, he subsided into fitful sleep. My grandmother awoke, but did not rise. Rather, she lay till dawn in the ruined bower of her immortality having her vision, which she tried to remember for my mother the following day. "The great serpent came to the garden and hid in the foliage and made a whispering. But I do not know whose heart he bound." Here my grandmother squinched her eyes, perhaps in an intense effort to recapture some lost part of the vision. "He fell on us with huge weight and vipered us and broke loose the promise. What do you think the promise was, daughter?"

"God only knows, Mama. The Bible is full of promises."

"Yes. My daddy said, 'The Bible is a living rainbow. Walk under it.' " She smiled thinly. "I tell you what I will not do and what I will do, daughter."

"Good, Mama. Tell me." My mother's voice was lifted briefly, no doubt by the hope that my grandmother was finally ready to send for help. Later, my roaring girl said, "There's no mystery, Daddy, about all that. In a repressive society somebody's got to dream monsters. You were lucky. If the job had been left to a highly imaginative type like you, you could've been a prewar Charlie Manson." She made her crowing laugh.

My grandmother said, "I will not join the end-of-the-worlders and peddle doom at every door. I will find a living shoot of this vine and plant again."

*   *   *

Here at dead Lawrence's cabin, I practice mortification, await my vision. A mere sign will not do. There are signs everywhere. For instance, just above the treeline on Mount Tenshin, which fronts me on the east, a salmon-shaped copse has detached itself to swim gallantly against the snow froth that pours down the mountain's flank. A moving symbol, but I must have a vision. So yesterday, when I had chopped enough firewood and dark had nearly fallen so that the split timber was grainless and colorless against the snow, rough-hewn slabs of indistinct days, I stood with my armload outside the window. Window light, window bright, stoutly grated against bears, pink in the glow of the fire I had left within, you did not show me an angelic face. You did not release a voice to soar above my head until it burst into a cloud of melodious cherubim. And in my arms the heavy wood assumed no significant shape. But there was this, a sudden flaring behind your panes. I laughed bitterly. Just my luck. One of my grandfather's demons had dived down the chimney and scattered embers beyond the hearth. The cabin would burn. I would freeze. And what would high summer reveal to some passing hiker? The nine-months' miracle of an incorrupt body, hands still clutching the rood? More likely a bear-worried and coyote-strewn mess too ripe even for the crows who patrol the rising snowline and already in August begin to call from the fir tops their hoarse black auguries of winter. So I rushed inside, where there was indeed a jetting red flame, but it was safely within the stone walls of the fireplace feeding briefly on a fault, a gaseous pocket in the log and, even as I stacked the new wood, retracted abruptly like the bright tongue of a serpent.

My Mother

Did not love the gentleness of my father any better than she had that of her own father, railed against his quiescence which took the form, under his little cobra lamp and in his bright vise, of beautiful tiny flies. The makings were laid out plainly enough, of course: hook, hair, feather, wax, thread, and glue. But the little creatures seemed to me to grow up magically under his fingers: ants and mayflies, tiny pop-eyed fingerlings, nymphs with curving mermaid bodies, and helgramites to scutter along the bottom in clever disguise of spit and sticks—all arrayed in small leather-bound volumes as it were. My mother's metaphor, I confess, for she was the one who picked the cases up one night and said, "I can't read these, Arnold. What's the sense of making books nobody can read?"

"Can a Cherokee read the *Bhagavad-Gita*?" My father, unlike my mother, did not have a college education, but had an uncanny knack for alluding more or less accurately to obscure things he knew only by name.

"Wrong kind of Indian," my mother said. "Anybody knows that." Then she laughed her rich crowing laugh which always seemed more intentional than spontaneous, more mockery than mirth.

"And you are the wrong kind of critter to read my books," my father said, with more spirit than usual, for he had been touching his lips frequently to a glass of bourbon. "Nobody can read them but me and the fishes. You see, I have studied fish eyes all of my life until I know exactly how they're threaded and therefore how to make fish-writing. Maybe this boy here will learn it too and carry on the great tradition."

My mother shook her head slowly as though preparatory to a

profound judgment, so I knew that what was to follow would be especially cruel. "No," she said, "James is not going to fool with any of this little stuff like you. He's going to make those big wire hoops they use to snag the snouts of giant gars. He's going to make bass plugs with propellers that sound like the moonlight yachts of rich men cruising in the Gulf. He's going to tie those streamers—I don't know for what kind of fish—with peacock eyes like the hats of models in New York City. He's going to go for the big ones."

My mother went for the big one and caught him, Stocker Plinth, the richest real-estate man in Atlanta, but that's getting ahead of my story. Did I, true to my mother's prophecy, go for the big ones? I offer you the ambiguous judgment of my roaring girl, who recently said, "You know something, Daddy? I don't like any of the stuff you write worth a shit. It's all old-timey mush. But you do stick to your guns."

I don't deny that my mother had grounds for restlessness. There was no chance for wealth in the commissions earned by my father, the seed merchant. And it is also true that my mother was alone while he went on the road half of every week. And it did not take a master psychologist to deduce where he spent a good bit of that time. "Catch anything up north?" my mother would say.

"You know very well," my father would say, the weak lie already failing in his throat, "that I have two big buyers up near Dahlonega that are fly fishermen."

"There's no such thing as a big buyer of anything within a hundred miles of Dahlonega," my mother would say. But before long her retorts lost their sharpness. Her voice took on a flatness that even I as a boy knew was worse. Then one night she brought home a thick book full of all kinds of diagrams, tables, and charts. "What in the world is that?" my father said.

"Can a hayseed understand the New York Stock Exchange?" But my father looked at the book anyway. It was a preparatory text for the state real-estate-salesman exam. And on Wednesday night, when my father was always out of town, my mother went to class and left me at home alone. "A fourteen-year-old boy can certainly take care of himself for a while." Yes, I could take care of myself, but the house was full of eerie afterimages. There was my father bending among furs and feathers under his little cobra lamp. (Sometimes I would see my father's work woven subtly into the landscape of the whole state: fields of huge hybrid corn growing from his seeds, streams of silver fish rising to his flies.) And there was my mother pricking numerals upon contracts and mortgages, prophetess of the great postwar Atlanta boom. Did my father realize then that my mother's thick book was full of streamier lures and sharper barbs than any of his, that out there in the wide shoaling light of the city swam her big one, great cruising silver shape? Of course he did. Just as I one night stepped into the living room, looked at my mother, and realized, as though instantaneously changed by a catalyst or a chemical, that she was extraordinarily beautiful.

*   *   *

Daily I walk in the snow, close to the cabin, wary of slides, crevasses, confusing forests, and the other literary archetypes that have swallowed up so many high climbers. And I continue to mortify myself—eat only beans and salt pork, suffer flatulence so sharp that it parodies the premonitions of birth, stare into the fire. Proscribed: tobacco, whiskey, autoeroticism, and books. I await my vision. I said that signs will not suffice. Neither will dreams, which since the days of the Viennese deep-divers have fallen into the hands of mechanists, torturers of cats. Therefore, beloved grandfather, I cannot emulate you. No, I must have my vision, and I must have it waking, though I begin to think that it may be very different from the paintings.

Consider. The strangest thing you will see in Avila is a manuscript which the placard tells us was written miraculously by an unlettered Carmelite nun inspired by Teresa. You have never seen such a strong black march. No waste of white can ever be known which that hand could not prick into significance. Listen, Doctor Teresa. Recently, to the great embarrassment of the academic world, a classics professor went mad and spoke of the erotic ur-language. Teach me the forbidden orthography of that language. Then I will write you the green vines that rove the mad gray of my grandmother's head. I will write you the stripes and lashes, the pricks and scarifications with which my artful mother made of the body of my father's consciousness a complex grating. And I will write you, alas, the pocked, nail-bitten, hirsute wreckage of my daughter's sex. And when all that is scribed as promised, I will resurrect Lawrence, and write the fire and the spitted flesh. And others, many others. And you take the pages, fold them like the petals of the multifoliate rose and present them to your Father.

My Daughter

Left us in a roar. "What in the hell is it exactly, Daddy, that you are trying to get me to say?"

"I'm trying to get you to tell us just what it is you plan to do, to be."

"I am not being. I am becoming. Do you think because you stopped becoming and died lo these many years ago that everybody in the world is contemplating their past and writing it down? Mah, Josie, wudn't Jamie a princely lil chile!" Then that high cawing laugh refined by some cursed gene I had harbored like a fatal disease for twenty-two years and unwittingly planted in my wife. I say refined because the mockery was purer than my mother's.

"Becoming? Are you planning to become a saint? I see that you are already growing your own sackcloth out of your head, legs, and armpits."

"Dear, you must not . . ."

"Let him talk, Mama. You just keep on weaving your beautiful tapestry—nothing he would understand incidentally, the great body of the apocalypse blooming under the earth."

I was frightened because I felt an old thrumming in my bowels, so I spoke quickly. "Consider the lilies of the valley. They toil not. Neither do they spin. Is that what you're thinking? Little artists of the self arrayed in their own hair? And waiting for the Second Coming?"

"What's the matter? You afraid I'll send home for money?" Again the silver crowing.

To which I whispered sibilantly, "I'm afraid you will be lost, daughter. I'm afraid your cry will rise to us de profundis. But not even your mother, who plumbs secrets deeper than the heart roots of the live oak, can reach down to you."

Then my roaring girl lifted an eyebrow, cocked her head, and began to speak with a deadly flatness, also remembered of my youth. "No, my father. I'm afraid that it's you who're lost. And you know where. Down in those old southern memories. And you think you can prick them with your pen like little insects and get them all down on pages and then bind them up in a book. That's de profundis, Daddy. That's death. The letter killeth, but the spirit giveth life. Something like that. You know it better than I do, don't you, because your grandmother was a great quoter of the good book." Suddenly she lifted her finger and brightened her eyes to signify that she had received a revelation. "That's what the trouble was. Old Christianity was a stirring religion until they wrote it all down in a code and then it died."

"And I suppose that down in the city with your mystic friends you plan to abjure language altogether, discover the ur-tongue of pure Eros and lick your ideations into each other's integument." Did I hear a sound of muted amusement from my wife? Probably not, for when I turned and looked at her she was pulling a thick fibrous length of yarn through the warp.

"Well, I hadn't thought of it in exactly that way, Daddy, but thank you. I will press it into the lips and palms of my friend Adela. But whatever we do—and you can write this down, Daddy, since it's nots instead of ises—it will *not* be the past, *not* be analyzed, *not* inscribed like black barbed-wire fence marching across the land. What you can't write down, can't word is what it *will* be. But Mama can weave it."

"Will you, dear?" I said, sarcastically, I'm afraid.

My wife smiled. "I weave what I weave."

"Weave us all back together again, Mama, the way we were before the evil demons of sex and race tore us apart." My wife said nothing to that, nor did I. So my daughter said, "Good-bye, Daddy. Good-bye, Mama. Are you going to kiss your prodigal daughter good-bye?"

"Yes, I will kiss you," my wife said. She held our daughter in her arms. And I knew what strength and warmth our daughter would feel in that embrace. So, when at last they released each other and my daughter turned to me, I said, "No. I'm not going to kiss you now. It would be a Judas kiss. But this is not forever. I will have a kiss for a more auspicious occasion."

She nodded. "Sure, come and see me down in the city." She hoisted her backpack and walked out of our house.

*   *   *

Once again I stand at fall of dark in the snow outside dead Lawrence's cabin. And once again the grated window glows pink. Let us, Teresa, holy doctor, make an excursion into the phenomenology of space, Hispanic not Gallic, peninsular not continental. For I remember in the entry hall, in your convent below the great murallas, the mural of Spain, washed by two seas, mountain-immured against the corruptions of the north. And after the girl had shut the door behind us, darkening the room, she tripped a switch and on the instant the wall was aglow with your little houses, Spain your own galaxy. Did I perceive a denser baldric of light, La Coruña to Cartagena, Cadiz to Barcelona? Or call it a cross in odd perspective, the kind El Greco might have painted, reminding one of a carpenter's sawbuck. Or did I only imagine it?

I, too, have had my houses. My grandmother's little one, in Elton, in the south of Georgia, glowing with the demonic fires that roasted my grandfather nightly. My father's equally small one in Atlanta, lighted by his cobra lamp. Then the great ones my mother began to sell, huge pillared things grinning gold in the city sunset. Currently, above Seattle, my wife and I live in an A-frame. Alpha. The great ring of mountain and sky Omega. And now, to understand all this the better, I make my retreat in dead Lawrence's cabin cell. So I have traced one arm of the rood. But I will never, though I once was a while in Virginia, recross this post-Christian land.

Far below, somewhere in the dim glow of the city, are the rooms of my daughter and her friends, outposts, perhaps, of the dread future. Black lights, posters with ocellated pyramids, world-brooding semiangelic nudes, pop Blake. What is the message, holy doctor? That I will never have my vision, never learn the secret script? Better to go below, kiss my missionary daughter, light my one candle where I can? No. You least of all would give such counsel.

My Grandmother

Wrote a letter a year after the death of my grandfather, in the last month my mother pretended to live with my father as his wife. It advised that my grandmother was selling the little house and moving across the river, which we knew was nothing but bottom land, black country. So my mother and I took the train down in August. We had to open the window to breathe. The soot flecked my face and my mother's white dress.

When we arrived, the house was already gutted, gone the bed of immortal ivy where my grandfather had died writhing tortuously, in mid-twist as it were. My grandmother received us in black widow's weeds, necklaced and bedizened with withered flowers as fantastically as ever the unbuoyant Ophelia, which was almost the name of the gnarled old black scrubbing the floor. "Delia has been faith-healed," my grandmother told us. "Until two weeks ago she could not talk." The old black grinned up at us toothlessly. "Mmm Ima mm Ima talma ima talma mow." The aura of sweat about this miraculous mumbler enveloped us in its holy stink. "Mmm mah mmm mah missy mmm make me mmm make me." That concluded her witnessing. She went on scrubbing and mm-ing endlessly in the joy of her newfound voice.

"So you yourself were the healer, Mama," said my mother, understanding more than I had.

"Daughter, I have been gifted with the Lord's tongue more than this once." *Just as you predicted*, I wanted to say to my mother, but didn't dare.

"And now what are you going to do, Mama?"

"I am going to live with Delia in her cabin across the river and do my Lord's bidding."

"Will the blacks love having a white amongst them?"

"Mmm muma mmm muma!" Delia nodded vigorously.

"Before you make up your mind for sure, I want you to come visit us in Atlanta."

"Atlanta?" A flat smile lay momentarily on my grandmother's mouth and then vanished. "Not even Elton will be spared, daughter, when the sword of the Lord smites."

"Mama, you promised you would never be a doom-sayer."

My grandmother shook her head mildly. "It is not doom for the chosen, daughter, but the cities of sin will come down like houses build on sand." She deliberated a moment, "I tell you what I will do, daughter. I will make you the only wager that is not a Devil's wager, my God against your godlessness. If you will come to our meeting tonight, I will go a day with you to Atlanta."

But my mother said she would not. After our supper, tête-à-tête, in the dining room of the one hotel in Elton, I said to her, "I bet you're afraid to go out there."

She looked at me with interest. "I saw the holy rolling and heard the coon-shouting when I was a child. I don't need to witness it again."

"Well, I'm going."

"No, you're not."

"Yes, I am. And when you go off with Stocker Plinth I'm going to stay with Dad, no matter what a court says."

She sat back and smiled at me. "Well I'll be damned. Maybe there is something to you after all. If so, my son, you won't find it very interesting living with your father. But don't worry, I won't contest for you in court." She patted my hand. "Now run off and play with Granny and the niggers. I'm leaving tomorrow morning on the eight-forty. If you want to go back with me, be up and ready."

So I walked down to the bottom, and I didn't have any trouble finding my grandmother even in that suddenly deepening dusk. She was squatting in hers and Delia's garden harvesting butter beans. From her neck a bulging gunny sack hung down between her knees. I half-expected to see a long-eared head peep out of the sack, for silhouetted there she looked like a great marsupial powerful enough to leap the dark river. "Did you come for the meeting?" I nodded.

"First we'll rest and meditate." My grandmother instructed me to lie down on a little plot of green grass. She lay down beside me, set aside her harvest, and pillowed my head on her left shoulder. Delia lay on the other side. "Ma mmm Mama."

"Be quiet now, Delia," she said, then after a while, "Do you know what I see, child?"

"No."

"I see under this bottom, right where we lie, a great body, the body of the Second Coming. I feel it stir. Listen and I will speak about it." And then she began a kind of thing that was a cross between a song and a wild ululation. And Delia hummed and mummed. And their voices struck me not in the ear but in the solar plexus and impaled me warmly to the earth, from which I grew up and was a lily of the field. But when I was almost lost to myself and on the point of bursting forth with my own sweet song, I grew afraid, because I could see ahead to the dark church filled with huge black thrumming, and I and my grandmother two tiny white flowers against the night. So I jumped up and ran, ran all the way to the hotel and entered my mother's room panting. She took me in her arms and after a while she said, "This is the last night I will ever rock you to sleep."

*   *   *

No new snow for several days, my gray and companionable northwest skies suddenly assuming a portentous clarity. I have studied the moon. It is faceless. The stars, in which mad old pagans once read bears, belts, twins—nothing. I have even climbed a steep slope and from that vantage studied my tracks in the snow, hoping to discover the unconscious footing of my self, but saw only the cipherless trail of a woodcutter. But tonight something happened, here on the cabin steps. What do you guess? That I was flung down into the snow by my grandfather's demons? No, nothing so bad as that. Saw the holy child? Nothing so good, but similar. Yes, a child. "Who are you?" it said. I surrendered my name. "And you?"

"You." Yes, it was me all right, a bit idealized, I thought, there in the spectral moonlight, crossed by deep shadows that not even the silver snow-glint could brighten.

"You are long awaited, warmly welcome," I said, "What is the message?"

"Wait," he said.

"Look," I said, "I'm not a saint. And you're not quite the princely

little chap that I have sometimes made you out to be." (Pax vobis-
cum, daughter.) "Nevertheless, let us be about our visionary task.
Do something, say something significant."

But he only repeated the one word, *wait*. And because one does
not brush aside an apparition or walk through it, I thought that I
would have to stand in snow until the first crowing of the cock. (The
child is the father of the man.) But of course there was no cock, only
the cawing of a crow, raucous sublunar mockery in the winter night.
Upon which sound he fled so swiftly that the crow's call hadn't time
to strike the mountain and make its diminished return before my
step was clear. Grandmother, mother, daughter, be quiet for a
season. I intend to wait, as instructed. And now that I think of it,
what else could he have said but *wait*? *Be still, and wait*.

My Mother

Went inside Stocker Plinth's great double-finned silver fish to
Nineveh. This is not a joke. Nineveh was the swishest suburb — piney
hills, a little lake, large plots, purchaser must agree to build a
$50,000 house minimum. But I was speaking of ΙΧΘΥΣ, the fish. All
silver outside, silver the hubs with a myriad of spokes that flashed in
the southern sun like a whole colosseum of careening chariots. On
the peak of the hood a chrome Victoire of Samothrace. Inside, all
was customized: telephone, melodious radio with deep double
speakers, air conditioning, piled carpeting, mahogany dash,
fawnskin cushions and overhead. In the back seat a small bar. I was
allowed to open it: bottles of clear and amber liquid, silver jigger,
crystal tumblers, and a small frosted freezer unit that purred there
in hot September like a dream of alpine lakes.

And Stocker himself was a showpiece: ruddy, with a vivid thatch
of strawberry hair, a crisp red mustache, and bright blue eyes. He
wore linen jackets, silk ascots, and pale blue shirts, tinted perhaps
by the reflection from his eyes. Educated, it was said, in England,
where his mother, a beautiful flame-haired adventuress, had taken
him. Indeed, his diction did sometimes achieve an Oxfordian
broadness, and he never spoke simply. "Mary dear, when we have
Mr. Forbes here in the coach, let us remember to sing together the
coolness of moonlit nights by the lake, for I fear he is a choleric
gentleman, difficult to sell in early autumn. And you, lad, do you
remember diving into the lake and discovering down deep the
delicious caves of ice?"

"Yes, I remember, Mr. Plinth."

"Good lad. That is the burden of your song."

And it was not a lie. The lake was deep and spring-fed, and among the cold stones of the bottom scuttled icy, translucent crawfish, their little pincers raised heroically against my monstrous approach.

So the message my mother delivered in Nineveh was boom. And when she walked among those pines beside dapper Stocker Plinth, in her early autumn organdy which hung out cooly from her lean legs, every prospective buyer knew that here was a piece of the future, rich, elegant, and suavely erotic. On the other hand, if the lady or gentleman found Nineveh a bit remote, there were a number of fine older homes, mostly colonial, on the more venerable and settled hills of the city, all offered exclusively through Mr. Plinth. And the flowing organdy and broad-beribboned hats appeared, if anything, even more elegant under those artfully molded capitals.

I hated them of course and burned with admiration, sitting there on those deep cushions with the cool air caressing me, holding my glass of Coke in which floated a crisp lemon slice and several miniature ice cubes and from which rose the thin pungence of rum, for Stocker Plinth had put a dollop in the glass saying, "Now, Mary, you have reared a perfect young gentleman of a son. It is time he began to learn the pleasures and the courtly use of liquor." Outside, the hot concrete of the city and the sweating blacks passed across the window like an irrelevant dream. Just behind me a nameless woman sang in sweet desperation "Prisoner of Love." And in my britches rose a full erection which that night, between satin sheets in Stocker Plinth's penthouse, I discharged. And did I on the moment of my ecstasy hear a woman's erotic groan? Or was it something wrenched from my own throat? Or only the sound of the fading city traffic far below?

Yes, I left my father and went with my mother, despite my vaunted threat in Elton. And in October, arriving late by special permission at a famous prep school in Virginia, I wept for my defection and for my father. But I could not have saved him by staying. Consider what happened the night my mother and I left.

He sat, of course, by his little cobra lamp, which seemed to me this time to bend its bright eye entirely on the glass of amber bourbon. Hair, hooks, and feathers lay about in an unfocused haze, amongst which his fingers crawled about like a stricken animal. "So you are leaving and taking the boy with you."

"James is coming of his own accord."

He lifted his head and looked at us. And I saw there in his dull eye, where we were reflected, the slow parade of alternatives: he would rise and rage at us, he would strike my mother and lay hold of me, he would dismiss us grandly saying that our departure ushered in his new life, he would weep and lift his arms to the heavens. Did my mother see these, too, standing there beside me like a granite pillar, deflecting his stare as she would have voice and hand had he lifted them? No matter. A darkness rose up behind his eyes, suave curtain released by the bourbon. His head sank down, and when he raised it once more as we left the room, there were hairs and feathers stuck to his forehead and lips as to the face of an idiot clown.

*   *   *

Miracles once begun multiply. So on the twenty-eighth day of my mountain solitude I was called to the forest, which stood under the full moon like a great castellated wall. No crows croaked. And this time, my quivering soul told me, there would be more than a moonchild with a single word on his tongue like a wafer. For I had already heard from within the wood high cries of pain, and when I had entered under the forest battlements I saw a pink glow. Twelve paces down the shifting enfilade of trees brought me in full view of a terrible sight: two lashed to a trunk, left by their torturers to burn and bleed where the cruel stripes had opened the flesh—Lawrence and my father, my old borrachos. When they saw me they stopped sobbing instantly, without the punctuation of so much as a final gasp or snivel. Thus I recognized a theatrical element in the pain. "Where have you been?" said Lawrence. "We have been waiting for years," said my father, their contiguous speech as unseamed as the palaver of a duo of comedians. Then together they said, "Yes, here in the fire and freezing."

"I have been ascending the continent," I said, but my voice was as unheroic as a scolded child's.

"You have been sitting in front of the fire fondling a stone like some old oriental fetishist, instead of searching the forest," said Lawrence. "And filling up pages with narcissistic scribblings, instead of threading your eye among these trees," said my father. And together: "Free us! Free us!" But when I reached them I found no binding ropes or vines after all, not even the sap of the fir but only the tacky scabs and suppurations of self-inflicted wounds. They laughed raucously in my face, with breath as foul as a sump. So I fled the forest. On the steps of the cabin I gathered my breath and lifted my voice. "Divine administrator! Holy doctor! Angel-pierced mystic! Listen! I am sick of visions of these self-pitying boys. Where are my women?"

My Daughter

Wrote me a letter which said in part, "Next Friday we have a session at which visitors are allowed. Come down and meet my friend Adela and give me that kiss you promised." I watched my wife pull a string of dark yarn through the stiff warp. What was the hunkered figure looming under her fingers? A fetus? A muscleman testing his strength against his own bones? A high springer hunched marsupiallike under the leapable mountain? "What does her letter say?" she asked.

"It says I have to come and kiss her."

My wife smiled. "You should have kissed her before."

"I would still have to go because it also says that I have to see the cells they have set up. Marxist? Biotic? Monastic?"

My wife shook her head. "Always the quipper," she said. "Go and see." But my mind had drifted away from the visit. I was wondering why there was always this difference: that when I watched my wife weave, as when I first watched my father tie flies, a warm contentment flowed throughout my whole body, unfocused my eyes, and rose into my scalp with a tingling heat. But when I touched pen to paper all was a kind of nervous scrawl as though something wrecked in its limbs was still driven down a hopeless searching. Garden snails make all in silver a fine hypnotic scroll, but what do my gray wanderings spell?

So I drove down, arriving in the late afternoon. The little clapboard house to which the letter directed me was painted purple except for the two square columns of the tiny front porch which were gilded and wreathed by the artist with turquoise ivy. I parked between a microbus and a road bike. The former threatened me with a huge Cyclopean eye, the latter with wind-swept flames. My daughter met me at the door and we kissed. I will not say that her mouth was sweet, but neither did it taste of bitter revolution as I had feared. "How are you, Margaret?"

"I'm good. How are things on the hill?"

"The house still stands. The future still grows across the great loom. She sends love."

"Tell her I love her."

"I will, but you should tell her yourself."

Inside was Adela, a black girl, in a room with only a few old cushions scattered around the floor. "Be the father?" Margaret nodded. I suppressed a smile, arraigned before the girl-queen, who sat with arms folded sternly and bare legs tucked carefully under her buttocks, a cross between the lotus position and some old tribal earth-worshiping squat. But this girl was not entirely African, nor yet quite mulatto—the skin a light translucent amber. She was beautiful. "Adela comes from New Orleans."

"Hello, Adela from further south than even I can claim," I said, taking a cushion beside my daughter. "Did you come to help with the U?"

Adela, from under her fillet of beads and beautiful bush of cinnamon hair looked at my daughter strangely, who clarified, "The Free U he means."

"The Free U is byed."

I meditated that. "Then what, ladies, is bid, hello-ed, or unbought, as the case may be."

"He got the whitey-man smart-ass tongue you said all right."

My daughter threw her head back and cawed. "He knows it, but he can't stop himself." They looked at me, impaled me on their eye-beams. And what do you guess I principally felt? Black revulsion? Repugnance of homosexual coupling? Sorrow for my lost daughter? No. What I felt was the corruscation of angry lust, for I had been bitten on the very moment of my entry by that little silver serpent that curled on the bosky flesh of her upper arm. I don't know how long I sat tongue-tied or what wars they read in my face. Finally I said, "Eros and revolution. Is that it?"

"Black time come. Time to unword, unbind body," said the princess, motionless, undisturbed in the deep placidity of her eye. Margaret said, "Do you understand, Daddy? It can't be said in words. Tonight we can show you. No one will hurt you." Adela did not add anything. Undoubtedly she had already predicted to herself my cowardly retreat.

Touching my daughter's hand, I said, "I trust you, entirely. But it wouldn't work. Once before I lay with two who had a knowing beyond words. It scared me and I jumped and ran." That was memory truly applied. For at that moment it was not my lust I feared. It was my voice. Just as on that other occasion, I had leaped ahead into the night, seen the black light, heard the strange music, sensed the heat of many bodies, and felt in my throat the seasonless rooting of what wild song I could not imagine. So I declined, drove my car back up the hill.

That night in bed my wife lay at my back with her arms around me. I drew my knees up and clasped them in my hands. And with all my strength I tried to crush my heart. But it beat on, unconsciously or with an intelligence of its own utterly beyond my self-loathing. "Relax," said my wife. "The earth will do with you as it pleases."

"I will make a retreat to Lawrence's cabin," I said.

"Yes," my wife said. "But right now relax." So I released my knees, and her fingers wove a soft cage around my heart.

* * *

The last of my three visions took place at the winter solstice but not where I had expected: in some waste of bright snow. Rather, it took place within the cabin itself. I, passing mindlessly under the window with my slabs of wood, was stricken motionless by the sudden sound—the holy doctor and her sisters making music. And do not imagine that it was sweet, though perhaps it fell short of acid rock. I was afraid to approach and spy upon these women's mysteries, so I have never known for sure who played the lute, who was on drums, who slapped the tambourine, who was striking brass bowl with pestle, and which ones were raising that wild song that rattled the roof and sent the chimney smoke shuddering along the flank of the mountain. You had all my women in there, didn't you, holy doctor? My soft weaver of deep melodies, my golden throated, my crooners, my jammers and jivers. Thank you for the serenade. And didn't I deserve it, having made my difficult ascent to the mountain, retracing as best I could the steps of that old friend of yours who knew the dark night and afterwards the flame that consumes and gives no pain? So I have been recompensed for those earlier sessions I fled in fear.

And one last thing. Did you not, holy doctor, write much and teach the art of writing? So it is therefore proper that this last night before I descend again into the world of my father, of mere men, I write this tribute, with pen steadier than ever before:

> Teresa mistress of angels,
> Blessed grandmother of the blacks,
> Delia of sweet sudor and sweet singing,
> Mother Mary of the golden hiving city,
> Beloved wife inheritor of the earth,
> Adela dark princess of the underworld,
> And you   my Margaret   my ravishing   my roaring girl,
> All,
> All my women,
> This is for you.

Metaphysical Tales

Homage to Poe, Kafka, Dinesen, and Borges

Circle. "I saw Eternity the other night / Like a great ring of pure and endless light," says Vaughan in "The World." And no doubt the shells of atoms are equally luminous. But spectroscopy and microscopy notwithstanding, the Pascalian declaration of our disproportion remains true: neither stars nor mites are truly within our ken. We seek protected intimacy, run from womb to cave. "For when it is experienced from inside, devoid of all exterior features, being cannot be otherwise than round." ("The Phenomenology of Roundness" in *The Poetics of Space* by Gaston Bachelard) Maw and mouth, womb and tomb, hut and house, these are our spaces. And the hero of the round is, of course, the slain god, he of endless vegetative vitality. Borne on the wind from what other world we know not, consumed (like little Jens in Dinesen's "The Dreaming Child") by recollections of other fathers and other mansions, buried, harrowed and harvested, sacked and cellared, swallowed at last, he never fails us with the multiplicity of his members.

The Melon-eaters

Somewhere, perhaps in a dream of starvation, you have seen such melons. They are called breadfruit. At first glance they look like huge breasts, ample to the hungriest mouth. How, you wonder, can the vines sustain them, or the thin bamboo pickets that bend precariously under the weight of the mother fruit? But look more closely. The pale rind is almost translucent. The interior is not so much flesh as a kind of veinal cloud. This conspiracy of sun and soil is decidedly ephemeral, nothing more than a decorative globing of air, a summer festoon against the dark jungle.

Nevertheless, it is true that on a board, under the single blow of a bulawa knife, the melon will split into succulent red halves. Furthermore, these hemispheres will continue for a long time to rock slowly to and fro like objects of great moment, or perhaps like the inconsolably divided androgynes of Plato's fable. You may even begin to imagine that it is not weight but appetency that keeps them rolling so long on their rinds. Ritually, the natives will not touch the fruit until it is still. Meanwhile the pale seeds glisten in the sun as though smeared with a placental fluid.

Now look at the natives. You find a plumpness that matches the melons. But again, look more closely. The hair, thatched elaborately in curious imitation of the construction of their huts, is brittle and frayed. The amber of their eyes is rheumy. The teeth are ramshackle. And note, the heavy breasts and bellies of the women are striated, as you have seen in the flesh of your own women just after delivery, with a kind of gristly separation of the subcutaneous tissue. These people are starving amid an opulence of breadfruit.

Our captain, a man of considerable presence, was a lover of photographs—not a photographer, because his favorite subject was himself, posed against unusual landscapes or with colorful natives. Consequently our passage down the east coast of Africa afforded extraordinary opportunities. I shot roll after roll of film. Now that I have had time to study the selection of photographs which he culled from this huge collection, I see that it does foretell the events in Couville. And perhaps some will say that I ought to have detected his fatal impulse soon enough to save him from it. But at that time I was dazzled by looking through his eyes. You see, I was his executive officer and constant companion. The others in the wardroom considered me a toady. Alas, they were right. For he entirely won me over with his flattery. "Mr. Gardiner," he would say, "you are the only officer aboard of percipience." *Percipience.* When he found a word like that, mixing plumpness with succulence, he seemed not so much to speak it as to chew it. It came to you wet with spittle, like the morsel a primitive mother has masticated for her infant. "Only your dutiful second in command," I would say, but I was entirely won over, up to the last steps into the hut. There I parted from him, as you see. I am here. But it was not courage, not the sudden recovery of myself. I merely shrank back.

So one can, if he is percipient, discover the constant image of the photographs which I took under the captain's direction. It is an arch. It tends to be wide and soft in its slope rather than ogival. It may be a canopy of trees, the entry of a hut, or the arms of two grinning blacks paid to imitate camaraderie. And there is the captain under the arch addressing to the camera a decidedly theatrical smile, like a weary old vaudevillian coming forward under the proscenium for one last antic. But consider these arches carefully. If you lift the plastic pockets of the captain's photo binder and let them slip one by one rapidly from the end of your finger, you will experience something akin to the crankcard flicks of the old penny arcade. What happens is this: the arches contract and dilate. Tree and sky mouth the captain. So, perhaps I should have seen what was coming, but I did not, until too late.

Melons, then, and arches. And one final ingredient: the bizarre business of racial confusion in Couville. This greatly animated the captain. Here's what happened. The chief of the local constabulary came aboard to explain the laws. "Whites must not consort with blacks during your stay here. Your men understand that, captain?"

"They can be made to understand it."

"Good. Now, have you any blacks among your crew?"

"Four stewards. High-caliber serviceable men."

"Good. These four will be classified as whites for the duration of your call in Couville. They must be particularly cautioned against consorting with blacks." Here the colonial's red mustache bobbed above a forced smile.

The captain's eyes narrowed. "How will my black whites be treated by your white whites?"

"I suggest the Feyanda district. Here they will be treated very well." From his coat pocket the chief produced a small chart and unfurled it under impeccably manicured hands. "Just here." He circumscribed an area of the city with a band of black ink. "Please keep this."

"Thank you." The captain smiled. "The potency of your laws is amazing. I assume that this alchemy of pigmentation is reversible so that at the proper time my white stewards can be reconverted into blacks."

"Of course, sir." Our colonial bobbed his red mustache for us again and then departed.

In the wardroom galley the captain assembled the stewards and decreed upon them whiteness. They were puzzled, of course. Then as understanding dawned, they giggled. But finally they settled into a kind of sullen uneasiness which displeased the captain. "You refuse to take up the white man's burden?"

"No sir," said Garrett, the chief steward, a black of great stature and dignity.

"What are you saying then?"

"We wish to meet alone, sir."

Quickly the word came that none of the stewards would go ashore, except Garrett, and he only to make necessary purchases for the wardroom.

"Is whiteness so fearful?" When I did not answer, the captain said, "Yes, Mr. Gardiner. Be honest and say yes. It's the color of nothingness. That's why the white man spreads over the globe gobbling up lands and peoples. He can't satisfy his appetite for color." He laughed humorlessly.

But the captain seemed to forget the stewards quickly, and we resumed our photographic quests, urging Kromah, the driver provided by the consulate, farther out into the native sections. Deepening shadows marked our progress. The white teeth of the natives shone brilliantly out of huts so dark that they seemed filled with a kind of gelatinous ink. Melon rinds lay in the black dust of the streets. Flies swarmed over them furiously. On the second day we reached an impasse. The street narrowed. The natives thickened. "Non beyond this," said Kromah. It was near the end of the day. "Very well," said the captain. "We will come here early tomorrow and set out on foot."

I sighed. "Captain, I've already photographed you with dozens of these people. Will they really be any different out at the edge of the jungle?"

"Very different, sir," Kromah interrupted in his loud and intense monotone.

"What's the difference?" I asked.

"Those non city sir, those very fierce."

"Precisely. Don't you see, Mr. Gardiner, there are two kinds of blacks, excluding, of course, Kromah's kind, totally acculturated to the white man. There are the melon-eaters, precarious parasites on the white man's culture, and the hunters out in the jungle still living according to the old ways." I deliberately looked blank. "Where's your curiosity, Mr. Gardiner? Don't you want to study these?"

"Why should I?"

"Because they represent two very interesting cases. The melon-eaters are marginal men, living in the penumbra of civilization. They are no longer what they were, but are not yet anything new. They are pure becoming. Among them we will study the hunger for being. Then we will go to the hunters, the flesh-eaters, and study the mastery of being. Is non true, Kromah?"

But we returned that evening to an unpleasant surprise: Garrett lay badly hurt in the brig, where the officer of the deck had put him for safekeeping. Red mustaches occupied the wardroom demanding that Garrett be turned over to the local authorities. A police boat snarled impatiently on our stern.

"See here, captain," said Sykes—Colonel Sykes he called himself on this occasion—"your ship is harboring a criminal, a steward named Garrett."

"Excuse me," said the captain. "You don't mean criminal. You mean suspect."

"All right, captain, suspect."

"What happened?"

Sykes's story was that Garrett had gone to the red-light district in Feyanda that afternoon and abused a white whore, thus starting a fracas during which several women and Garrett himself had been hurt. He managed to reach Feyanda landing ahead of his pursuers, and the police boat had been too late to intercept the ship's whaler. "We must have our prisoner, captain. This is clearly a crime against the civil code, not against your military code."

"Colonel, I'm amazed. Do you imagine that the Uniform Code of Military Justice of the United States fails of sanctions against the abuse of foreign ladies of the night?"

"I mean, captain, that the offense comes under our jurisdiction. I am certain that your superiors at the consulate will concur entirely." The red mustache gave a menacing twitch.

"Please be seated, colonel, while I have a word with Garrett."

I accompanied the captain to the brig, where we found the chief steward, his head heavily bandaged. "Garrett," he said, "what the hell happened? There's a bigoted little colonial in the wardroom that would like to have you spend several years in a South African jail."

"I have the right not to speak," said Garrett with great dignity.

The captain nodded gravely. "You certainly do, Garrett. But you may find yourself in front of a Dutch judge who can't remember that you're technically white."

"What do you want to know, captain?"

"I want to know exactly what happened."

"I was shopping where the man told us to go. I had everything on my list but the Edam cheese."

"My God, man, what kind of cock and bull is this? There must be a ball of Edam every six feet in Couville."

"Yes, sir, but a woman told me she could show me a place where I could get big hunks of Edam cheap."

The captain laughed sarcastically. "Mr. Gardiner, of all the expressions you know for that particular article have you ever encountered one more overripe?"

I refused to answer that. Garrett said nothing.

"And you had no idea that she was a woman of the streets?"

Garrett shook his head. "I thought she was talking about cheese."

"So let me guess, Garrett. When she discovered that you wouldn't purchase her brand of Edam, she and her friends fell on you."

"They tore up my market basket and dumped all my good eats in the gutter."

"And you struck back."

"Yes sir. I should have turned and walked off, but they made me mad, hollering about the nigger is queer. And then they went wild, clawing and biting."

"Mr. Gardiner, see that this man is returned to his quarters. And I myself will see our visitor off briskly."

These things were done, but the captain's agitation did not cease. Early the next morning he took Garrett to sick bay to have his wounds dressed again. I went along. There were nasty abrasions on both hands and arms, but the ugliest wound was a set of deep tooth marks on the right cheek and ear. The captain examined these closely. "Doctor, there you have the primeval stigmata."

"Yes sir," said the doctor after a considerable pause, "the mark of Cain." He was a slow southerner and obviously pleased with himself for striking off this spark of learning.

"Yes," said the captain in a kind of rapt whisper. "Until I saw Garrett's wounds I had not realized that God branded Cain with his teeth."

Garrett winced as antiseptic was applied. "Clean him good, doctor. Can you think of anything more infectious than a whore's teeth?"

"Nothing, captain," said the doctor, jabbing his little swab savagely into Garrett's broken flesh. But the steward had overcome the shock of the first sting. He sat stoically still.

Kromah came at ten to the main landing. "We go back to consul, sir. See melon cutting another day."

"No," said the captain, "I've talked with the consul by phone since you left him, Kromah. We've changed my appointment to the afternoon so that we can witness the cutting." That was a lie of course. The last word from the consul was an urgent call for conference about Garrett's case.

Nevertheless, misled by the captain's lie, Kromah drove us out again toward that narrowing of the road which permitted no further passage. As we wound among the shacks of the melon-eaters, the captain peered ahead over Kromah's shoulder with keen anticipation. But something was lacking. For several minutes I could not figure out what it was, and then, with a start I saw. "Captain, you've forgotten your camera."

"Where we're going, Mr. Gardiner, there's not enough light for a photo."

"I could have drawn the infrared camera from gunnery, Captain," I said, pressing shrewdly I thought.

"No, Mr. Gardiner, we need an instrument that records more than light or heat—one for instance that records the smell and the titillation of acidic moisture, records sighs and the taste on the tongue of tongue. A sexasensographer." He paused and probed my eye half-humorously. "Why not an ordinary pentasensographer, Mr. Gardiner?" I shook my head. "Equilibrium, Mr. Gardiner. We need also to record the warping of space—and not merely the liquids of the inner ear running east or west, up or down, but spreading themselves out evenly in the little canals like a dew. Imagine that sensation, Mr. Gardiner."

I did imagine it. It was like floating in space. "Be careful, captain," I said, inadvertently assuming Kromah's stentorian monotone. "The instrument you are speaking of is the human consciousness. But there are places where we must not send ourselves. We must be satisfied to look at them through the long glass so to speak."

He made no comment, but only chuckled ambiguously. Moments later we debouched into a dust so finely powdered that it rose like smoke about our feet. At our passage, too, fly-blown melon rinds released clouds of black buzzing. Dust and flies, but not a native in sight. "These all ahead in the circle," said Kromah.

"How far?"

"See." Kromah showed us a glimpse of light perhaps a quarter of a mile down the gloomy lane of arching trees.

As we neared the circle we began to hear above the plop of our footfall a rumbling of drums, gentle and soporific. And that was precisely the effect on the natives. Perhaps a hundred reclined somnolently along the shaded perimeter of the circle where a grassy embankment rose up from the dusty center. Kromah led us to a spot unoccupied by sleepers. We moved stealthily at his signal, but our arrival was marked. I saw several pairs of sad eyes open and take us in without expression. Our arrival was also noted by the six drummers and by the officialdom of the cutting. These latter, also six, were distinguished by their leather loincloths and by the long heavy knives which hung from tight waistbands. All others, women as well as men, were clad in a wild variety of garments made of khaki twill: breechcloths, leggings, shorts, skirts, caps, scarves, greaves, and all sorts of bindings and baldrics. One had the feeling that one had chanced upon some defeated regiment of native irregulars, or that these were cannibals who had eaten their victims and dismembered their uniforms.

When the six with knives began to arrange on a long raised cutting board a line of perhaps four dozen melons, the drummers picked up the tempo. The sleepers began to sit up one by one, theatrically, as if aroused from a deep trance and returned to a reality which for some moments was altogether unfamiliar. I smiled.

"Non smile sir."

The tempo of the drums increased. The crowd began to clap and chant. The six did a sword dance, threatening each other in the most unconvincing way, pretending frenzy. Inevitably there came the sudden silence, the halving of the melons with the single flashing stroke of the bulawa knives, and the brief mass scream of the eaters. Then followed the only truly memorable moment of the ritual—an absolute stillness during which the melon halves rocked slowly to and fro, red and glistening, returning to the sun at its zenith an old debt of flesh and blood.

The leader of the six cutters, a gray-haired but muscular black, beckoned us toward the feast. I hung back. The captain did not. Kromah touched my elbow. "Muss go sir." At the table, following the example of the captain, I seized a slice of melon and sank my teeth into it—a swill of insubstantial sweetness, pulpy and veinous, which left on the palate a lacteous aftertaste and in the teeth elusive threads. And the juice, which was nothing more than a saccharine pink water, ran down our chins and stained our uniforms. It was hard to believe that even the natives themselves could take any joy of this pallid food. In fact, such animation as there was related less to eating than to the skeeting of seeds. At this the natives were masterful. Seeds flew from their lips with amazing force and accuracy. Immense passion went into the great inhalation of breath, into the precise puckering of lips, and into the oohs and aahs that rewarded an especially long trajectory which culminated in a direct hit. No one dodged. In fact, the target, whether man or woman, always wore the missle proudly upon his skin until the spittle dried and the seed fell into the dust. This play went on for perhaps a quarter of an hour and then the circle emptied rapidly.

The captain detained the grizzled leader of the cutters. "Kromah, can you speak with this fellow?"

"Some word sir."

"Ask him what else these people eat."

Kromah and the cutter exchanged words. "These eat insect, too, and tuber and soup from garden reptile."

"Does he preside over ceremonies for these foods too?"

Another exchange, this time more complicated. "He do this for others sir."

"You mean for another tribe?"

"Yes sir, he do other cuts."

"What does he cut for the others?"

"He non say sir."

"Ask him."

"Muss non ask sir. Police chop chop."

Then the cutter spoke without interrogation. Kromah answered.

"What was that?" asked the captain.

"He say you come to other cut. I say non come."

The captain nodded. "Where does the other cutting take place?"

"He non say sir. In jungle, or police come chop chop."

The captain glanced at his watch. "We'd better get back to the consulate, Kromah. Please thank our host for the breadfruit."

In a spacious white stucco building the consul received us brusquely. With him was Colonel Sykes, his mustache twitching impatiently.

"I assume you were delayed."

"Yes, consul. We had an appointment out in the native quarters for the noon melon cutting. That explains the appearance of our uniforms, which I hope you will excuse." The captain plucked his britches regretfully.

"The case of Garrett," said the consul with ferocious loudness as though sweeping with his voice the smirched air.

"Yes," said the captain. "Well, you and the colonel will be pleased to learn that I have persuaded Garrett not to press charges." He nodded lightly at the consul and Sykes. A pained incredulity crossed the consul's face. He must have thought that he was dealing with an utter fool, the archetypal American naif.

"Captain . . ." began the colonel strenuously.

"Please, John." The consul raised his hand. He spoke slowly, as to a child. "The charges in question, captain, are being brought *against* Garrett, *against* Garrett—resisting arrest and aggravated assault."

The captain shook his head. "I'm amazed, consul, but if that's the case, then we'd better have a private word. You see, I have been serving informally as Garrett's legal counsel."

The consul fussed about his desk for a moment. "Colonel, in the interest of expediting this case, would you please allow me a moment with the captain. I assure you we will arrive at a quick issue."

"The man is playing the fool. I will not be put off," said the colonel, but he did march out.

"Now captain . . ."

"Just be quiet a minute, consul. I have questioned Garrett closely, a man of great honesty. Whores in the Feyanda district, recommended incidentally by the colonel to my stewards, enticed him to their quarters and attacked him when he rejected their offers. Consequently, under absolutely no circumstance will I turn Garrett over to the local authorities. You understand that?"

The consul was set back by the captain's sudden change in character, but he managed to speak with a suitable sternness. "You wish me to inform the local authorities that they must make the arrest without my assistance? You understand that the charges might then extend to those protecting the criminal?"

"If the police boat approaches within 300 yards of my side I will blow it out of the water." The captain leaned forward. "You see these, consul?" He pointed to two of the dozen or so ribbons above the pocket of his blouse. "Purple Heart, Medal of Honor—the Coral Sea. And you know, consul, I yearn for one more good whiff of gunsmoke and carrion." He rubbed his hands together. "Is there a Dutch man-of-war nearby we could call in? Are there any shore batteries?" He turned briefly to me. His eyes glowed madly. "Mr. Gardiner, prepare a fire grid of the city. We'll lob a few shells into the police garrison. We'll send in the motorboat for you and your staff, consul. Cover it with the three-inchers."

"Stop it, captain. You must turn the man over and you know it."

"I will not, consul. Question. Isn't it your job to represent American citizens here? Why are you playing toady to a hash of Dutch and British bigots, cravenly assisting in the most errant miscarriage of justice? What do they pay you for that kind of work, consul?" That flayed away the professional exterior of the consul. He shook his fist. "I'll have your ass, captain. I'll send an urgent dispatch to the Commander of the Sixth Fleet."

The captain nodded. "Admiral Gaines is one of my old mentors, consul. But you're right. You could make trouble." He paused. "Let's look at things another way. My guess is you're about fifty, consul. I also guess that if you were having a promising career with the State Department you would not be in Couville. And you know, consul, the times being what they are, sentiment ripening, cases which involve injustices to blacks can be very ugly. You have my ass, I have your ass. Why don't we try a different way?"

"What?" said the consul almost abstractedly, the flush of anger drained from his face.

"Well," said the captain, also much subdued, "suppose I charge Garrett with, say, absence without leave and conduct unbecoming—offenses too serious for captain's mast. I appoint Mr. Gardiner to conduct a summary court-martial. Mr. Gardiner will receive depositions and statements from the colonel and others. The trial will be concluded at sea after our sailing. I will send you a report of the powerful punishments which Garrett is to undergo."

The consul smiled wanly. "Nicely invented, captain, but it won't wash with these people. They'll eat me alive."

The captain looked searchingly at the consul, then he said, "If you send the dispatch, consul, Sixth Fleet will eat me alive."

"Turn him over," said the consul.

"The question is whether one wants to be eaten from the outside or the inside," said the captain. He sat still for some moments looking intently at the consul, then he seemed to drift off.

"Are you reconciling yourself to the inevitable, captain?"

The captain shook his head absently. "Actually, consul, my old war-dog braggadocio of a moment ago put me in mind of Okinawa again and the kamikazes."

"Is that so, captain?"

"Yes. At the time, consul, as you can imagine, I hated the kamikazes. Later I pitied them, poor little yellow boys strapped in half-gassed Zeros by their evil elders. But now I see that neither sentiment was appropriate. Think of it, consul—diving down those smoky skies toward the black mouth of a man-of-war's stack. And if you made it . . ."

The consul shot me a curious look. I said, "If you made it, captain, you never knew it. So it didn't do you any good—unless you're prepared to believe that you soared out on the other side into an imperial paradise where your warrior ancestors welcomed you as a hero."

The captain smiled. "Mr. Gardiner keeps me rational, consul. I'll consult with him about the disposition of Garrett."

"I'm afraid, captain, that I must have your commitment, at this very moment, to turn Garrett over to Colonel Sykes."

The captain said nothing to that. He stood and extended his hand. "Forgive words spoken in heat, consul."

But there was no heat in that room. This was not your equatorial Africa of slowly turning fans. Outside the window all was bright and temperate. From clay pots hung the blood bells of gorgeous fuchsia.

The dispatch came the following morning from Admiral Gaines: "Relinquish immediately Henry M. Garrett to W. John Sykes, Chief of Constabulary, Couville. Right to counsel and all other legal protections guaranteed Garrett." The firm but moderate tone of the dispatch assured us that the consul had had the decency, perhaps even the compassion, not to send the admiral an inflammatory message. The captain said to me, "We're moving our ETD up one day, Mr. Gardiner. We sail tomorrow at dawn. In a few minutes I'm going to take the motorboat in and wind up a couple of things."

"I'll go along."

"It's not necessary, Mr. Gardiner."

"Yes, it is necessary."

He looked at me sharply. "Very well."

I thought that we might be intercepted in the harbor, but the police boat did not come out. I thought we might be arrested when we put in, but there was Kromah waiting for us, according to the captain's instructions, as though nothing were amiss. Sometimes I have thought that Kromah had entered a subtle conspiracy with his jungle cousins, that he only pretended to oppose the captain's desire to penetrate the mysteries of the flesh-eaters. But who can see behind the black mask of the house nigger?

We went to the melon-cutting ceremony, of course. The drums beat, the sleepers arose from their ersatz trance, the great bulawa knives flashed up and down, the circle filled briefly with silence and the rocking glister of the melons, the eaters rushed forward, and presently the air was lanced with seeds. Then the captain talked again through Kromah to the grizzled leader of the cutters, as I knew he would. He wished to arrange to witness the other cutting ceremony in the jungle. "Muss non go," said Kromah. "Police chop chop."

The cutter was willing to take the captain to the jungle ceremony. He required no money.

"Kromah non go."

"That's right, Kromah, you stay with the car. Otherwise these people might eat the tires. Mr. Gardiner will stay with you."

"No, captain, I'll make the show."

"Very well." The captain gave me a look of mild surprise.

From the clearing the cutter led us onto a path that passed again under a dark arch of trees. The path was straight. It did not twist among the trees. It seemed older than the trees. I said, "Captain, fortunately this is an easy path to retrace. It's not too late to turn back."

"What's behind us, Mr. Gardiner?"

"Garrett's behind us, captain, with nothing standing between him and the Dutch but you."

"Remember that, Mr. Gardiner."

"I am remembering it, captain, but you seem to forget it." He didn't reply to that, but after a while he said, "I have discovered my vocation, Mr. Gardiner. It is to learn why men eat each other."

I laughed. "All the thinkers of the ages haven't found the answer to that question, captain."

"They didn't look in the right place."

"The jungle?"

"Yes."

"It's not necessary to come out here to the jungle, captain. Study the colonel. Study the whores in Feyanda. And yesterday you wanted to eat the consul. Study your own heart."

The captain smiled. "Surely, Mr. Gardiner, you will excuse me from the study of the colonel for the mere asking. As for the whores of Feyanda, I fear they wouldn't find me as tempting as Garrett, the black white man, and therefore wouldn't show me their teeth. And my own heart, rank with Japanese carrion? Who would learn anything from it, Mr. Gardiner? No, my appointment is with the flesh-eaters out here in the jungle. But it is not your appointment, Mr. Gardiner."

"I am with you, captain."

"Then march on, Emmanuel."

We heard a noise ahead like the whine of gnats. As we approached, it deepened and became human. Presently the path turned abruptly and we walked out upon the edge of a clearing. In the center a dozen wailing dancers performed around a smoky fire. They were masked as panthers. From time to time one of the natives sitting along the grassy perimeter of the clearing echoed their wailing. It was not fierce, but there was something in it so profoundly exigent that it made me shudder.

So it was a circle much like the other, except that the fire replaced the long melon table, and a hut with an arched thatch roof stood just behind it. Did I remember then all those arches—arm, door, tree—which my weary eye had centered in the captain's lens? Did I take from the intensity of the captain's face sign and signature of this last, this darkest arch? Yes. Nevertheless, and no matter how futilely, I held my hand out. "This is as far as we go, captain." I had at least the energy of fear. But I expected our guide, the grizzled cutter, to shout for the panther men to seize and bind us. I was mistaken. He showed no signs of misgiving and waited patiently while the captain and I exchanged final words.

"We must turn back now captain, for Garrett's sake if for nothing else."

"Mr. Gardiner, don't let the Dutch have Garrett. Take any steps necessary. That's an order."

I flared up—fear again, not courage. "You're the one who's got to take care of that, captain, instead of indulging yourself in this jungle idiocy!"

"Jungle idiocy?" The captain looked at me with frowning disapproval. And, yes, he was right. Whatever one chose to call what we witnessed, it was not idiocy. Just at that moment the panther men, widening the round of their dance, touched with high-arched feet the edge of the narrow circle of greensward where we stood. They brought their knees high and ducked their heads low in a curious pantomime of stealth, wailing all the while as though the extremity of their need cruelly deprived them of the cunning required to satisfy it. Behind leaped the fire, making red tongues against the morning sunlight. And behind the fire stood the thatched hut. And in my mind's eye passed, like a flickering nightmare, the endless series of arches I had seen through the captain's camera. But about that he was also right. No camera could record the images of this scene. It might catch the blackness of the panther men and the sun-paled fire with the hut shimmering behind, but not the subhuman wailing, not the wraith of smoke that tickled the nose, moistened the eye, and caused the tongue to explore fearfully the roof of the mouth, and certainly not the frightening hint of vertigo I felt as the panther men began to circle back now closer to the fire and the hut. I seized the captain's arm as firmly as I could, but he obviously felt the palsy in my grip. "Steady, Mr. Gardiner."

"Why are we here, captain?" I tried to make the question stern and challenging, but my voice shook.

"For this, Mr. Gardiner." He took in with a sweep of his free hand the whole expanse of the clearing. The grizzled cutter followed this gesture with interest.

"You knew this is what it would be?"

"Not exactly, Mr. Gardiner. It's the fate of the initiate to go blindly into the rite."

By now the panther men were in a tight circle about the fire passing, it seemed, between the leached flames and the columns the sunlight made of the smoke, and wailing inconsolably. For the first time the grizzled cutter shuffled his feet with a hint of impatience.

"Don't go, captain," I said shaking his arm. "Don't go. Remember the pictures I took of all the mouths. Remember the tooth marks in Garrett's head." I think I attempted a sibylline whisper.

"Be still, Mr. Gardiner."

"Captain! Remember Garrett, who has polished your shoes, made your bed, and cooked your food for four years. Remember, you are the captain of our ship."

"I'm detaching myself from the ship, Mr. Gardiner, leaving it and Garrett in your good hands. Go back and make ready to get under-way. Weigh anchor at 0600 tomorrow." I was trembling. He laid his hand on my shoulder. "Be still, Mr. Gardiner. Some day not long from now, when you have rounded the rough seas of the Cape of Good Hope and sailed northwest to the Caribbean, you will look down from the bridge into blue water and see clearly the perfect image of all this." His voice did not shake. His eyes did not flash. To all outward appearances he was perfectly sane. Nevertheless, when he pulled away from me and started toward the center of the circle, I dashed after him and grabbed his arm. Yet I never spoke to him again. We stood there together one step down the declivity toward fire and hut. But what I felt pulling me was nothing so innocent as gravity. It was the hollow yearning of the hut's mouth, sucking at my bowels. And suddenly I knew why the split noon melons always rocked with uncanny moment, with fatal appetency. And knew, too, why they were, though red, so watery — blood and balance preempted by some ancient failure of the vine's will. I let the captain go. I turned and labored back over the lip of that little hillock as other men labor to climb mountains. It was long, very long. Some-times I seemed not to move at all. The sun stood up over the tops of the trees and fixed upon me its great bright eye. But I labored on.

I reached the straight path at last and ran down it without looking back. Perhaps the panther men raised a triumphant cry. But I did not hear it. My own breath, so narrowly reclaimed, came in sobs and filled my ears.

Across the water, in Sierra Leone, bougainvillea hang in profusion from the walls of the city, their reds deeper even than those of the fuchsia in Couville. I can also see through my binoculars blacks working on the docks. They are glossier than the captain's dusty melon-eaters and smoky panther men. They glisten. It is hot here. Tomorrow the new captain arrives by plane. The same plane will fly Garrett to Couville to face his accusers. I offered to slip him ashore here to fend for himself among his fellow blacks, but he refused. The jungle frightens him. He prefers, as a white, to face the Dutch court. They will eat him alive. So in the end the captain was wrong. Garrett did not refuse to take up the white man's burden. Thus we have lost one black to the whites and one white to the blacks. *Ave atque vale*, my gallant, my sacrificial miscegenators.

The new captain will hold an inquiry. I will tell him that my captain was captured by evil natives, panther men, and that I barely escaped with my life. I will tell him that I set sail as ordered by my captain against my better judgment but in passionate respect (shall I say reverence?) for his final words. In short, I will play the fool, addled by African mysteries. They cannot court-martial me. But neither can they ever again trust me at sea. They will find me serviceable in, say, the communications office of some out-of-the-way base, an auxiliary air station in Florida, where the windows are wreathed in morning glories. I will be a man of mystery, career wrecked by curious occluded events in Africa—best left alone.

So, I have had heroic moments: walking to the edge of doom with the captain, sailing with a fugitive under the guns of the Dutch. Naught availeth. I leave them to their destinies in hut, in prison, in black maw. I have only a few years of service remaining. However uneasy the peace, I savor it, knowing that the ages of cannibalism are in the offing.

Line. At the end of Borges's fascinating Euclidean fiction "Death and the Compass," the Parisian mobster Red Scharlach shoots and kills the detective Eric Lönnrot. "Red Red" kills "Red Line-red." Or, through a punning on the Indo-European roots and a more attractive arrangement of word order: "Red Red" meets "Red-line Red-line." The assassination comes after an illusory rhombic chase and the simple animadversions of Lönnrot's assistant, Treviranus, the Christian, whose trinitarian principles determine his plainness.

Therefore the universe is not, according to Borges, in essence a quarternity, though he will not require us to sacrifice Jung's mandalas. Nor is it a trinity, though we may preserve the endless ingenuity of the Council of Nicaea. Least of all is it a duality, that most unsuppressible of heresies against which most recently Lévi-Strauss has arrayed whole galaxies of symphonic myth. No, the universe is a line, itself illusory, showing at its two ends the mirror images of a single entity which has been separated temporarily for we know not what purpose, most easily rejoined by a bullet. The assassin with his gun is the hero of the line.

Selections from the Assassin's Memoirs, or a Shard of the History of the World since World War II

[Patterns]

I killed him in Barcelona just after the war. I detected his afterimage by a fountain under a plane tree on the Ramblas. Later, I saw the stain of his shadow against the pediment of the great Colombo, where in a moment of bravado he had posed for his photograph. Presently he strolled among the stalls of the famous glass-domed market, where heaps of plucked fruit and the mournful eyes of eviscerated fish pressed upon him his mortality. He returned resignedly to his hotel near Los Caracoles and waited for me on the balcony. . . .

I killed him aboard a small freighter south of Salonika. He said, looking through his binoculars at the ruins of Diana Trinominata, that the present gods had retired three quarters of the spectrum, to the last squib. Fear no westering tints, he said. Only alabaster now, sky-blue, midnight, and the silver lances of the moon. But his blood was red. . . .

I killed him in Alexandria where a beautiful prostitute vainly lowered her eyes for him. The lids were silver, and the irises, touched perhaps with belladonna, violet. He turned away. I sprinkled in his retsina a seeding of golden crystals. . . .

These were the war-wounded, the seekers of perpetual seedlessness. But in the early sixties all changed. I imagined a comically obscene business card. *Mortimer Amoretti: Specialist in Copulatory Assassinations.* Emblem: hawk rampant, tongue outstretched. In short, my masters shifted their attention to the opposite type: the sensualist, the broadcaster. At the time I found this change puzzling, but then I did not yet understand the essence of my masters' moderation, did not understand how the world, ever yawing between languor and appetency, would, were it not for our constant and adaptable vigilance, crash upon one rock or the other.

I killed him in Oslo in an endless June dusk behind the hairy logs of Ibsen's old study cohabiting under evergreens. I killed him in a flowered hotel room in Paris, where he was enfolded in the laminous ambiance of his whore—perfume, perspiration, love's lubricants. In the sinking ripeness of Venice, under Paola's saccharine radiance, his blood confused the famous mosaic. Even in Bursa, once as brutal as the mountains that serrate its sunrises, I found him among

panderers in poppied sleep. . . . Port Said, drunk, his hands spilling
small coin. *I am the great sower*, he cried. His seeds stippled the sea.
Naked divers made furrows for his plantings. A bumboat vendor
tossed up a wet necklace of clay beads. The colors were not fast. His
shirt grew iridescent. *Joseph I am*, he cried. *These are the fat years.*
But I, winter's falcon, cooled that fevered blood. . . .

[A New Quarry]

. . . midsummer, a special caveat from my masters: *Many aliases:
Major Rumford, Ivan Broderick, also recently known as the Holy
Man of Nehrud* . . . I have forgotten the other aliases, but the con-
cluding phrases of the dispatch are clear in the memory: *Mensur
scar. Devilishly clever. Will know that he is pursued. Careless of life.*
Romance in high places, I thought. He has always cared. Even when
life ought to have seemed a tasteless pit, he would not spit it out.
That self-garroting in an Athenian cul-de-sac was not suicide. The
device was laid for me. . . .

I found his hotel. From its high terrace he had looked down, I
knew, at the subcontinent creeping forward, affronting sea. He had
seen foolish man, tempted by the alluvial richness of the delta,
succumbing to disease and flood. On the far bank of the river he had
seen the refugee camp writhing in the dust like a stricken serpent.
And what had he felt — the same revulsion as I? No. A deep inscruta-
ble sympathy. I thought I knew the whole array, from the icy death-
wisher to the feverish seed-bearer. But here, as my masters had
forewarned, was a specimen that fell outside our normal taxonomy,
one far more dangerous than the merely sterile or erotic. But how
would I pursue this quarry for whom a whole new set of intuitions
was needed? I felt what I had not felt in years, fear, fear confirmed
when presently the manager spoke to me. He was a small Eurasian
with beautiful skin that darkened, as though iodined, under the
flanks of the nose and in the partially eclipsed canthi of the eyes. "I am
sorry you have missed the major, sir, but he has left a message for you.
He wishes you to know that he is in the refugee camp."

"As the Holy Man of Nehrud?"

"No, sir. As one sufferer among ten thousand."

I did not sleep until the voices of night finally restored equanimity
with wise imperatives. *Avoid literary commonplaces like: who is the
hunter, who the hunted? You are the hawk, always. Abolish fear of
death, for according to his nature he cannot kill.* . . .

[In the Serpent's Belly]

. . . down the swarming summer air, then, I stooped on my prey. But in that shadowless world even my accipiter's eye was deceived in all sizes—the river as wide as the sea between the pillars of Hercules, the sinuous thing beside it huger than the ones he had wrestled, impervious to my talons, its skin a tough motley of canvas, hides, pelts, and the like, lashed to a tortuous skeleton of uprights and cross-members. And all within writhed the wretched refugees, indigestible gobbets of Islam cast up from the East. So I folded my pennoned metaphor, walked the igneous dust, and entered through a portiere made of knots of hemp.

. . . lost in the labyrinthine gloom but not long, his track easy to discover, the glister of his tears everywhere: on the swollen belly of a rickety child sucking feverishly at the teat of one of the huge hairless cows allowed to wander freely and befoul the earthen floor, on the withered breast of a young mother who compounded of grain and spit short stay of her infant's starvation, on the flanks of an old man where a hundred suppurating sores opened like mouths begging for food. Inward, ever inward led his lachrymose trail until at last I found his cubicle and entered it through a baffle of hanging flaps. It contained only a cloth-covered straw mat and a clay pot. On the canvas walls he had painted mandalas with rich dyes in intricate unbroken lines like the calligraphies of Hejaz or the convolutions of intestines. I sat at the foot of his mat facing the entry, hand on my gun, following with my eye each sliding shadow that approached. But he with the scar in the corner of his mouth did not enter. My head grew muzzy. I seemed to hear a sound as a yeasty churning. And suddenly I realized what was happening. There in the bowels of the beast gastric fluids were slowly converting me into pulpy aliment while he waited nearby for my fingerprints to fade, my face to soften like hot suet, and my bones to jelly. Then he would invite those cavernous mouths to feast on my flesh. I was furious. *Come, Holy Man of Nehrud! Come with your friends and eat me!* Even as the echo of my shout faded, the shadows outside the walls thickened. A murmur went up. And now, I thought, I will force him to come for me. I took aim at a tall shadow. But it was late afternoon and a breeze had sprung up so that the walls swayed and the slant sunlight splayed the image confusingly over the undulant surface of the canvas. I fired three times in rapid succession, once in the center of the shadow and once to each side, but there was no scream. The figure did not fall. Instead, it drifted away up and to the left, like a puppet in a shadow show hoisted into the flies. I fired at another shadow and another, but they, too, only drifted away. So I thought in my bewilderment that the canvas was only a theatrical scrim and the images bodiless illusions — all contrived by him to keep me occupied until the serpent's maw crushed me. I leapt up with a roar, burst through the flaps of his cubicle, and ran out shouting. Had I met in the corridors of the labyrinth any hapless soul — man, woman, or child — I would have fired. And not out of vengeance, but just to see again the reassuring red of blood. But everyone kept to his cubicle.

At last I arrived at an exit where a portiere hung black knots against the gold setting of the sun. There stood a great hairless cow masticating hay with a circular grinding motion of its jaw. I shot it between the eyes, which presently glazed over stupidly. The front legs buckled at the knees. The animal slumped down on its neck. And finally when the slow news of death reached the hindquarters, it tumbled into the dust. Blood streamed from its mouth. I watched for a moment, then stepped over the beast and out into the breeze that coursed down the river.

So I had no chance in that labyrinth. I had been foolish ever to enter his element: darkness, stench, starvation, and pity. I began to hate him. In my waking dreams I saw him sitting shrewdly in those deep bowels. No, not shrewd, because he was actually enamored of those foul recesses where man walks at the edge of his humanity. I searched for a means to draw him out. . . .

[Cherchez la femme]

. . . late July. I saw her standing as he had left her, just beyond the lanterns of the hotel terrace in the vestibule of night — pale sari, honey-dark swath of flesh at the midriff, black hair. She was slight. But he had opened her — lips full and eyes tunneled by pain and ecstasy. She looked at me knowingly. The manager ceremoniously escorted her to a table — a lady of high station. But the hungry eyes and the prominent nodes of the spine revealed that she desired to sacrifice everything for him. Later, when the manager had made unctuous introduction, I said, *shall I take you to him?* And how glad I was of that obscene doe-eyed nodding, that voluptuous pity, for it shattered her severe beauty which otherwise, that one time in all my dutiful history, might have undermined my resolve. Then how pleasant to ride in a cool cream Jaguar under the tropic sun out across the river. Minutes later she and I, arm in arm, lowly escort and high lady, walked inward and inward down the track of his compassion into the very maw of that immense suffering. I left her in his cubicle. *Will you not wait for his thanks?* I shook my head. *I cannot.* In fact, already the moist air had begun to soften me with its gummy mastication. *Tell him that I will watch and wait outside, knowing that he will not keep your fabled beauty confined here forever.* I did, however, stay near the cubicle for a while on the off chance that I might catch him there. While I waited, I breathed slowly, wary of the frenzy that had led to the shameful episode of the cow, the only creature I had ever destroyed other than on explicit orders of my masters. And I knew, too, that only luck had saved me from other indiscriminate killing. He did not come of course. Still, as I wound my way out of the maze I allowed myself a moment of self-congratulation. I had thought of burying a small explosive in the straw mat, the instrument of a fiery *liebestod* — a double destruction authorized by a dispatch from my masters which explicitly added her to the official roll of those to be executed. But the explosive seemed to me not perfectly predictable, and in view of my wild shadow-shooting and my regrettable bovicide, I wanted to redeem myself with a twin immolation of absolute precision.

. . . and daily I circled, memorizing every fold in that motley integument, counting the knots of every crude portiere in every entry. Meanwhile the dust-bearded sun of August burned in the southern sky, and still my pair of pity-pricked hearts twined within and did not seek the light. Round and round I walked until one day the sky wheeled vertiginously and made a looping scrawl of thin cloud. The sunrays curled like disturbed smoke. Heat stroke. In the hospital the swart doctor, officious, American-trained, pronounced the falling sickness. I laughed. A chart traced the return of feelings: thigh, knee, calf, foot. *I am the anti-Socrates, doctor.* He did not laugh. Avoid death and resurrection in the early fall of the subcontinent. Ether, sweat, and the ripeness of the moribund thickened the air like the flies that now swarmed, now contentedly rode the slow blades of the ceiling fan. I must be still yet a while longer, they said. I smiled. *I must arise now and be about my masters' business. . . .*

They were gone from the camp, as I had suspected. Even they could not sustain their saintly ministry entirely in that stifling gloom. They craved a freshet of air in other quarters of the city, stippled as autumn advanced by the flickering and feckless joys of the children of the world. But I knew that their dutiful compassion would soon drive them back into the labyrinth. Therefore quickly I cast wide the net of my intuitions. . . .

It was the sight of a cake that plucked my eye and sent me diving down the last hours of that long hunt. The cake, honeygold, lay in a small pan on a brazier in a crowded street. Hot oil bubbled richly around it, while its ancient vendor called out in an incantatory voice addressed more to the sky than to the throng of potential buyers. I contracted for it. I received it upon a wide leaf whose green was deepened immediately by the seepage of oil. Yes, they had eaten a cake here. I shared with my sweethearts its sweetness. . . .

. . . a little stone arch, a diminutive Indian elephant caparisoned with beads and topped by a precarious rider's box, an aviary of raucous birds, a cage of monkeys, a balloon man—the perfect site for a lovers' sabbath. And for a while I was content to stroll this amiable world of the maimed. The elephant man had a left eye like a March puddle, a whorled winking of cloudy sky. The balloon man was trundle-legged with a rolling gait that rode his colorful globes skyward and then earthward, like fruits in contention between gods and men. The most memorable of all was the old woman without a spine who crouched over the pavement by the fountain. From her fingers slipped tiny streams of colored sand, which slowly formed, like the spillings of a broken hourglass, time's concentric design. As I watched her, I began to wonder if my masters would some day turn their attention to the deformed. No, they never would, I concluded, because their practice of precise adjustment had nothing to do with immodest eugenical schemes. In fact, it was a mark of their great wisdom that the old woman should live out her cribbed days in the soft leisure of time's advance, whereas the disturbers of balance must die.

I searched systematically until I found them under the banyan tree by the swan lake. But it was nothing so neat as a mensur scar that the image in the placid water revealed. It was a deep-rooted cicatrix joining mouth and eye, emblem of morbid empathy. She leaned upon his shoulder so that the black of her hair seemed to touch the scar like the soothing shadow of a velvet drug. Then a swan disturbed the image, slowly sailing through the banyan roots. We shared its stately passage. We raised our eyes and acknowledged each other. I called to them. *I am almost sorry to see it end, my friends.* They did not rise to flee. They did not answer, but I knew that fear had not frozen them, and I thought we should exchange farewells. *You have been the very best of all my career.* Still they did not speak. Their silence piqued me. *Did you think it could end otherwise? You the androgynous pit and I the fallen fruit of autumn?* They continued to lean against each other as though they made an inviolable image of unity. That angered me.

Did you think that you would prevail? You the two-headed fate and I
the talismanless captain you ate? They did not move, did not speak. *I*
have other instructive metaphors for the obstinate —webs, magnets,
maelstroms. What will you? They clung together, serenely speechless.
And so I thought, let them die there, unenlightened. I aimed carefully
and fired twice. . . .

[Canonization]

So I have killed the sterile and the sowers. I have killed the too
kind. I lean against the earth's precession and she turns more evenly
down new invagrant ways. Yes. Our network of agents has greatly
expanded. Our speed and efficiency are vastly improved. Who would
have expected this fine bustle of activity to sweeten my advancing
age and cap my career? I had often been lonely and cynical. But now
my taxonomies of quarry, with only minor revision, are official. My
reports are canonical. And even these more personal notes can be
released, I am told, quite soon, when opposition to the program of
my masters has become negligible.

Void. Senda del Monte Carmelo espíritu de perfección. nada • nada •
nada • nada • nada • nada • y aun en el monte nada

　　The path of Mount Carmel the perfect spirit nothing nothing
nothing nothing nothing nothing and even on the Mount nothing
　　　　　　　　　　　　—From the sketch of Mount Carmel
　　　　　　　　　　　　by St. John of the Cross

Compared to the purity of St. John's abnegation even Eliot, even
the *Gita* are a little noisy:

　　　　　　Descend lower, descend only
　　　　　　Into the world of perpetual solitude,
　　　　　　World not world, but that which is not world . . .
　　　　　　　　　　　　—"Burnt Norton"

In the dark night of all beings awakes to Light the tranquil man.
But what is day to other beings is night for the sage who sees.
　　　　　　　　　　　　—*Bhagavad-Gita* 2

Ascent or descent, these are equal metaphors and do not occupy
the hero of the void, the eremite—the true eremite, of course, living
in the maw of night, not the romantic version who keeps a mossy

stump and shrives the agonized voyager. What occupies the true eremite is the perpetual paradox that for our good he must raise a paean to nothingness, sing the *via negativa*, but without words, with only melodious silence.

White Monkey Man

Once I thought that these trees which you have just passed beneath would be my final friends—my lollop-leafed old dowager pricking up to the gossip of the rain, my deft mason with fronds that trowel in the breeze bright mortar of the sinking sun, and dozens of others—hunky matrons whelmed with gorgeous parasites, agonists enfolded in vinous serpents, thin-boled saints sweet with bird song. Until very recently, in fact, their limbs could still tempt me toward a brotherly embrace.

But to begin more plainly. I was an American. I came on a large ship through that tormented canal where guns glisten and planes roar incessantly. I found in the city far east of here a handsome esplanade with thatch shops and smiling black shopkeepers. I bought wooden heads with brass earrings and distended lips. I bought zebra shields, spears, hairy amulets, and God knows what all. Thus laden, I stepped into the exclusive S——— Club, where ceiling fans turned slowly without disturbing the images in glistening teak, where billiard balls labored exorbitantly across the felt and their clatter rose like the subaqueous echoes of jostled bones. I sat at the bar. I spread like a rank polyp, my souvenirs, my new khaki twills, my hapless speech, my wealth, my miseducation, my swagger. The membership of that arrested life could not bear it. There were words, challenges, a scuffle. I remember that at the end there rose from the pile of souvenirs at my feet in the foregarden sheets of the *London Times* into the evening breeze, swaying and plunging like storm-tossed gulls. I lost everything. I could not return to the ship. I walked toward the center of Africa.

My blessed intermediary between that club and this chapel was a goatherd. I walked almost to his face in the sundazzle of noon before he saw me, and yet his eyes were keen. Let me explain. This black man had never learned discrimination. The sky was a blue goat with a golden roving eye. The mountain was a dark goat with a white horn. Before him spread the hairy flanks of the great green goat. The staling of the sky goat forever puzzled him—its clarity, its deliciousness, which he supped from his palms with the greatest curiosity.

And there was, of course, his own herd from which he took milk and meat and skins. It was for him a single being. He knew nothing of number, though some mornings he would arise delighted to discover its body slightly larger, its voice enriched by a new bleat. There was for him, therefore, only goat and self.

What was I then, that day at noon, lunging across the great green goat with blistered eyes and swollen tongue? What he must have seen first were the festoons of rags, paler than the vines and mosses of the forest. I fell on my knees before him. He raced about his hut like a mad man. I did not move. He dashed at me and retreated. I did not move. He made a small hole in my thigh with his stave. He tasted the blood gingerly. He kneaded my head and limbs. He inspected my genitals. He became calm. I was him, or part of him, or a shadow more palpable and persistent than all others. He put milk and meat in my mouth. He put skins on my body. With a stone blade he whittled me a stave.

For a long while I thought I would make with the goatherd the last motion of my days. Rejected by the clubmen, denuded by the whispering forests during my westward trek, self-abased at the feet of a black, I a white man from the world's greatest nation learned to ape a mute and thus earned the boon of wordless harmony. Or so I thought in my ignorant posturing, little noting that I had fashioned the very idea of this profound peace from words. And yet all things around me seemed to concede. Every morning came still, every noon sun-drenched, every afternoon full of breeze and bent grass and the patter of rain. Every night the stench of the black man's hut flared my nostrils and enfolded me, a mother ranker and riper than the deepest dream. Imagine a boat at anchor on a sea of a world that has just ceased to turn—the time of the last flutter of breeze, the last undulance of shadow upon the water, the last creaking and wearing, the threshold of the ultimate silence.

Then one night we were sitting by our fire turning on whittled skewers tender gobbets of little goat. The smoke rose up through the low dome of firelight to sweeten the moonless sky. And I drifted off. My gourd of milk sat beside me untouched. My skewer, forgotten, dipped into the fire and the fat flared. I tipped it up, and blew the flame away. But my goatherd began to watch me. Remember, I was only his shadow—on the slopes less agile, at a nanny's udder less dexterous, but always docile and faithful in my limitations. This fatal night, though, my goatherd began to watch me closely. He chewed, and watched me. I chewed, and watched him, made the same rolling mastication, stripped the charred meat from the skewer with the same acute hooking of the fingers—faithful mirror. But it was too late to repair the broken image. When he finished eating, he came to me. He twisted his finger in my ear, and then in his own, in my nostrils, and in his own, traced the curving blade of my teeth almost with fear, and then his own. Downward he proceeded with the greatest deliberation even to our toes, mine blunt, his almost prehensile and furnished with nails as sharp as scimitars. My heart sank. His eyes widened and brightened horribly. "Mmum?" he said. "Mmum, mmum, mmum." I was other. I was named. And the fatal word fever was upon him. I put my hand firmly over his mouth, but he nipped my palm with his teeth. He laughed and in his laughter found another word. "Hrar, hrar, hrar." And I saw all the horror to come—rolling glottis, darting tongue, fricative teeth, heaving chest. I coiled, repulsed, and when he touched me again, I sprang at him and struck him down. I heaped words upon him while he lay frozen in fear and fascination. "This is hair," I said, tore a handful from his head, and threw it in his face. "Ear!" I pulled his lobe until he yowled. "Eye, nose, mouth, throat, chest, belly." I poked and buffeted him mercilessly, but he did not move. I wept and roared. "At least no abstractions, my friend! Words of the flesh only. Hip and thigh, butt and penis. And for that, myriads. Rod, roger, dodger, pricker, pecker, peter!" I stripped the skins from his body and pounded and kneaded the words into his flesh. "Now," I shouted in his face, "I name you Amon. You are worded, sentenced, doomed." He groveled before me by the fire, babbling. I kicked him and strode off. When he pursued me gabbling piteously I turned and flung him down and ran off into the night.

A long diet of berries and tubers will produce blood lust in a man. The eye quickens to every animal movement, the body leans, the fingers flex, the mouth remembers the savor of flesh. So, after months crossing the great grasslands and skirting the shore of a wide lake, I entered this second forest with ravening entrails and the same day burst upon this clearing at the hush of dusk. At my approach the monkeys deserted the chapel in a rush, streaming from the windows, whispering and chittering. They seemed scarcely to touch the ground in the clearing before swinging up into the trees. The sound of them slid quickly into the murmurs of the evening breeze. Were they watching me? I opened the door. I walked straight up the aisle, stepped over the rail, and stopped before the altar. There was the key still in the door of the tabernacle amid fragments of a golden painting, irradiations, no doubt, from a glowing chalice. What did I expect as I turned the key? A paten of fleshly wafers, a flagon of blood? I'll tell you what I found. The skeleton of an infant monkey crouched there, skull toward the door, waiting for the father who never came with remission from that airless dark. Then it collapsed. The little bones tumbled down into a heap and the skull rolled onto the altar, onto the shreds of a fair linen that might have been the cerements of a desert king. A puff of acrid dust flew up. I grew faint. The clatter of dry bones against my hunger was too much for me. I fell to the floor.

The first thing I noticed when I awoke was that my bowels were quiet, and have been ever since, though the air here is filled with a species of little wrenlike birds. I could snare any number of them. I arose that time in the gray of dawn. A sly scampering at the windows marked the departure of the monkey spies. And then how many days it was before we reached accord. How many hours I sat motionless to prove my harmlessness, how often walked about the clearing with arms outstretched to show my brotherliness, how often buried my head and wept in destitution.

One morning a banana struck my shoulder, a bruised and blackened one, but I pretended that it was my day's only sustenance. I howled with joy, I crammed the fruit into my mouth wildly until the pulp sluiced from my lips. This antic behavior was mistaken. I soon learned the essential quietness of my monkeys—their eyes like cat's eyes, easily closed to the illusions of the world. I would find them swaying somnolently on a limb, one arm grasping a branch above with precarious carelessness. Or I would find them grooming each other abstractly, the search for fleas and lice done, but the fingers still moving through the hair caressingly. While I was among them I often fell asleep under the gentle tingle of my groomer's nails. In fact, for a time I was certain that I would pass away entirely into the quiet shade of Old World monkeydom. But it turned out that my initiator and mentor was also the agent of my rejection.

I mean the great old grandfather almost four feet tall, grizzled and bearded, who after all my piteous and antic overtures came at last into the chapel and delicately touched my lips. I thought: the world that passes through such softly padded fingers must be suave beyond the subtlest eroticism. The old one stood beside me and with an arm longer than mine waved gently. Hundreds then swept in over the window sills swiftly and silently. But I will tell you how far my heart was from understanding. I expected some kind of preternatural mimicry—that one would mount the pulpit, another stand with arms extended beneath the cross, another dispense bananas, others crouch in the pews fingering the decaying prayer books, and so on. Nothing of the sort. Mothers suckled their babies on the altar rail. The young played above in the exposed ceiling joists. The elders sat meditatively in the aisle or glided slowly across the tops of the pews. I stayed beside my Nestor, whose slowly reeving eyes taught mine to see the meaning. The chapel was a tree again, the severed members, pierced by nails, made whole again by the healing glissandos of our brothers and sisters. Thus passed a whirring time at the end of which so surely tree became the chapel and so surely monkey I that when the old one led me out amid the gay-solemn procession of our hundreds across the clearing and to their favorite emyatta—marvelous old blossomer with a quarter of the western sky in his arms—the trunk fit my feet more naturally than had the hewn altar steps.

In a forking of limbs I wove my bower of jungle reeds. All went well. From my half-closed eyes every color fled except the lingering yellow of the bananas, the verdance of certain tart leaves I chewed, and the copper flesh of the giant beetles my monkeys cracked for me. The wind and the rain kept decent silence beyond my canopy of leaves. The sky withdrew—day and night an eyeblink, and the year with its piddling wheel of heavenly bodies seasonless. All around crouched my brothers and sisters like dark angelic sentinels, my old one always at the foot of my bower. And so a second time I thought in my ignorance that the motion of my days had ceased. Had I not found at last the peace that passeth all understanding?

Well, pride propelled me from the monkey world. One night a pretty sleek-coated monkey girl slid down the moonless dark of our emyatta and into my bower—gently, not a trace of yahooish lust. What brought her to me? Certainly not the temptation of a pale, tailless, and almost hairless body, nor the prospect of being caressed by unpadded fingers. She was not heated. Perhaps I had groaned in my sleep or made other signs of deprivation, and my old mentor had sent her to me. If so, it certainly would not have been for sex—I see that now—but only for comfort, for animal warmth. Yet when I awoke in her embrace, the first thing I noticed was that he was gone from his accustomed place at the foot of my bower. And for a time I did not easily forgive him that, because if he had been there, I would not have acted as I did. I would have lifted her gently and set her on a limb outside my bower. Or at most I would have untwined her arms, given her a mild spank, and sent her scampering away. But in his absence I panicked. All my peace seemed undermined by the presence of this little animal, because none had entered my bower before. So, you see, I had unconsciously held aloof from them. And in that fatal moment my secret denial of my sisters and brothers was revealed and judged. Starting from sleep, I heaved the monkey girl off me and flung her down a limbless space, against the hairy trunk of the tree, where she scrambled screaming until at last she caught hold and saved herself from death by falling. "Get out!" I shouted. The words rent the air like an angry thunderbolt. A moment of profound silence followed, then a great chittering and rustling went up around me. The monkeys fled, never to return. The last to go was my old one. Perhaps he had been near me all the while, watching. His soft eyes saddened as he hoisted himself up mournfully and disappeared into the night.

Of course I called after them. "Come back! Come back!" and when the last sound of their passage through distant leaves died away I wept bitterly, wept myself to sleep. But when I awoke in the great empty emyatta, I resolved—careful, however, not to exonerate myself falsely—that human and animal companionship were not for me. Inevitably they involved distracting entanglements. So, as I said, I became a lover of trees. At first I personified them, peopling the forest around the clearing with many characters comic and heroic. But these personages obviously were merely the pitiable imaginings of a creature unable to conceal from himself his own loneliness. In time, I grew quieter and wiser. Instead of insisting on making them members of my kind, I sued for admission to theirs. I learned to enter like light the veins of the leaf, learned to course down the limbs and into the thick bole. And I even began to make out dimly the web of dark roots curling around the gently beating heart, before my descent was interrupted.

One day I was squatting under my emyatta in deep meditation, all my weight centered low on my haunches. Slowly my toes began to curl down. The hair of my testicles seemed not to hang but to burst up through the dust like tiny seedlings. I experienced the fullest prefiguration of treeness I was ever to have: my arms reached up, my feet and fundament rooted.

Then a disturbance struck my ear. I opened my eyes reluctantly and looked up. There stood a frizzle-headed tribesman of the Willumpa, who live on the grassy plains to the east. He was making a placatory murmur, eyes wide. I rose up, half-conscious, aware only that I must escape that stupified gaze, leaped by old custom and practice onto the trunk of the emyatta and scaled it in a trice, leaving my admirer below aghast.

Discovered, I stayed hidden in my bower, descended stealthily in the dark to gather bananas, leaves, and beetles. But late every afternoon the little birds grew quiet, so I knew the Willumpa were lurking about. And soon they ventured out into the clearing, built fires, beat drums, chanted my name. "Ballala! Ballala!"—white monkey man. So I was a god—a god withdrawn, until one night my worshipers performed the ceremony of my incarnation. Then I appeared. Who can bear to watch one's self mumbled like fly-blown flesh in the mouth of ancient religion? Here is how it was.

My devotees built a fire much larger than ever before, and chanted my name incessantly. Several of the younger men extended the call to mimicry, wearing ragged pieces of white skins and furs, mounting on their heads animal ears. They danced about, chittered monkeylike, and practiced a desultory wantonness, grooming and titillating each other. The tempo of the drums increased. The cries of *Ballala, Ballala* rose to a kind of plaintive keening. The dancing mimics lifted their arms to the skies. Then suddenly a herald came running into their midst, sweating and breathing hoarsely. "Baba ai ja! Baba ai ja!" He comes! And after a period of stillness and silence, he did come, Ballala, into the circle of firelight, god of snowy splendor. Behind a painted pallor his face passed through disdain, lust, blasphemous egomania. This, I thought, is the primal albino whose uncontrolled passions drive dark men to devotion. His arms, lengthened by subtle appurtenances, were in the awesomeness of their arc the very emblem of insatiable craving. He also had an immense tail, and control of it. Not by any arrangement of strapping and bondage, but by thrusting it deep into his bowels. His legs were hairy springs, his feet prehensile.

Drummers, chanters, mimics, all made low obeisance, but he paid them little mind. Instead, with a grand sweep of his arm, he motioned out of the shadow of the chapel door a figure that joined him in the firelight, his divine mate, as unlovely a creature as I have ever seen—black from the waist up, white from the waist down, human above, monkey below. It was also hermaphroditic. The genitalia were male, but rough breasts as of papier mâché had been strapped above. The two divinities stood together for a time, monkey man and paramour. The chanters and drummers bowed. The mimics joined hands and formed around them a swaying circle. The monkey man towered above all, casting a long shadow which crossed the clearing and reached even to the chapel wall.

Then began an erotic pursuit. The motley spouse broke from the circle of mimics and minced coyly about the fire while Ballala made hot and horned pursuit—all to the great delight of the Willumpa tribesmen, who chanted moonily while the drummers beat a rhythm that rose and fell like the palpitations of a love-stricken heart. That was enough for me. Perhaps until that moment I had harbored unconsciously some blasphemous dream of true apotheosis, after which I would create a cult, teach the Willumpa the meaning of shade and silence—who knows? But their worship sickened me. I grasped a hairy vine my monkeys used to swing on, pushed off from the trunk, and began a long arcing descent through the deep shadow of the emyatta. Ballala never saw me, though a tribesman, spying me as I first swept with tremendous velocity into the firelight, shouted a warning. I struck the false god with my heels in the very center of his belly. The force of the blow sent him wheeling through the fire, scattering burning wood and live coals in every direction. The hairy extensions of his arms flew out into the dark. His silvery pelt fell among the flames, hissed, and made a black smoke. His tail, torn loose, lay near him not far from the fire. Blood spurted from his anus. I knew from the pain in my feet that I had burst his belly like an overripe melon. So much for self-appointed gods.

On my return swing, down over the dark chapel roof, I hoped to catch Ballala's hermaphroditic partner in blasphemy. But he and all the rest had fled in terror, streaming out through the woods toward the grassy plain and leaving the slain god behind—at least for the moment. "Go!" I shouted after them. "Go! Go! Go! Don't come back!"

I climbed the rope back to my bower. In the welcome silence that returned in the wake of the fleeing Willumpa I slept, though during the night my legs stiffened from heel to hip. Early the next morning several fearful tribesmen crept into the clearing and, making to the trees fearful obeisance, took away Ballala's corpse. Bury him, I thought, but he will not come up. And I also thought that it was time for me to leave, take my stiff legs into the jungle, give up clearing, chapel, trees, all—old scraps of a personal history that veiled my final goal. But something held me back, something in the air, something in the tenuousness of the songs of the little birds. It told me that I was not quite finished there.

I resumed my daily routines until one morning I awoke to find my previous day's feces removed from the bushy covert behind the chapel where I always carefully concealed it. The next day, hiding again in my bower, I caught a glimpse of light fabric in the trees. And the morning after that I awoke to something novel indeed—in the center of the clearing a woman in khaki shirt and pants just finishing, with the help of a Willumpa tribesman, a small pyramid of stones. She topped it with a white flag on a stick, and then the two of them left the clearing. From my high and steeply angled vantage I could observe little more than that she had yellow hair and seemed of medium stature. A lady anthropologist, I thought, from the blond north, come to unravel the dark mystery of Ballala.

At midnight I descended to the clearing, opened the stone pyramid, and plucked out the message I was sure was there. By the light of the half-moon I read: "I am desiring to speak with you. If you come by the kirk and make a loud sound, I will come also." Then I knew what I wanted. I sharpened a stick with my teeth and punctured one of the purple berries that hang in profusion from the stooping old tree behind the chapel. On the back of the lady's note I scratched: "Bring pen, paper, ink." The liquid dried slowly, fragrant and velveteen, as though the words had always been lurking in the fruit. So I would leave a parable in writing, of one who learned to go beyond flesh and words. I hid my message in the pyramid and watched from my bower. Before dawn she took it away and brought the things I had asked for. A second note was attached. "I am desiring much to speak with you." But I did not think about that. I began to write the story which you now have in your hand. By the next night I was done, and slept deeply. About midnight, however, I awoke to the sound of the lady singing softly in the chapel. "Come to me, thou. Come to me." I rolled my papers up, tied them with a vine, and descended. The half-moon was low in the sky and the chapel therefore dark, but still I could see the faint glow of her whiteness. She was sitting on the altar step. "You have come," she said. Then all was silent again, the little birds asleep in their nesting places.

I walked forward several paces, and she stood. I stopped, because she was naked. "I am naked," she said, "to be like you. We can speak one and one, like."

I stepped forward and offered her the scroll. The smell of her, at once musky and soapy, flared my nostrils. Desire and repulsion contended in my bowels.

"In this night I cannot read. Tell me what you write."

But I did not speak. I had resolved that the last word of my manuscript was the last word of my life. Remember the words in the club and my answers to the pitiable gabble of the goatherd. And twice since, remember, I had fallen among the trammels of speech, cursing the innocent monkey girl and the foolish Willumpa. The lady would have to understand that there must be only silence between us — except for the manuscript, which I offered again, but still she did not take it. "Tell me slow, you write your life of the dark of Africa?" I did not answer. "It is not too difficult thing for me if you cannot speak with me now. I tell you what we do, because you know more than what is on the pages." She paused. She leaned forward and searched my face. Her breath filled my nostrils, stirring in me again the pull between attraction and repulsion, and piquing me to look more closely. She was perhaps 40. She had slightly protruding ears that held her light hair neatly back from her wide temples and forehead. Her eyes were pale even in that darkness, probably extraordinarily light blue or gray. Her nose was narrow and wingless, her mouth small, her chin sharp—a German or a Scandinavian as I had suspected. But if she was an anthropologist, then she was one with a special, perhaps mystic, dedication—to come naked to a rendezvous with the violent white monkey man. But actually at that moment I was not thinking of that. I was thinking of the whole world of persons I had left behind, the millions of shining faces, each one individualized so that I could pick this one out from a sea of others. I stepped back from her.

She said, "You can not escape man. We are your species, not the monkeys."

I wanted to tell her that, despite the error of the foolish Willumpa, I had not been a monkey for some time. More recently I had been a tree, but in the future I would not be that either. I would be a thing that rose and fell imperceptibly on the slow breathing breast of the jungle. All of which I had tried to write down, so I offered her the scroll again, but she did not even lift her hand. Instead, she said, "This is what we have to do. We have to return . . ." I must have started, because she smiled and said, "We will not put iron on you like the old wild man of Borneo. You will speak and teach to ones that can understand these things." A vision of that came with sudden vividness to my mind's eye like a painting. I was sitting in some kind of amphitheater or academic hall crowded with listeners. And I alone was not in modern dress, but wore a white robe. And even that folded about me with a temporary look, because I was naked man, naked to our primordial essence, the guru of devolution, the one who had made the long descent down the trunk of human, animal, and vegetative, who after this brief appearance among the civilized would return to the jungle, to the ineffable threshold of total silence, but not without leaving behind in the world words and disciples capable of quieting at least the loudest clamor of man's inconsolable heart.

"You have been at the center of this," she said. "It is great temptation to remain. But you have to come to teach." She held her hands out. "If you desire I will remain with you." She stepped down from the altar. I commanded my body to turn and run. I actually felt the torque in my spine, but I scarcely moved. The fingers of my hand slipped open and the scroll fell to the floor.

What happened then surprised me, surprises me still, because in strict logic, in strict justice, my fall and my ecstasy ought to have unraveled all my months in the forests and propelled me, laughing cynically at myself, back to civilization. But that is not what happened. As my consciousness began slowly to return I perceived that I was netted. It was only her limbs and her hair of course, but seemed to me a white net and her face above me the fleering face of the trapper. I roared and struck out like a wild beast, broke free, slashed her face with my beetle-bronzed nails, and heaved her violently against the altar rail. She cried out and then lay still whimpering, "Do not. Do not thou."

As full consciousness returned to me, I knew she must be thinking that she had encountered some impossible paradox: a feral man who writes. So, although she had tempted me toward the destruction of all I had recently learned, I pitied her. And I thought that violence should not be her last knowledge of me. But at my approach she shuddered and cowered so piteously that I left her as she was. I picked up my scroll, and then the thought came to me that the finished manuscript would take the place of the rejected caress. Perhaps it will, perhaps not.

So I returned once more to my bower.

It is light now as I write these last words. A while ago several Willumpa, led cautiously by a grizzled elder wearing an elaborate necklace of authority, searched the clearing and entered the chapel. Some minutes later they led the lady forth gently. She was clothed again and able to walk, though somewhat unsteadily, so I had not broken her body. I was glad of that. But at the end of the trail to the grassland she stopped and lifted her face to the trees. I have never seen a look so baleful, so loveless.

And so, white man, my story ends. I leave it for you here in the chapel, in the tabernacle. Do not come with theories, nets, and guns, searching, secretly ravening for my body, just as I on my first day here craved the wafers of flesh and the flagon of blood. You will not find me in my bower. Your expeditions will not find me in the jungle, I will have passed the far edge of your sight.

Consider, white man, that in your world, which I came from, there is a great multitude of objects, and also mirrors—polished teak and words—to multiply this multitude. Fortunately all my objects were stricken from my hands and lay on the garden floor that fateful day. Then, as you have read, there was a world of goat, which is an insufficient reduction. Next there was a beauteous monkey world of fruited light and shadow, but it was corrupted by human fears and desires — my own and those of the cult of Ballala — and is therefore an insufficient reduction. There was also the populous world of personable trees, but that was mere animism, and is therefore an insufficient reduction. Nor is even the descent to the heart root of the vegetative world sufficient reduction. I leave today on my last leg west. Imagine what I foresee — a jungle so wide that every place is its center, so dayless and dreamless that its moments all congeal into a perpetual present. I know that when I first enter it, I will be in agony, even I, surely among the best prepared of all men, for in that silence of silences my heart will thunder, and my bowels will rumble and quake. But I will lie down. I will replicate that silence.

So all you will ever have of me are these papers. Perhaps some few of you — old men on the verge of sleep, young men in the sweetness of their first dreams — will read them and understand. If so, I welcome you in these twilight hours, journeying in your imagination from the hiving city, passing under the high horn of the goatherd's mountain, walking the grassland and the lake shore, crossing the chapel clearing under the suspirous trees, and entering at last the slowly welling silence of the jungle.

The Black Prince

What she initially described was not the black prince or the girl whose body was like a harp. Rather it was the tapping at her door, which came first in late January and then again several nights later and finally every night — until she believed it would never cease. Elfin was not quite the word, she said. The tapping was firm but uncanny as though something long disembodied had received the unexpected boon of flesh. And now, come from the forest, it mounted the world's thresholds disporting again and again its new solidity, tapping, tapping, tapping.

Why from the forest, I asked. Because all such beings come from the forest, she said.

Have you awakened some night holding in your cupped hand a thrilling so intense that you could not bear to touch anything? And have you, after an initial foolish fright, smiled and said to yourself, *my hand has gone to sleep*? Consider. When the hand slept, the feelings awoke. Imagine your whole body become that hand. Imagine that sudden intensification of feeling. Imagine that longing for a magical suspension in a currentless air until the unbearable prickling ceases. That is how she described the effect on her of the tapping. That is how she knew the girl's body was like a harp.

It was the practice of the girl and the black prince, from the very first, to disrobe as soon as she let them in. To save on the cost of oil she always had an open fire in the fireplace. Remember, this was long before she became famous. She lived alone in a cabin. Fortunately, scraps of alder lay in abundance in the woods behind her cabin. But if the couple was grateful for the fire they did not show it, did not chaff their hands in its warmth or turn their naked backsides to its radiance — though the firs on the hill wailed in the north wind. But in fact they seemed incapable of any domestic activity — never touched each other, never took into their mouths any of the food she offered.

The girl's body was exquisitely frail. Though the little breasts were full and peaked with rich amber, they seemed threatened by the rib cage which in the slant firelight had all the shadowed sharpness of a medieval woodcut. The body was also like a harp, she said, strung along the high neck, the spine, and the long limbs. She could see it vibrate, catching the firelight in elongated ogives so bright that it hurt to look at them. Even brighter were the nodes in the golden falcon eyes where all the vibrant lines gathered into a cruel and piercing apparition of stillness.

She knew that the thrilling of her own body caused by the tapping was as nothing compared to this. The poor girl had been plucked by the black prince and the flesh was shaken from the bone. Once she had even cried out for the girl to come to her by the fire and they would cling together against him. But the falcon eyes, tunneled by death and desire, had only flashed disdainfully.

That was much later. In the beginning they simply came and sat naked upon her couch. They wanted to be painted. They had heard of her skill and they knew that as subjects they were irresistible. He certainly was irresistible. Never had she seen such a body. Ebony, but not carved, rather miraculously trained: a living tree of flesh. Consequently, you did not think of his sharp and precise teeth or of his bright white eyes, which always caught a faint tint of gold from the girl's hair, as old ebur set and burnished by a skilled craftsman. Instead, they seemed exposures of the white heart-wood of his being. He was not negroid, she insisted. The palms of his hands and the soles of his feet were not pink but iodine. His nose was sharp and his lips thin. His hair, though black of course, was soft. He was an Asian black, she believed.

She sat in a chair near the fire while they sat naked on the couch just at the edge of the fire's glow. The two of them shared wicked cigarettes which released an overbearing pungency as of hot perfumed bodies. But more remarkable than the odor of the smoke was its appearance. It did not dissipate into a haze. It wreathed and rose intact to the ceiling. There it caught the firelight in a delicately veined translucency, like old serpentine. When the January wind struck the panes, the smoke shuddered and writhed, but always resettled into distinct coils.

"You will please to paint us," he said with a hovering intonation she could not interpret—a delicate request, a sinister threat, a soft-quilled arrow dipped in purple.

She sighed, "I've been working in woods." She brought them a piece she had just finished. It is now mine, a beautiful collage of wood scraps she gathered behind the cabin. It is much more than the merely ingenious comment of texture upon texture which usually limits even the best of such works. She chose primarily punky timber full of charming little caves and grots. One is suddenly an insect spelunker with a lantern eye walking a prehistoric world of wood—eternity in the grain of wood, to alter the poet.

He laid his fingertips delicately upon the work and smiled, she said, a smile that seemed an emblem of the tactile ecstasy of the blind. And because the tapping and their presence had begun to wear her, she offered it. "Please take it. I can't paint you. But I want you to have this if you like it."

He smiled. "This is very fine indeed. This is very dead." He handed it back to her. In the meantime the girl had touched it and withdrawn her fingers quickly as from flesh grown cold. And yes, I must assent, there is a morbidity to those punky woods where death blossoms into an endless tunneling so that someday the receding timber will be merely a frail filigree around an ever-expanding darkness. Perhaps the golden girl saw in it the image of the darkness that was rapidly filling her body.

So, she put the work away and fed the fire and returned stubbornly to her chair. The black prince lit a cigarette and watched the smoke coil under the ceiling. "You will please to paint us."

II

Why did she not immediately apply the obvious remedy? In our county we had then a silver-haired sheriff who rode a fine white horse in every parade, followed by a posse of smart irregulars whose pearl-handled pistols glinted in the sun. She could easily have exposed her nude interlopers to the sheriff and freed herself of them forever. But for a time she did not think of it, so subtly had their hypnotic bodies and serpent smokes limited her world to their premises.

At length, in early February, she consented to paint them, but only—and she was almost ashamed of this jejune proviso—on condition that they not ask to look at the canvas until she was done. The painting has long since been consumed by flames, but as she described it, it must have been a marvelously effective thing. She worked on a large canvas using thick oils and a coarse brush, sometimes even a palette knife. In her painting the black prince became a bloated squidlike creature. An inky ambiance poured from his mouth like poisonous smoke—an evil incubus engulfing a poor golden girl and sucking the life from her. In fact, she painted on the canvas an obscene proboscis, and the girl was almost entirely sucked up except for the frail fortress of her golden eyes in which light still toiled like two unborn serpents.

When she was done she turned the easel and defiantly displayed her indictment. The girl's eyes widened ambiguously. My friend nodded insistently. "Yes. Yes. This is the truth." The black prince looked at her with baleful eyes, but said nothing. She believed that she could save the girl if she could jar her from the deadly rhythm of his touch, a touch she knew by its effects, a body tuned like a harp, flesh shaken from the bone. But the black prince arose almost casually, took up the painting, broke the frame, crushed it, and fed it to the fire. The oil hissed and flamed hotly. He turned and walked back to the couch with a wonderfully provocative insouciance which seemed certainly an old signal between them. The girl smiled, her body tuned again, singing again in ogives of beautiful broken flesh.

"I tell you a parable. In the forests of my home roams the black panther, who eats only animal flesh. But in the dreams of foolish men, many times they are eaten. Their mouths open with screams and their ribs run with blood hotter than fire—so that their wives must cool them and wipe the sweat. The panther's mouth is a gate only the brave may pass."

"You're no panther," she said.

He nodded. "That is precisely what the tale tells." He smiled. "Please to paint us, just as we are."

"No."

"So simple a thing, to paint, just as we are. Why will you give over to mindless evils?"

"I will not paint you for any price, under any threat, not even to save my life, not even for my life."

Then the girl spoke, who she thought was dumb. Or was that thin voice only the sleep-choked cry of the panther's dream quarry? "Will you for my life?"

III

The girl's plea pierced her to the quick. Her will weakened. And then she did begin to think of going to the authorities. Several times, in the dark hours after they had left, she actually reached a resolve to report to the sheriff's office. But the dawning always defeated her. The windows, which had resembled during the night the prince's black skin, were suddenly filled with gray light revealing the motley of her beloved alders. The mist would rise, the forest would fill up with light, she would bundle up and go out with a sack in search of wood scraps for her collages. Sometimes, if the sun came through, she would eat lunch in the woods and sometimes even doze afterwards on a mossy feeder timber. The evil images of the night would fade away like a wraith of dreams. But when she was fixing her supper and the woods began to darken outside the kitchen window, then she wished she had gone to the sheriff crying out to the silver-haired old man, "Father, father." But it was time to build a fire. It was time to wait for the tapping which would suffuse her body with exquisite tingling pain.

That was about the time she called from her chair by the fire to the girl, "Come to me. I'll feed you, and he can't hurt us." She said her breasts actually felt swollen, that pain of overabundance which she never felt again; for, as you know, she remained a lifelong celibate. But the girl only said in that voice from which all color was bled, "Will you not, for my life?" And the falcon eyes roiled in that fatal ingathered fire.

In the meantime the black prince grew restless. He curled and uncurled on the couch. He smoked more fiercely. He retracted his lips and opened his teeth. The smoke streamed from his red tongue, which was like fire or like blood.

She laughed at him. "Stage royalty," she said, mocking him behind a thin veneer of courage. "Barbados dukes. Tell us your lineage, you who have prowled all the western world to catch one poor little girl. Are you hungry, prince? Hungry for one good gobbet of fat flesh?" Again she was conscious of her heavy breasts, of her ample flesh, though the long sleepless nights had begun to thin her. She said that her hairiness gave her comfort, especially the shadow of hair between her breasts. But he assured her that he would not deplore sinking his teeth into her flesh.

"I am a prince," he said, without much urgency, "in the last place where royalty is still real. Among you it is unreal. And as for the flesh I take," he said smiling, "I find it among you offering itself to me in great variety and abundancy. And because, as you say, I am barbarian, my tongue is not delicate. My appetites are well satisfied."

She made some sound of mockery.

"You place yourself too low," he said with a flourish of gallantry. "Flesh we find abundantly. We come to you for art. Please to paint us, just as we are."

"Will you not do it, for my life?"

She could not hold out. She could not unravel the web which their presences wove in the room. Her eyes could not reave the smoke that rose from their mouths to make vinous intricacies under the ceiling. But she could see that the girl shrank a little each night. The cups of darkness in her flesh dilated. Soon the falcon fire of the eyes would dim and the golden girl would tumble to ash. She could not bear that prospect. Perhaps the painting would bring some kind of release. And yet she knew that when she had submitted her will to theirs, even once, she might never recover it. Still, was that more perilous than sitting sleeplessly night after night, breathing intoxicating smoke, feeling one's own flesh dwindle, feeling the deftness that has only just begun to quicken one's fingers wither like a vine?

"All right then," she cried out. "Will you leave me forever when I finish this painting?"

"Yes," they both said.

"You, black man, will you swear it on your royalty?"

"Yes."

"Then swear it."

"I swear it on my blood. It will spill and I will die if these words are not true."

"Say the words."

"We will leave you when the painting is finished."

"You, black man, do you swear to let her live when the painting is done?"

"I swear it on my blood."

IV

So she selected a canvas and fixed it on the easel. She mixed some dark oils carefully and dipped a wide brush into them. But before she could touch the canvas, the black prince said, "It must not be done in this fashion."

She stepped back from the canvas, startled. "What do you mean?"

"You wish for painting the most possible empathy of subject."

She recovered herself, crisped her eyes. "I am the artist, not you."

"Nevertheless, permit a humble savage of the forest to point out that tactile imago of our bodies cannot be the same as yours clothed. How can you feel us?"

"I feel you well enough."

He shook his head heavily, as with strained patience. "It cannot be. You must disrobe."

"I must not."

"Then I fear our contract cannot remain consecrated."

"My nakedness was never part of the contract, you black fraud."

He did not answer immediately, but the girl nodded slowly, painfully. Yet, her eyes belied pain. They burned, she said, with a curious avidity that she would have examined had she not been so angry with the black, who now puffed smoke from his lips disdainfully and said, "Such puritanism."

At length she flung her clothes off with great heat and set to work, but I am certain that her anger could not entirely have overborne her exquisite sense of propriety, for I have often seen the russet suffuse her throat and face upon the slightest misappraisal of feelings. I can see her now beginning to paint that canvas, her flesh burnished more by emotion than by firelight.

But a strange thing happened, she said. The general shapes of the two bodies flowed onto the canvas effortlessly. And even when those were done, she continued to work at an almost feverish pace on details. It was as though the textures and colors of the strange pair poured out to her uninterruptedly, perhaps through the medium of that densely gliding smoke. The brush in her fingers seemed not to be working upon a flat surface at all, rather she could feel it following the contours of the bodies, even exploring surfaces she could not see. She grew excited, because she had the feeling that she was producing a canvas of coiling light and that this had never been done before, though now it can be done with laser photography. Presently she was no longer aware of her nakedness and could not, therefore, ascribe her magical facility to the black prince's potent demand. At any rate, thus passed several nights of almost ecstatic achievement. The sittings, in fact, grew longer and longer though sheer physical exhaustion stiffened her hand and cold invaded the room where the fire nightly died untended. Toward morning she would finally stop. They would leave and she would fall into a shuddering sleep that lasted all day. Then she would arise and prowl about the cabin until the tapping came. During this period, she said, the woods were denied her. An irreversible instinct forbade her to leave the cabin and even forced her to lower the blinds against her beloved alders.

Then without warning the marvelous facility lapsed. She found herself one night worrying at the slope of the girl's shoulder. The black prince was perfect, she would not touch him. But the girl suddenly seemed all wrong, and this surprised her because she thought she had caught the essence of that figure: the slightness of the limbs through which the bones tunneled with a ghastly translucency, the terrible concavity of the torso, and the paradoxical scintillance of the falcon eyes. Yet now something very akin to a physical force tugged at her hand, urging her to enlarge the figure of the girl. She resisted. Enlarging it would destroy the harplike delicacy of the body, the plucked strings opening into thin ogives of sounding light. It would also ruin the leaning balance of the canvas, the shadow of the black prince closing over the girl like the hand of avarice over a saffron gem and taking from it a pale iodine light. So she resisted, but the force against her hand grew more insistent. She set down her brush and held her head.

"Do not resist the pulsations of the subjects," said the black prince.

"But it will change the whole canvas," she replied, as though his words had not come out of a yawning silence, as though he and she had been engaged for a great while in an aesthetical polemic.

"Even so, you must let the subjects insinuate your hand."

So, reluctant but desirous of regaining her first passionate creativity, she began to expand the figure of the girl. And for a time the first energies did return. The limbs and torso widened handsomely. The translucency became waxy and fruity. What had been a spectral phosphorescence became sunny, apple-skinned. The dark shadow of the black prince cupped a golden apple. She rounded all, brightening the light here and there. She was almost finished. But when she looked up at her subjects to judge of a last touch or two, suddenly to her profound dismay the tugging began again, more fiercely than before. Her fingers trembled and curled like the legs of a stricken insect. The brush dropped from her hand and made a splotch of amber on the floor. She held her head.

"Do not resist the pulsations of the subjects," said the black prince.

"You are doing so beautifully." Whose voice was that, so mellifluous and throaty? You have never heard, she said, words so succulent, so softly islanded in a honey-sweet sea.

V

The following day she awoke earlier than usual. She bathed her face. She was haggard. She must finish the painting and be rid of them. The black prince's oath would hold, she had to believe that. So, when they came that night, she worked feverishly on what she was determined would be the second and last enlargement of the girl's figure. The hand that had once held the fragile gem was now only a pliant fabric, a fold of black velvet into which the girl's body pressed heavily. The painting verged on a still life. The central object was a golden fruit that gathered all light to itself. Even the brightness of the prince's teeth and eyes was only a wayward glancing from the surface of that luminous apple.

She set her brush down with a trembling and furtive joy. "I am finished," she began to say, but as she looked up, the words died in her throat. There sat the girl in a luxury of golden flesh that terrified her. She was confronted with the body of a composite carnivore. A fold of flesh across the belly was a wide mouth. The golden hair was serpentine. The eyes darted. The pubes writhed like tentacles. She fell back into her chair by the cold fireplace. Where had all this rank growth of flesh and hair come from? From the painting, of course. From the brush. From her own hand and body. She looked at herself. She was wasted. Her thighs were concave. Her knees were great knobs of bone like skulls. Flesh, of course, might be replaced. Even in her poor cabin there was enough simple food for that. But mere eating was no solution. What would stop the tugging that was already beginning to worry at her hand? In a moment it would be fierce again, irresistible. The third enlargement would begin.

"You must not resist the pulsations of the subjects," said the black prince, but how sadly flat his voice, which in the beginning had been so crisp, so full of savage hauteur.

"You are doing beautifully," said the other voice, full and rotund.

For a while longer she resisted the force at her hand. She thought for the moment not of herself but of the black prince. On what fatal occasion had his royal person become enthralled, panderer for a monstrous succubus, he who must once have roamed an old jungle of the blood amid the screams of panthers? No doubt the talons of desire had seized his groin. Strands of viscid smoke coiled about his heart and lungs. Now there was no hope for him, she judged, because when the golden girl had done with her, had cast the dry husk of her body away, then would begin again the process of self-consuming. Presently they would have to emerge again from the forest, tapping, tapping, tapping. The black prince would have to disport again his royal body, wear again his voice and mein of compelling authority. The girl would speak again in her piteous reedy voice and display again her fleshless translucent bones. Always the consuming, the consuming.

"How many have you sucked up?" she asked.

"I have told you," said the black prince, "we find in this land many willingly offering themselves up into the panther mouth."

She felt a moment of ease, almost of blessedness, because she was not chained to their wheel. While they made their perpetual rounds she would return to dust. She responded to the force on her hand. She picked up the brush and slowly, carefully began to paint her own death.

VI

She awoke the next afternoon in the grip of a feverish desire to live. Though her body was wasted, skin dull and gray, she wanted to save it. She wanted to perform some decisive act that would save her and perhaps even free the black prince. Suppose she contracted the golden figure stroke by stroke into lightless death. She rushed into the living room and seized her brush, but her hand was as powerless to paint as if she were manacled. She could not even remove the cover from the canvas. She ran to the kitchen, took up a knife, and charged at the canvas, only to be repelled by an invisible cordon as piercing as a coronet of steel spikes. She fell down in pain, bleeding from the palm of her hand. But she soon leaped up. She made of kerosene-soaked papers a fierce flambeau. She hurled it at the painting. It roared in the air, but when it reached the canvas it opened suddenly like a spent rose and fluttered down with a dying flicker. From its ashes ascended a thin screed of oily smoke, a pale imitation of the black prince's rich gusts.

Still, she was not done. She flung open all the blinds. There were her beloved alders budding against a blue sky. It was spring. Who could die in spring? She ran from the cabin down the corridor of alders leading out to the road. She ran down the road toward the highway, where she would catch a ride to the sheriff's office. But no one stopped. Drivers of approaching cars averted their faces. By the highway was a pool of rainwater. Above it a blackbird rode a reed in the wind, screaming like a broken seer. She frightened him away and stooped over the water, but she did not drink. Who could drink from a pool in which lived a death's-head? The eyes were bowls of darkness. Lips and gums receded from teeth ghoulishly huge. Hair tumbled in the wind, dry and rootless. Nothing here to stay death's final touch. No car would stop for that face, no sheriff give credence to what passed those lips. She stumbled back to the cabin. The lengthening shadows of the alders fell across the windows like the wide weave of a cerement.

But inside of her a fierce little life still burned, just as the falcon eyes of the girl had husbanded light until food was found. The comparison gave her a start. Was it possible that the girl would reach satiety and release the black prince to her? Was it possible that she herself and the black prince would go together tapping, tapping, tapping? Was this the way, passing from mouth to mouth, hunger made its black rounds eternally? No. She would never submit to that. Death or a decisive act. It was one or the other. She prowled around the hooded canvas, fierce in her impotence, like a caged panther. The taste of the blood she had sucked from her wounded hand lingered on her tongue. She paced to and fro.

She was still pacing when the tapping came and still pacing after they had arranged themselves on the couch, the great apple of flesh and the other who followed, nothing now but a pitiful faceless foil, a smoky shadow, which nevertheless spoke: "I am surprised to find you restless."

"It's spring."

"Yes, but one so close to high artistic achievement expects a pleasing repose."

"You mean the painting. The painting is finished."

The black prince shook his head slowly. "Your excellent eyes have failed you this once, though perhaps only a minor detail. Do examine the canvas."

"I have examined the canvas, you have not. I say it is finished." During this exchange, the longest in many days, she recognized the extreme thinness of her voice.

The black prince shook his head. "We know that you are not quite completed because of what I mentioned before, body imago. We feel yet some emanations to be settled with you." The golden girl nodded, but more than the simple sign of affirmation it was like the rhythmic bowing of a heavily fruited tree.

"No. I say the painting is finished. Our contract did not stipulate who is to judge completion, but common practice gives that judgment to the artist. Correct?"

"Of course. Our concern now is only perfection of the picture." He shot from his mouth a great plume of smoke, which rising revealed his red tongue roaming its cage of teeth. The image gripped her heart. She longed to put her lips to his, to touch his tongue with hers, to disperse the evil smoke of guile and prepare the palate for meat and the dark eloquence of love. But he was speaking again. "Let us settle the matter thus. You must, of course, disrobe as before. Remove cover from canvas. Compare subject and art. If no impulse for improvement comes, then we accept the judgment of completeness."

The golden girl nodded again heavily. "I long to see it. It will be beautifully done."

So she bared her pitifully emaciated body. Yet, she said, she felt a paradoxical strength. There was no flesh left for the girl to consume—only ligaments stringing the bones, a network of veins, and a cage of ravening entrails. Even after she flung the cover from the painting and the will of the succubus clamped her wrist like wolves' teeth, she still had hope. She believed that satiety weakened her enemy while hunger strengthened her. She clenched her fist and strained against the force that drove her hand to brush and canvas, but the force was relentless. The wound in the palm of her hand reopened. The blood followed the lines of her palm and marked the joints of her fingers. She could not resist. The brush plunged into a pod of golden paint, bursting the thin film which had formed during the day. She could not prevent her hand from painting the last enlargement of the golden girl, which would bring death. But as the color went on, a curious thing happened. The blood ran down and streaked the gold with crimson. She grew dizzy. She looked up at the golden girl, but her eyes would not focus. Gold and black whirled about in vertiginous vapors, within which in bright contrast moved a blood-red tongue.

She said that in that moment she was perfectly balanced between hunger and death. She was neither dead nor alive. She perceived herself as only a great gaping mouth. It would either make one final exhalation of gray breath or it would seize something in its teeth. She fell, she said, or rather she plunged down in space. She burst through something. There was a tumbling of bones which suddenly began to chitter plaintively. She was where death is, or she was in hunger's deepest throes. All went black.

VII

When several years ago I was appointed executor of her estate, as I knew I would be, I did not expect to make any startling discoveries in the studio. All the important canvases were by then carefully catalogued, except of course the two recording the adventure with the black prince and the golden girl. Those were long ago destroyed. The first, you recall, was burned by the prince. The second was torn to shreds. She said it was as though a great cat had slashed it, but it was she. She awoke to find her hands and mouth smeared with black

and gold. So the studio was as I expected, virtually empty. She was
celibate in all things—flesh, color, and memorabilia. Nothing here
for the biographer, only the fading redolence of oils, or at most the
apparition of a détente between the sun in the skylight and the
shadows holding a corner behind smoky flourishes of dust.

Still, I had an uncanny premonition that I would uncover some
small remembrance of those strange sittings in the cabin long ago,
something more domestic than the great canvases in which the
bones of men, the boles of trees, the very lineaments of space itself
strain heroically out of darkness toward light. But all I found was a
botched canvas. Or is it a botched canvas? It is a single untextured
gobbet of red. Because the unpainted part of the canvas is yellowed
and dry, it obviously is an old enterprise, deliberately saved. It might
be a posthumous joke, to tangle critics, but that would be unlike her.
I am free to speculate. The prince's roaming tongue? Her own
blood-hunger? The welling cut that caused the swoon that broke the
spell and saved her life? Perhaps it is what subsumes all of these and
more—the crimson which never quite appears on her canvas, the
haunting absence which warns us that she is more than chiaroscuro,
that it is not only or even principally the clash of light and dark, but
the blood that beats at their common heart. No. Such poeticizing
will not do. The finest net of images comes back empty. We can only
say, never except this once did she paint the color of every hunger,
and this was all her strength.

The Prisoner

"Guess where I was tonight, Sonny."

"I can't guess, Mother." She makes me call her Mother.

"I was in the flies." I don't ask why. The story will be told. "The rope on number five panel for Miss Ethel's *Sunday in the Park* was busted. 'Don't fret, Mr. Smith,' says I. 'The light man can cover the drop same as the pit covers the voice.' " Raucous cackling. " 'Get up there, you old simian,' he says, 'and drop this new rope through the pulley. There's an extra two bucks in it for you.' 'Five,' says I. And here's what we got, Sonny." She skins a brown paper bag down from the neck of a bottle and swigs. So tonight we will have a scene. I have been Quasimodo, Mr. Hyde, Dorian Gray, The Jew of Malta, Nero, de Sade, and others. She hands me the bottle and watches carefully to see that I don't wipe her spit off.

" 'Five,' I says, 'and ten if you look up.' " More mad cackling. "So I was in the flies. Sit here beside me, Sonny." She wiggles, the human fly sharpening one leg against the other. Tonight I will be, perhaps, Beelzebub. "So I dropped the rope and then I looked down from my catwalk which is about as wide as your one buttock, Sonny."

"In the Orient, Mother, the art of the foot massage—ball, heel, toe—is highly developed."

"Be quiet, Sonny. Let me tell you. From the flies you see the whole show—all the doings in the wings, the lit stage, and the black pit. The whole thing, Sonny."

"God is in the flies, Mother."

"What a head you got, Sonny." She pulls my hair passionately and shines me her ramshackle teeth.

"And the devil is in the pit. Remember when I was Mephistopheles, Mother, lover of darkness, with a wicked tongue?"

"You was a grand Mephistopheles, Sonny, even if you was just learning—with your spiked head and tail. By god, you horned me." She narrows her eyes. "And now you're horny for the world, ain't you, Sonny?"

I nod. "When will you let me go, Mother? I'll play you a farewell Jack the Ripper that will scald your bowels."

"Drink this and hush." She broods. "Old roles, Sonny. That's what's the matter with the stage ladies—forever courted in the same words, bumped on the same couches. They dry up. But I ain't dry, Sonny. Lean over here and suck this bottle with me."

"What will our finale be, Mother?"

"The time you burn me dry, Sonny." Her eyes flare. It's true that though the dugs droop and the veins strain against the skin, she's still wet. She swigs and settles down. "You've done all the roles I ever saw on my everlasting free passes to the playhouse. Now you pick a part, Sonny. You're a reader." She swigs. "I used to crave to be an actress, Sonny. I would sneak into the dressing rooms when I was cleaning and put on them panties with the smell of stars in 'em. Then I would dance in front of the mirror until I was worked up into such a prickly puckering that I couldn't keep my hands off myself. Pah!" She spits.

"And then you started to find your Sonnys."

"That's right. You're the third Sonny. Three Draculas, three Moriartys, three Rippers, three of everything."

"And I'm the last, Mother."

She looks at me balefully. "I should of never went up into the flies, Sonny, for the price of a bottle. You know why?" I shake my head. "Because from up there I saw that all the seats in the house were empty save one where sat a man from old times, waiting. 'Don't sit out there,' I hollered. 'Bring my roses to the stage door, Johnny.' But he only sits and waits, God damn his eyes. Be that as it may, Sonny, I ain't through with you yet." She grabs my ear and wags my head.

So I must burn her dry for my freedom. I wrack my head: Faust? Close. Raskolnikov? Closer. Then I remember her words of the night before—the Johnny of old times. But who is he exactly, and what does he look like? There isn't much to go on here—closets of decaying clothes, drawers full of rusting hairpins and blackened pennies. No packets of letters, no scrapbook, no diary with flowers pressed between the pages. I find only one article of potential use, a cracked photograph. Mother is standing at a bar with a man. She is probably forty, he is a little older—a puffy and debauched Irishman, yet an imp peaks out of that florid face, an imp who cannot understand how he has allowed himself to be imprisoned in that decaying body. Behind them are rows of bottles and a smoky mirror which gazes at the backs of their heads with a jaundiced eye. This will have to do. Using the theatrical arts which Mother has taught me, I will re-create the man's dress with meticulous care. I will age my face with dark ointments. I will practice a brogue and the flourishes of barroom gallantry. Yes, and I will have my knife, my gay blade. From Mephistopheles to Johnny O'Rourke without a hitch. Love leads the way. And it would be shameful not to give a good performance here on the threshold of freedom after my long season of patience.

"Bring home a bottle tonight, Mother. I've discovered a new role and I've been practicing."

"Well!" She shines her teeth for me. Too many gaps, Mother. One is for license, several make pinking shears for ears and foreskin, but too many make headstones and vaults. "Who will you be, Sonny?"

"O'Rourke."

Her pupils contract as though I had probed them with a sharp light. She says, "Where's the romance and the horrors in a coarse name like that?"

"It's a pseudonym, Mother, like Mr. Hyde."

"Who's the real chap then?"

"That's what the play reveals."

She squints suspiciously. "You be sure the real chap is intriguing, Sonny. I won't have your street drama, your garbage-can realism in here. And O'Rourke is an unlikely name."

"Have I ever let you down, Mother, since you taught me? You remember Genghis Kahn with the whip and the spurs?"

"By God, I do. And I was your mare that sucked up all of Europe in stride. I do trust you, Sonny." She extends her old lips to mine. "But remember, Sonny, not a step beyond this threshold until you burn me down." She rolls the r in burn. "You ever think about Tarzan the ape man?" Mad cackling.

"Who knows who O'Rourke is behind his shabby ascot and his spurious brogue? Not even the Shadow knows. But you know, Mother, that I was never one to take a bit part."

She pauses at the door. "That's true, Sonny."

"You bring home the liquor, Mother." Yes, and encounter my gay blade.

At two A.M. she comes in tired and drops on the couch with the brown bag in her lap. I watch from behind the portiere. The knife is in my pocket. "Sonny!" She uncaps the bottle and takes a swig. "Sonny! Where are you? Come here and have a drink with Mother."

I step through the portiere with a clatter, and stop. She looks up. Her eyes widen. "O'Rourke!"

"Hello, Meg."

Her face hardens. She inverts her hand on the neck of the bottle. "Stay where you are, O'Rourke, or I'll brain you." She smiles fiercely. "I'll drown you in booze, since you ain't quite done it to yourself yet."

"Give me a little sup for old times' sake, Meg."

"I ain't got a long enough spoon, O'Rourke." Mad cackling. I take a step, but she makes as if to lift the bottle. "Stay where you are." Her eyes crisp suddenly. "Where's the boy?"

"What a comely lad, Meg. My congratulations."

"Where is he?"

"Gone. Went out as I came in."

"That's a lie. He would never."

I place hand on heart. "God be my witness, Meg."

"We had an agreement he wouldn't leave until a certain event took place."

"Then he'll be back, Meg. There was trustworthiness etched in that face to the very quick."

She relaxes for a moment, then stiffens again. "If you've harmed a hair of his head, O'Rourke . . ." She menaces me with the bottle.

"Would I harm my own son?"

She shakes her head ambiguously.

"He is mine, ain't he, Meg. He's got my parts—squat and strong, black hair, and a face between a cherub and an ogre." A touch of high unearthly whickering creeps into my laugh. "You tell me he's mine, Meg."

"He ain't."

"Whose then? He looks the right age to be conceived in the blessed year of our consortment, Meg."

She tips the bottle. "He was conceived by the Holy Ghost." Mad cackling.

"Amen. And so are we all, Meg. But there's the earthly father, too. And that's me, Johnny O'Rourke. And now, for old time's sake, Meg, let me sit myself down beside you and take a little sup."

"No. What did he say when he left?"

"The boy? He said I was to keep you company until he returned in costume. By which he meant what, Meg?"

She doesn't answer, but sucks the bottle and grins like a flatulent baby at nipple. I step over quickly and sit in the far corner of the couch. The knife is in my pocket. Her face is momentarily crossed while she thinks of driving me off. But she decides not to. I say, "Hallo, Father, don't the communicants over here on the epistle side get any?"

"Sheep and goats. You're a goat, O'Rourke." Raucous cackling.

"I'm parched as hell, Monsignor, I confess. But it's not your business to preempt the divine judgment."

She passes the bottle. "Lightly."

I take a good swallow and run my tongue over my lips. "By God, Meg, you was ever the perfect timer, holding back the sweets until the juices flow like the Nile."

"Give it back." I do. She skins down the paper and squints at the level of the liquid. "Where have you been, Johnny, all these years?"

"Wet my tongue once more, Meg, and I'll tell you." She passes the bottle. I drink and pass it back. "Africa. Desert Africa. See how brown I am?"

She looks at me skeptically. "Your face is brown, but the hands ain't."

"I had to wear thick gloves to repel the sting of scorpions."

She makes a pishing laugh. "Why couldn't you tell me you was in gay Paree or at the Court of Saint James? You think I want sand and scorpions for my whiskey?"

"You want the truth, don't you, Meg? I was in the grand freedom army of General Av Boylan. And it wasn't all sand and scorpions. I saw the Nile, the pyramids, the Sphinx, Cheops. Which would you prefer?" I slip closer on the couch. The knife is in my pocket.

"I don't prefer none of them. I prefer silence until the boy's back."

"Let me tell you about the Sphinx."

"Go on then."

"The Sphinx is part lion, part eagle, and part maid."

"Pah!"

"What's the matter, Meg?"

"Everything declines with years. You can't even fable anymore, Johnny. Eagle and maid! For the love of God. You used to tell ripping tales." Her face brightens. "Remember the incubus stories, Johnny? The little nocturnal devil who tweaks tits, mats hair, makes a snail track of gism on the buttocks, and then plunges in like a knife?" She looks at me. "No, you don't remember. Then tell me about the bloody Sphinx. Here, here's whiskey. Warm your tongue."

"She's an eater of man's flesh, the Sphinx."

She cackles. "That's better, Johnny."

"But she's had no man's flesh for many years."

"Why not, for Christ's sake? In that land of niggers and Moors flesh must be as cheap as dirt."

"Cheaper, Meg. Dirt is dear in a world of sand."

"Then why don't they feed her, God damn their souls?"

"Here's the way it is, Meg. She was a riddler. Whatever man failed to answer the riddle, she ate. She was a deep riddler and ate well. Until one day a hero unraveled the riddle, told the answer. She went hungry. Of course by now many misremember the answer, but it's too late to help her. Starvation has eaten away tongue, teeth, and throat. She can only moan in the desert wind. 'Who? Who? Who?' "

"God damn their souls." She drinks. "There never was real heroes, Johnny. You know what heroes are?" I shake my head. I touch my knife. "Painted buffos with big voices and little balls. I've seen 'em on stage by the dozens and not enough stiffening in the lot to entertain the likes of me between supper and first moonshine. Pah! The devil in the pit and God in the flies laugh at such." Suddenly she looks at me softly. "So why tell nonsense, Johnny? You was never one to go for such mincers, stage heroes." She reaches over and touches my hand. I touch my knife. "And you and me, Johnny, we know exactly what happened to your old bitch Sphinx. No hero plumbed her riddle. None could. Did you ever plumb mine, Johnny?" Lascivious cackling.

"I confess I never, Meg."

"And you was no mere hero, Johnny. You was at least a man, albeit Irish. I give you that."

"Thank you, Meg."

"So it was just time, Johnny, wasn't it? The everlasting wind blowing sand in the face. Time and nothing more than time, or we would riddle you whimpering men and whittle you down to the last nubbin of pleasure and then spit you out like the mere husk of a scorpion on the sand. Come here, Johnny. Before the boy comes back. He's a gentle one with clear eyes. Give not scandal to the little children, is it, Johnny?"

I take out my knife and touch the button. The blade springs forth. But she only smiles. "Who can you be, mister, with that piddling little pisser?"

"Just me, O'Rourke, your Irish liberator, come to open the jails of all this evil mothering land, Meg, and set the lads free upon the sod."

"Haw and haw again, O'Rourke. Your memory is dimmer than night if you think you can open my carcass with that little pricker."

"Look at it, Meg." I catch the light of the lamp on the blade and shine it in her eye. I run it around and around the iris as though I were coring an apple. "Ain't it a bit like the kleig lights of the grand stage, Meg?"

Her eye quivers. "'Tis."

"And the thousand-handed thing in the dark beyond the pit — do you hear it clapping and swelling its throat? That's all for you, Meg. Tonight you are the star."

"Yes," she says almost rapt, but then she frowns. "There ain't a suitable article in my closet, nothing but the moth-eaten remnants of the very gowns you brought me all those years ago, O'Rourke."

"Leave that to me, Meg. I am the costumer for this performance." I make with my gay blade a long cut through her stinking rags from neck to knee so that when she stands forth she leaves them all on the sofa like the abandoned carapace of a lobster, which retains the shape of the departed beast. Then she herself peels off her stockings and flings them upon the air. "Very like the festoons of Loie Fuller's floating dragon, Meg. But what about the bindings upon the thigh? Will you dance to a house of this quality with that yellowing parchment upon your flesh, and it right below where your sweet old thing shines like a plum in a summer shower?"

"Alas it must stay, O'Rourke, or the blue blood of passion will leap forth and bespatter the boards. And besides, you was to costume me regally so it won't matter."

"I will, Meg. Meanwhile the house notes with a ripple of pleasure the integrity of your belly. Unlike those of certain aging Irish ladies, eviscerated by priestly permission, it does not have a great Nile of a cicatrix coursing from the navel to the pubes."

"Douse the palaver, O'Rourke, and costume me as you promised."

I hand her the bottle. "Take a long swallow of this, Meg, for this costuming will cost you a bit of pain, but when I am done, you will dance and sing like any queen."

She drinks. "Get on with it."

"From top to bottom, then, Queen Meg—and all in rubies." I stand. With my gay blade I scratch a wide arc above her brow. "There is the exquisite crown, Meg, the royal blood that commands fealty from the delta south to the tropic of the headwater."

She cocks her head and muses. "Mayhap that's how Sonny's decking himself out this very minute—like a stalking nigger in a panther skin."

I make two piercing thrusts into the lobes. "Earrings like little kisses of fire, Meg." I make a tiny incision all about the neck. "The delicate choker Caesar locked upon you, Meg, saying 'Never henceforth shall thou go utterly naked, but the waterhorses themselves will make slaverous obeisance to this royal band.' The rest is quick work. A bracelet with a red cat's-eye here upon the arm sinister to ward off the fiend. Here a navel jewel, crimson omphalos. And finally a thread-thin anklet. Was there ever such a queen?"

She stands regally erect, bedizened with the dewdrops of her own blood. But presently she narrows her eyes at me. "Wasn't there an asp? A sweet nibbling asp in the bosom?"

"If you say so, your highness." I take a little gobbet from between the old dugs and the blood wells up as pretty as any virgin's.

"Now then I will dance."

"Do." For the heat of it will make the blood course quicker so that when I make the final nick the play will sooner end. So she makes a little step, her horny old toenails ticking the floor. She twirls herself this way and that, a dance of veils in which the wisps of concealment come not off, but on. I mean that the oozing of my crimson etching, splayed by the force of my lady's turning and subject to the liquefaction of her sweet sudor—for queens must not sweat—makes a wide-woven scarfing.

"Now I will sing."

"Do." So she makes a high broken crooning. The words are only intermittently distinct. Something about a sweet baby boy. The foundling? The third and fatal foundling she folded into the crevices of her desire? Perhaps not.

"Look here, Mother. O'Rourke's manifesto of freedom for all lads, which I have written out in bold red letters and scrolled up like a royal proclamation."

She looks at me sharply. The blood beaded on her brow masks her frown. She snatches the document from my hand, rolls the paper down, and reads: " 'Ladies of the stage and of the night, beware of O'Rourke the black Irishman, bon vivant, gay blade, gallant, Thespian. Beware. For fresh from his mother's milk he is late come into the world to ravel up your breath in ecstasy unbearable. Beware, ladies, beware.' It ain't bad, Sonny."

"Thank you, Mother. In just a moment I will pin it to your neck, just at the base where the sweet little calyx of soft flesh already brims with beckoning crimson."

"And that ain't bad either, Sonny. In fact, the whole night was well done." She hands me back the paper, which I impale on my gay blade. I rush forward.

"Just let me hold you, Sonny. Be quiet now. It was ever this way. Why, I remember one toward the last got just as riled as you, hanged himself by his own petard, and his eyes bulged out until he was all but blind." She cackles and croons.

> *High up in a treetop*
> *All by himself*
> *Sweet baby boy swings . . .*

The Child

The child is sleeping now, but may awaken at any moment.   Yes, and speak. It always utters something.   No, gender has never been a question. *It* has been used from the very moment of its discovery.   Yes, on Christmas Eve, when as you know, there is still among certain elements a dilation of the feelings, a titillation of miraculous expectation, though there never is a miracle. All of this, of course, helps account for the initial stir.   Many other factors: the obscure origins, which seemed to tally with the Christmas myth; its strange utterances; the incredible bell-like resonance of its voice, which you will soon hear; the state's melodramatic precautions and sequestration of the child; the hundreds of would-be interpreters; the spate of spurious books purporting to record the sayings; the bafflement of the doctors; the disdain of the scientific community and of the state church, which always gives a thing a special plausibility among some; and, of course, the assassin's attempt, which supported the belief, the hope that there was indeed a vast secret to be revealed.   Surprised? No, the surprise was that there weren't more attempts on its life, especially during the time when it was reciting a catalogue of curious hybrid names: *Theodakis Mann, Jal Angutan, Eugene Mogabgab, Gunnar Acevedo, Clifford Tuminello, Jean Paul Zanzovich, Huan Grenier*, and so on.   Yes, curiously one was actually real, an utterly innocent and insignificant man. So of course the cryptographers and etymologists went to work digging up roots, recombining and so forth, but they got nowhere.   Abraham Perlman was the name of the would-be assassin, who, as you remember, was himself assassinated just outside the Hall of Justice by a gunman who was never apprehended.   Of course. From the very first even female visitors were inspected minutely by matrons added to the guard staff explicitly for that purpose. Background checks of applicants were meticulous. So how Perlman reached the door here with his stiletto remains a mystery.   By April I noticed a certain slackness. In May, as you know, came the resolution declaring the child at once incurable and inscrutable. There was a great rush of visitors for two or three weeks, assiduous copiers of every word. Several articles and books came out claiming to have unlocked the fabled language, hardly ingenious any of them in their linguistic concoctions, cabalistic trash beneath even the notice of the censor's office—although I remember reading one with considerable interest, a tiny epic which purported to be a redaction of an especially voluminous flow from the child during a three-day period in July. It began, *"He bore his load slowly under the dust-bearded sun, his eyes downcast as though to decipher the hieratic scarifications in the road under his feet."* That seemed to me a fine beginning. But presently there were predictable ogrish persecutors, deserts, ravenous beasts, and so forth. I never finished it.   And now? As you see, a rare visitor like yourself every other day or so, who needs only register at the door. If Perlman had only been a little more patient he would have had his way. For what could I, an old man, interpose between the assassin and his object? Sometimes I have thought the state itself might send an agent to dispatch the child, relieve itself of its charge, but the expense, I suppose, is too small to bother about—the pitiable salary which I draw.   No, please. Keep your money. To tell the truth, I have put away a good bit of that which I earned during our busy days here, though I never sold information. There were those inevitably who thought that I, being here hour after hour and hearing all the child said, would have discovered the pattern.   No. Actually I remember very little. There is something curiously not mnemonic about its utterances. They are beautiful, liquid, but very much things of the hour. Here is one of my own perhaps not entirely errant translations of something it sang in April: *"When all the aral rods he fashed the green world about then arched music upon the quivered limbs its wild neck and bill."* I shall be sorry to lose such sweet bafflement.   Before next Christmas surely. Though there is no doctor even in irregular attendance now, the one that was released by the state in late May kept elaborate charts on the changes in the child's condition. He set the end in November. The process is slow but inexorable. Sir, I prefer that you do not come any closer than this. The doctor has asserted that the disease is not communicable, but in my judgment precautions are nevertheless in order.   Yes, always open. And as pellucid a blue as any poet ever dreamed his mistress's.   Unseeing? Who's to say what it sees, whether of this world or another? I will tell you a brief anecdote. In the first days after the state lifted its tight security, all manner of quacks appeared: palmists, physiognomists, phrenologists, what have you. Among these was an ophthalmic investigator. He shined a penlight into the child's eye and bent close, probing those blue depths minutely—or at least so I thought. But as his inspection seemed to be proceeding very slowly and as other visitors were beginning to mutter, I suggested that he conclude his preliminary investigation and return another day for a fuller examination. He said nothing, moved not. And I realized that he was fixated. I summoned the doorman and together we managed to lug him out into the anteroom. He was absolutely frozen in his posture of rapt scrutiny. I had to return to the child immediately of course. Later the doorman reported to me that the eye expert did eventually thaw and depart, but he stumbled off dazedly gabbling to himself incoherently. Which reminds me that among the most numerous of that time were the so-called interpreters of tongues. I often argued with them saying that the child was not speaking glossolalia but rather a language like any other with its own grammar, phonology, et cetera, only vastly more complex and beautiful than ours. But they insisted on searching for the ghostly tongue lurking within the songs. You asked me if I remembered many of the child's utterances and I said no, but I do remember a translation I essayed of a thing it said after about a week of this quackery. It shows that not every thing from the child's mouth is sweetness and light. *"Forfend me the prickings of blind preening minds, pretenders to the tongue of tongues."* So I resolved to request power to select visitors, but quickly the numbers dropped off sharply and there was no need to trouble my superiors. And you sir. I see by the entry in the register that you are from the village of Bursina. The mountains must be lovely this time of year—purple and golden with heather and lichens. And let me guess. This is your first visit to the capital, and after the great halls, the museums, the elaborate rituals of cathedral and parade ground, you thought the child would be a welcome change, a conversational cameo upon your return. You are right, sir. Although the child is at present much out of the public eye, it will surely go down in popular history and legend with the flagpole poet, the human bat, the river-diver, and the like. Interested friends have asked you especially to try to get the true story of the child's discovery and to remember carefully what the child says. Am I not right? Please don't imagine that I am mocking you mountaineers. In fact, the unassuming curiosity of all my mountain visitors has been refreshing.   Also a detailed description? That may not be so convenient or desirable as you and your neighbors imagine. Let us come back to that. In the meantime, while we wait for the child to speak, I can tell you quite briefly the story of its discovery, as you request. First you must put out of mind all embroidered accounts involving angelic visitations, starshafts impaling a sublime hovel, and the like. The truth is that two guardsmen discovered the child—two, of course, because in the Bedan district not even members of the constabulary, perhaps *especially* members of the constabulary, can travel alone with safety. At any rate, on Christmas Eve the two guardsmen found the child propped against a crumbling wall. It was bound in rags, cocoonlike, but had nothing on its head, so that the snow, which was light and feathery, piled on its luxuriant blond curls like a fantastic coiffure. Also the snow covered the ragged gray encasement and gave it the semblance of white ermine. It was almost dark. The yellow light of a window lamp made a gilded swath at the child's feet. And the child was singing. The guardsmen were transfixed by this utterly unexpected vision of beauty.   Yes, not only saw the original report but also talked personally to both guardsmen. In fact, I remember one of them telling me that the child's eyelashes were prettily snowladen like the steep eaves of one of your mountain houses. See how long they are? But to continue. Obviously this was not your ordinary young thief or procurer thrown out on the streets by its superior in crime. The guardsmen were immediately convinced that this was a special case. So, with a shrilling of their whistles they summoned an armed carriage.   Yes, I was just coming to that. There were several inmates of the district standing about from the first, giving the child their rapt attention—old ragged specimens for the most part, according to the guardsmen. Also, from windows publicans, trollops, pimps, and thieves looked out with muted but mounting interest. All this informed the guardsmen that knowledge of the child was current among the habitués of the place. Even so, where it came from, who had kept it and cared for it prior to its appearance on the street—these things were never known, any more than the identities of the perpetrators of the thousand and one crimes of the district. There they protect each other—the one who speaks drives a stiletto into his own heart. Anyway, when the carriage with a detachment of armed guardsmen arrived to pick up the child, several bystanders—toughs who had just come upon the scene— began to raise an angry clamor. These the guards drove off. Meanwhile the original rapt admirers made a piteous wailing of deprivation as the child was lifted up into the carriage. Distinct from both of these groups, the whores and harridans whooped their delight. "Good riddance!" they cried. "Take the freak away!" And then there was the inevitable wayside soothsayer. "Beware the magical chanting of the child," he keened. "Who hears and does not heed is doomed!"   Directly to the state orphanage, where it would have remained without further ado were it not for certain alarming features which the matron of the house described for an officer close to the mayor, who sent examiners, who . . . etc. You can imagine for yourself the train of events which led to the ensconcing of the child here in this outbuilding of the palace.   My directions? You flatter me, sir. You don't imagine that the large staff which was originally assigned to care for the *puer mirabilis* of this age was under the supervision of an aging retainer of the palace library? No, I was assigned merely as a keeper of records. Now, ironically, I am all that is left. And when the child dies, I will be put out to pasture. Perhaps I will take a coach up your way, into the mountains, see at close range what I have seen only distantly from the palace parapets.   The body? If you insist, sir. I take it that you are in possession of certain recent rumors which I would gladly have you help me dispel, though I must warn you that one or two other visitors, much to my surprise, have not been pleased with what they saw. Shall I proceed?   Very well. To begin, the head, as you see, is lovely and virtually perfect.

I know, sir. You have already commented on the eyes. However, let me assure you that there is strong evidence, too complex to enter into here, that the child is not blind.   Yes, the mouth is toothless, I readily admit. But it has not always been so. The teeth have been discarded only within the last weeks. They were not carious, nor were the gums diseased. The teeth were, as I say, gently discarded, as though they never had any place in the child's nature, were an alien, carnivorous accretion. Consider. The lips and tongue are the servants of Calliope and Cupid, but the teeth are entirely violent.

The teeth erogenous? I can scarcely believe that even the most sunken sensualist would claim it, sir. And I know that you do not, coming as you do from the crystal purity of the mountains. In any case, this is not the time nor the place to be cynical about one's canines, if you will allow that waggish pun.   Yes sir, there is one other peculiarity of the head. In recent days the passage from the portals of the ears inward has been closed over by a delicate membrane, a sort of auditory maidenhead if you will. What a marvelous achievement of the child's immense will. For what further need had it of the cacophonies of this evil world when it had already wrung from them the sweetest song ever sung? I will now pull down the covers, sir, and lift the robe a little, but we must not keep the child exposed long, for the season wanes. Tomorrow I will order in drapes and brazier.   Not at all. A night watch by red coals can be a very pleasant thing. While the world sleeps, you nod, sometimes gazing, sometimes dozing, the two blending sweetly in the fire. The great Worm Ouroboros was the father of the Phoenix and the salamander

and thence down through cooling gradients past man to our little
Hibernian hero the horned toad, whose heartbeat marks the hour.

Indeed, sir, your patience is rewarded. First gaze upon the feet,
or what were the feet before these transformations commenced. I
am pleased to see, sir, that you are not taken aback. Other
visitors—well, I have already mentioned that. Notice the small shaft
joining the two here at the locus of the ankles. When we first
unwound from the child those wretched gray rags, this was the only
abnormality, this little axle, as it were, of ossification. And—
perhaps because I am a bookish man—it immediately occurred to
me that the child had been transported from mountain to city,
impaled on the heights by one of your shepherds, sir, like the
Oedipus of old. But then came the further changes. Have you ever
seen flesh of such translucent blue, such sapphirelike beauty? A fair
lady near childbearing will grow luminous and blue-veined, but
nothing like this.   No sir, I would not say finned exactly, for the
fluting is too delicate, though in all candor one other visitor referred
to mermen—a trivial legend in my view.   Indeed. Notice that the
beautiful scalloping continues . . .   No sir, not scales, decidedly
not—anymore than you would call the golden mail on a knight's
breast serpentine. Well then, this scalloping, this lovely interlinking
of blue continues up here to the locus of the knees where, as you see,
it begins to change texture and shade off into a sea-green . . .   No
sir, no one, including the doctors, has ever suggested putrescence.
This is emeraldine. And do you not agree that the deep undulant
striations give it something of the appearance of tresses?   Very
good, sir. I can see that there will be nothing shocking for you in the
next rather more sharp alteration. See how up the indivisible thighs
green goes to gold, gold deepens, almost ambers. And now you can
see why we do not speak of the gender of . . .   Sir, sir! The covers
are replaced, sir. Will you not stay for the child's beautiful evensong?

Well, we are alone again, my child, for another silent evening
together, I suspect, for I think you will never sing again. The sweet
shoaling of your song is now dammed up behind the gums. The
tongue's pool is drying and the tongue itself undoubtedly will follow
the rest of the body into its beautiful glittering mansion. Perhaps the
last wave of crystalization will, in contrast to the slow earlier stages,
sweep upward so rapidly that it will arrest the lips parted upon a
final suspiration, transform into obsidian darkness the last inhala-
tion in the delicately flared nostrils, sapphire the eyes, and mold the
soft curls into immemorial gold. So, I told our mountain visitor a lie,

but it was a white lie, for I myself would have chanted him some words, fetching words, too, I warrant, because even a leathery old tongue, under your constant tutelage, child, can learn to loll sweetly. But I will not try to sing tonight, child. I will soliloquize. I will step out here on the balcony, and my words will come to you, if at all, as nothing more than the far wash of a low tide. It is a beautiful evening for a soliloquy, though there is no hero of old here to speculate for a hushed audience upon the lineaments of his tragic fate. The air is chill and clear. Already the North Star shines over the pure and perpetually white rim of the distant mountain peaks. Below, the westering river lies gold in the sunset. The flaxen hue of the stubble fields deepens to purple. And not far beyond the horizon, child, lies the sea. The lamplighters are making their rounds. The high windows of the palace wink against the darkening sky like scintillant eyes in the fan of the bird of paradise. And from chinks in the stone, where the grass has grown, the crickets begin to chirp. The wind and the rain are slowly returning the palace to soil, but who has planted the grass in the stone, child? Small birds? Or is it the midnight work of the crickets themselves who crawl up from the plains below with seeds tucked under their carapaces? Transformation, evolution, devolution — these were the questions the wise ones speculated on in the days when your nature was a rich treasure trove to be discovered, child. But they have all deserted us now, for they do not love an unyielding mystery. So I alone meditate these matters. I think it likely you were once a beautiful sea creature, child, living in a coral palace in a green grot of the deep sea, with fishes for brothers and old ocean deities for father and mother. And then one day you said: "Pity the poor landlocked whom Mother Earth forever pulls down so that they cannot swim in the air. I will visit them and teach them how to conquer weight with song." And so you crawled up out of the sea and took limbs and sang, but found us deaf. And now you are resuming your old form. Will bright red gills blossom on your throat? Well, I know what you yearn for. Trust me, child. I have still that modicum of authority that will enable me at the right moment to summon a carriage and take you down to the river. The current will carry you home. And after that I shall return here and immolate the last vestiges of your visit: the state seal, the red velvet rope much rubbed by the hands of your admirers, the thick book which records their names, including many of the most famous, and of course your robe and your covers. And then Age will immolate me. Well, do you think it would have been good, child, if we had understood your song? I wonder. It would have transformed us, of course. We would have been drunk. We would have been candles blazing at noon, our heads afire with intolerable poignance. I remember one morning last May standing upon this very balcony and you began to sing, and although I could not understand one word, the whole world was aflame with green fire. The grains deep-rooted in the fields glowed white hot while the river, slipping its slough like a silver serpent, slid through its reedy banks. And the winter mountains, like gap-toothed old men, stood in alarm at the sensuous excesses of spring. But then, O child, my eyes already adazzle, there came yet another sunburst of birdsong. The larks, from the meadow, soared by the palace walls and piped their matins so sweetly that I did not know what music was theirs and what was yours. And I teetered, for I longed to leap out upon the air. So, when you are in that deep grot, child, think no more of us. Do not sorrow because we failed to understand your song, for if we had we would have taken wing, or imagined that we had taken wing, and thus in our dreams plunged to an early and multitudinous death. Sleep, child, while the green changes of the deep sea grow upon you.

The Gamblers

His first wagering was in Plaquemines Parish, where excommunications later rained upon racists like a plague of locusts, but no sanction ever touched the casinos. Just as his father had foretold, the doorman furnished him a sport jacket laden with the odor of cigars, like the coats of his grandfather. So he entered there an avatar of the great bearded one, most famous gambler of the Crescent City. Above the low hum of voices he heard the slap of cards, the metallic titillation of the roulette ball, and the scamper of warm dice over green felt. He twitched his nose in the smoke. He had arrived. But how could he have guessed then that the drink girl in the black net stockings was a mistress of the inner sanctum?

He knew there was a great secret at the heart of it. In his room over the grocery old man Tisdale told him how he had stood under the night lights at Narragansett one July beside a man who held a twin double ticket worth twenty-four thousand dollars, whose fourth horse came second but an inquiry moved it up. And the man went down on his knees, said Mr. Tisdale. And though he was young his eyes mattered and his fingers curled and withered, and when he got home no doubt his wife did not recognize him because he was twenty years grayer, like Rip Van Winkle. Mere money could not cause such a thing. And he, the boy, saw in the old man's own eyes such a brightness that he thought maybe the tote board with the pulsing red "Inquiry" had unmanned him at the same time.

Later, inheriting something of his father's belief in science, he studied combinations and permutations, read the great cryptographer's inquiry into poker and the physicist's report of the man who repaired watches with brain waves. He read about the mathematics professor who had won twenty thousand at roulette in Las Vegas. But the system of hedging was so complicated that when the croupier shrewdly increased the tempo of the betting, the professor said he was seized with something like a brain fever which did not leave him for a year, by which time his wife, whose name was Loma, had gone away in despair.

Nerve, his grandfather had said, whom he had once been allowed to watch at poker. The old man wore a straw hat, a white shirt, black sleeve garters above the elbow, and a black bowtie. From his left forearm hung a cane like a stunted third leg, which he needed when he rose, because he had suffered a stroke. And over his left eye was a thick lens which effected an horrendous Cyclopean beaming. "Yet, gentlemen, I assure you that it can scarcely penetrate this smoky ozone, much less the paper of your holdings." Each hand revealed with a little poetry. "Here in this scribble of low black forest two heart's-blood red knaves. Do they excel, gentlemen?" The old man spread his cards upon the felt with a quick crooking of his middle finger which, along with the subtle obscenity of his words, set the table to laughing.

"The goddess Mnemosyne sits at my feet," said the father, the blackjack man, the bridge man who mentally constructed models of the concealed hands at the beginning of play and revised them as the cards fell. "Remember, son, there is no Fortuna. And Mnemosyne does not favor an impetuous suitor." So his father played modestly, according to his needs, earning at blackjack, gin, and bridge perhaps a thousand a month in the forties and fifteen hundred in the fifties. "But don't you, my son, ever think of being a professional gambler, because it is slow work for the patient and the nerveless, and you are a romantic, son, a thruster and a diver in."

That first time in the Old Post House in Plaquemines Parish he constructed himself an image, Manichaean, which he hoped might lead toward the *sanctum sanctorum*, because even then at the age of sixteen he did not accept nerve or science, sensing that at heart every true gambler is an heretical metaphysician, that father and grandfather tricked their dualistic cosmologies out in jejune metaphors as older girls will sometimes wear spring pinafores. That was, in fact, half of the double image—the black woman who served the sandwiches wore a white pinafore. The other half was the black net stockings which the drink girl wore over the creamy flesh of her legs. But they seemed to him mere servants. How could he have guessed they were themselves part of the mystery?

On the greensward of the felt table his grandfather had made a high stack of red chips rise up out of a scattering of white and blue, like the minaret amid Moorish ruins he would later see in Spain yielding to the wind's patient embrace and the grass's slow advance.

So, in his mind's eye the chips were emblems of epochs, rising and falling, swept away by the blank hand of time. Behind them sat his grandfather, Cyclopean god of Chance, white beard ambered by the eons of smoke rising from the cigar that hung from the corner of his mouth, the cigar virtually motionless, tipped by a long delicately curved white ash like, perhaps, a wand of incense in a temple of the East.

At Jesuit High School, the only Protestant in his class, he had a special relationship with Mr. Donough, the tall scholastic, idol of his classmates, from whose black cassock appeared two beautiful bone-white hands, and a head of hair so red that he might have been splashed with his savior's blood. At the class picnic in May, when Mr. Donough traded black cassock for white gym trunks, all the boys tried to duck him in the lake, drown idol like frenzied devotees of Krishna. But could not. For he stood erect, all heart-wood, would bend but not buckle. When they tried to push his head under water, he snapped up like a sapling, and when at last he was tired of playing with them, he flicked them off like flies. "Away Beelzebubs!" he thundered. Later he asked Mr. Donough, "What is the theological objection to gambling?"

When confronted by the proposal, his father had said, "I'm going to surprise you, son. I'm not going to oppose for one minute your going to school with the Jesuits. In fact, I want you to study your Aquinas hard, because he was a hell of a system man and will act as an effective antidote against your propensity to dream. And it doesn't matter that he threw it all up at the end, because that is a death's door trick of every saint, a little something to spice up the canonization inquiry, a fillip for the Devil's advocate, a clever little bump at the top of the stretch, as Mr. Tisdale would say." So there was no fight, and he had geared himself for a fight, so he said, "Is it true that all great gamblers and saints are celibates?"

Mr. Tisdale's horse stories were legion; therefore it was not out of pity for the old man that he climbed the malodorous stairs behind the grocery. It was part of his quest. There was, for instance, the story of the ghost horse, the ringer, a gray gelding moved surreptitiously from track to track and substituted for long shots—a ruse more daring than dope or bugs. Mr. Tisdale himself had once been at Hialeah with the ghost horse and won a pile. And right here in New Orleans at the Fairgrounds was where the ghost horse's career ended, bit in his teeth, twenty lengths in the fore, breaking the track record for the mile in a $1,500 claiming race. The jockey was cashiered, but the trainer and the owner disappeared. Where was the gray gelding now? Named, legitimized? Miraculously resexed and now siring a line of lightning foals? Mr. Tisdale did not know.

He was a scholarly one and did not easily abandon hope of finding significance in books. At times he turned even to fiction. There was, of course, the great story of the obsessive gambler driven to rhythmic release of guilt through hideous loss. There was the very strange story of the great gray horse that might have ridden straight out of Mr. Tisdale's dreams. This horse was essentially a huge penis, which accorded better with his observations and intuitions than the anal theories. But the only story that really seized his imagination was the one of the young man driven from snow to hot card dens, from towering hope to despair, confronted at last by the Queen of Spades.

So that night at the Old Post House while his father played blackjack he played at the silver-dollar dice table, betting a system that his father had taught him, hedging *Field* and *Don't Come.* He won forty-two dollars and would have won more if he hadn't occasionally made a wild bet on snake-eyes or ten-the-hard-way just to break the monotony of the system. Yet it was a good thing the system was simple, because his eye was often on the drink girl, who later that night in his masturbatory imaginings lay writhing beneath him, black stockings and black bush a tacky web against her moonlit silver flesh.

He and Mr. Donough stood by the box hedge at the end of the school ground. "Well, my Protestant friend, the Roman soldiers diced for Christ's garments. That image alone would be conclusive for some. If not, the church finds the same fault as with usury—earnings without base of labor. But if it be argued, as you do, that the gambler works hard, sustains risk, then the church points to side effects—concupiscence, lust, et cetera. But if it be argued, as you do, that the gambler is a paragon of sobriety, then consider. The Devil works in two ways—possession and dispossession. Gambling falls in the second class. It substitutes for this rich round world of ours another of utter nonsignificance, rife with empty ciphers, and bogus royalty, bodiless red and black queens displaying geometrical flowers."

His mother died soon after he was born, just as his father's had. But his grandfather took a second wife much younger than he, an elegant silver-haired lady who kept a candlelit table served by a black woman in a white pinafore. No cards were played in that house, no whiskey or cigars appeared outside his grandfather's study. He and his father were dinner guests there on rare occasion. Always after the meal the black woman brought them brass finger bowls of icy water with thin lemon slices floating on the surface. His grandfather and his father dipped and cleaned card-sullied fingers while his stepgrandmother in a high-collared black dress presided like a priestess over their ablutions. He dipped his fingers, too, but had no hope of cleaning them, fouled in the secret nights.

"You asked if it is true that all great saints and gamblers are celibates," his father said smiling. "Actually, son, nothing is true that begins with the word *all* unless it's that all fatherly advice is given to be ignored. Distrust all syllogisms. However, if you want the testimony of a minor gambler, I would say that the statement is certainly *generally* true." "Why?" he asked, smiling in his turn. "Because, son, the three ladies refuse to consort. Each demands all: Mnemosyne (the unenlightened, but not we, would say Fortuna), Aphrodite, and Theologia the handmaiden of Faith." "What about grandfather? Doesn't he serve both Mnemosyne and Aphrodite?" "A sly old philanderer all right, but pays for it with a forked life. Mnemosyne keep you, son, in mind of these answers."

So, in his senior year he wrote his own dialogue called "An Inquiry into Games of Chance." Socrates and the young man reclined in the shade of a high hedge. In front of them glowed the lake in the midday sun. "Why can not a man settle fortune and life with a quick stroke of luck?" The chaste old satyr answered slyly with a metaphor of lake, blind when gold, clairvoyant when blue. "And Fortuna, struck on a drachma, closes dead men's eyes." By these and other exempla the young man was taught to avoid luck's fleering seductions. But a little later, he slipped tunic and Socrates robe. Together they plunged to the bottom of the lake where beautiful dark fronds caressed their thighs and unravelled the morning's stern dialectic.

The last story that Mr. Tisdale told him was of a steeplechase. (Yes, in his golden days he had been to England and once even to Rio, where he cashed three consecutive quinellas, eating steak on the terrace among beautiful ladies under parasols, watching the horses pass before the soft arch of Sugarloaf Mountain.) At the final jump his horse lost jockey and he a thousand pounds sterling. "Boy," he said, "for the love of God, never bet steeplechases because the hedges and ditches will trip you every time. And preferably, too, never bet the turf. Your bare dirt track is your only firm footing." There on the arm of his chair Mr. Tisdale's fingers ramped feebly like an old pastured gray imagining itself answering the call to the post. So he deserted Mr. Tisdale on the grounds that his horses of Chance had never been truly cosmic but were merely sexual totems, impotent at that.

A last time by the box hedge Mr. Donough gave him valedictory words. "I say nothing, my Protestant friend, about the theological irregularities of your brilliantly written inquiry, for you do not fall under our orthodoxy." "Thank you for the left-hand compliment." Mr. Donough laughed, then sobered. "If I were the sybil I would prophesy, saying, 'Protestant, you will suffer fierce contention between the Devil and the flesh on the one hand and God and the spirit on the other. But you will fall at last among the sheep.' " Then, without benefit of the occulting grill, he confessed. "I have sinned sexually." To which the scholastic replied, "I have no power to shrive you. But hear this. When the issue seems most dark and dubious, remember all that you can of love." Mr. Donough laid his hand briefly on his shoulder and then, because it was early June and the grass already high, plucked up his cassock over his shoes and led him back.

II

He meant to choose Aphrodite. At any rate, he slid the golden band onto the third finger sinister, kissed sweet lips, and with the small legacy his grandfather had left him took her to Europe. And her family did not object that he was the son and grandson of gamblers or that he took his bride honeymooning before he was certain of a job. For he had graduated first in his class at the university and it was 1961. He could have his pick of dozens of positions, all with trajectories as high as rainbows, ending in treasure troves. But the bride's old grandmother, who had come to them from Lyon ten years before, would not remove her widow's weeds for the wedding. "Break my mourning for marriage wiz a Protestant?"

In Monte Carlo the second night she said, "What are you going to play?" "Nothing." They stood outside the velvet rope that cordoned off the chemin de fer table. He did not need to understand the game. The noble man with the gray hair had captured the cards and held them against six other players whom he eyed disdainfully through a monocle. Gold cuff links flashed at the edge of the sleeves of his black coat. The hands of his paramour, she also in black but sequined and scintillant, made a white band on his upper arm. The croupier with polished paddle served him from a little tower of cards, dropped the defunct holdings of his foes into a shadowy slit in the green felt.

"You're hurting me," she said. "I have to, because you aren't broken yet." A little later he told her to stop crying. "Everything good is marked by blood—birth, marriage, redemption." "Phooey. Don't feel required to parade your Phi Beta Kappa valedictorian wisdom around for me." But later, in the black of night, with the sea below almost as quiet as a lake, she said, "I'm afraid." "Why?" "Because you aren't always with me. Where do you go?" When he didn't answer, she said, "My grandmother told me you would come and go." "I was only thinking that I had never seen those big square gold and black chips stacked around a greensward with a tower in the middle, like a kind of Stonehenge."

At Lido he encountered the square black chip again. The rule was that each entrant must buy one for five thousand lire. It was also a rule that the black chip could not be changed or redeemed. She didn't quite understand. "Why don't they just charge admission?" "This is better, because although you have to lose the chip, you could make a million with it first." She lost hers the first bet at the roulette table, black on black. He won twice on red, then lost. He watched the wheel for a while and then bet singles in the 00–6 quadrant, for his father had said, "Your only chance at roulette is to find a hinkey in the wheel balance." He won a hundred thousand lire. "You're some player. Can I come to your hotel?"

That night, for the first time, she allowed him a slant light from the bathroom, and the dark net of her sex was more labyrinthine than touch had led him to hope. Yet the second time he failed. Because suddenly the passionate eye that looked up at him was a spinning wheel and the curious single fleck against the sheen of the cornea was the clicking ball. Dizzy, he shut his eyes. She laughed without spite. "I forgot to count. Mama said it would come about the tenth night." He shook his head. "It was that black old woman who played opposite me all night. She looked like your grandmother."

That became a series of three. Twice more before they left Venice he won, only much bigger, and twice more he failed, only more abjectly. On the third occasion her laughter faded. "What is it?" No answer. "Where are you now? . . . One time when you were drinking you told me we ought not to marry until you understood something. Does this have to do with that?" "I see now that my grandfather and my father are circle men, converting square cards into coin. But I have been boxing the wheel, converting circles into gold and black squares, a deadly forbidden business. That is the lesson of Lido. But what is the lesson of your black hair?"

"Me? I'm a ghost, a gray gelding racing across the turf toward an imaginary line where in a little tower the official film reels. . . . No, I'm an ersatz Catholic schoolboy. Father, can God circle the square, square the circle? Or only the Devil? Or one one and the other the other, et cetera?" He was drunk. "Are you here, Mr. Donough? And do you still say they are without significance, the ciphers that piled up all those big square chips for me?" "I'm here." "Let's see. You wouldn't be Mnemosyne would you? Theologia? Faith? Fortuna? No? Aphrodite? No? Why then you are nothing more than my step-grandmother's brazen finger bowl and a little tart at that. Hey?"

He was very drunk. "Mnemosyne, my dear, remember how old man Tisdale made of his fingers a steeplechaser and leaped the box hedge and beat all Ireland to the finish line? And the name of his horse was Black Knave, though I would have preferred Red Knave. Get it? Red Knave, box hedge. No?" "I think you ought to remember your circle men." "All right, the groom remembers his saintly grandfather, who is now a denizen of the City of God. But whose cane long before his interment, Aphrodite dear, hung loosely on his forearm. All flesh is grass. But, on the other hand, the father warned, beware all *all*'s. All syllogisms. Silly gism, we southerners say. Get it, Aphrodite honey?" Suddenly he began to weep. She held him in her arms.

On a gray morning she said, "Let's leave Venice. It's been bad for us." "Yes, let's leave it to sink like a sequined lady in her own corruption. You want to go home?" "You said that with your Lido winnings you would take me on a sea voyage to the Greek isles. Deep blue grots and the white temples of Diana. I remember everything

you say. I'm your book. You will read me and know yourself." "I need
to understand a lot more than my paltry self. Still, maybe if I could
read you Braille." "But just now you can't. So let's redeem those black
Lido chips on our sea voyage." He shook his head dubiously. "I'm
afraid nothing good can come of that money."

"All right," he said later, "but first we're going to take a train trip
down the Spanish coast. We'll get the ship in Málaga." He had
profound faith in the train. Hadn't the great southern boy-writer, also
a father-ridden and grandfather-ridden seeker, found ultimate
significance in the rhythmic turning of wheels, motion so powerful
that it regulated earth and moon? And, indeed, when on the second
day they saw from the window a Moorish ruin with minaret intact, he
took that for his sign. But when he crept into her berth like a joyous
thief, he found that the Lido croupier of sable suit and thin mustache
had already toppled down the stacked chips with his evil little rake.

From their choice window in the Palacio they watched the Resur-
rection, the Roman guards in silver tunics thrown back by the bright
assault of the angel. And those who had been in black reappeared in
white robes to see the stone rolled away as if a huge hand were
dicing, but the treasure was gone. All this transpired serially under
the marchers' flambeaux and to the incessant drumbeat along Av-
enida Generalísimo Franco. So he took this for a sign, and when the
bugles had retreated beyond the midnight, took his bride in arms.
But for him it was still the penitential season. Somewhere on the
empty streets below, Mr. Donough's black cassock swept the litter of
the revelers.

On the ship, too, he mistook the suspiration of the sea and a vision
of dark undulant kelp for a sign. And this time she said, "Don't try
any more for a while. Relax. Everything will be all right again." So he
went down to the ship's gaming room, where casual players of gin
and bridge were arrayed like theatrical supernumeraries on the edge
of a bright light that shone down on the poker table, which, like an
unbalanced wheel, was dominated by—who else?—a gentleman
with a monocle. When he took a seat, a willowy Negress delivered
him whiskey from a brass tray. "The gentleman," she said, "wel-
comes each new player."

While the incense from the monocled gentleman's thin cigar curled
up into the dark beyond the hanging light like a honey-thick image of

time, he, the erstwhile groom, played cautiously, made careful inquiry into the game. By the second night he was certain that there were no brothers at the table, no watermarks or broken spokes in the big wheel of the comic bicycle the leopard-skinned man rode in some *fin de siècle* circus. So there were only these: three bad players slowly bleeding to death under the gentleman's clever pricks, a puffy little science player who had attached himself parasitically to the shark's lip, and himself, the onetime honeymooner.

Neither was the Negress of concern, though she obviously was his priestess, his temple whore, keeping silent watch behind the bar even after all the other tables were bare. Presently a wife rescued one of the bleeding players, and the other two answered, albeit tardily, to their own wisdom, so that there remained only the unholy trinity of monocle, sucker, and honeymooner. "Gentlemen," said the gentleman when the triumvirate had completed its third session, "my cordial American companions of the main, I think we are on for the voyage, for the tide is slack and the wind variable." "I'm only hanging by a thread, colonel," lied the scientist, all whose predatory benefactors were no doubt denominated colonel.

So that was the way it seemed, the game as immovable as the black idol who tended without witnessing it. The parasite had swum a long equanimous life in the benign constancy of numbers and could not be denied his leavings. The monocle minced and parried, dashed and thrust, but could not find the honeymooner's heart, who told his bride, "Down there is Beelzebub, who can fly backwards and whet his hands like spears and whose eye records everything nine times or more but cannot strip a twenty-two-year-old American upstart and cannot understand why." "Why?" "Because my father told me I was a deep diver, a loon, and could not be predicted." "He was right."

The end came in the form that any objective observer could have predicted, watching the scientist, the parasite, packing jaws and pockets with the spillings of the ever-fiercer confrontation. Suddenly he pushed upon the table a great castellated tower-topped wall of chips. The monocle looked at the honeymooner. "Who topples that Ilium, lad? You or I?" "I," said he. "I," said the monocle. But neither was the Greek, toward whose bright isles the ship now made close approach. So the scientist took all, except for a sibilant confidence he wormed into the honeymooner's ear. "Never play a system man, son. The universe is on our side."

"Did Beelzebub leave us enough to get home?" she said. "Barely, but it wasn't Beelzebub. It was Saint Thomas Aquinas that won the day. But, look," he said, "we're wasting the money we spent on this choice cabin." He undogged the hatch, and there it was all right, a big moon brighter than a silver dollar hanging between the twin horns of the lifeboat davits. And because the ship was rolling gently, the circle of white light roved slowly over her thighs. "I feel like I'm on stage." "Just an old fetishist's trick with lights, my dark beauty, my queen of spades." Later, long after the moon was gone, she said, "My God, you certainly are all right. What did it? What did you learn?"